INCARNATE

JAMES KAHN

PUBLISHED BY PREMIERE

Published by Premiere
307 Orchard City Drive
Suite 210
Campbell CA 95008 USA
info@fastpencil.com
(408) 540-7571
(408) 540-7572 (Fax)
http://premiere.fastpencil.com

Printed in the United States of America.

First Edition

favorite Oldies station, back when Vicky was ten. *She'll have fun fun fun 'til her daddy takes her T-Bird away.*

That was one of her dreams and she'd always believed a girl had to make her own dreams real. Everyone believes that, of course – but she really <u>believed</u> it. And always worked toward it. Unlocking the door of her dream car that morning, that's when she saw the bad thing happening.

Standing across Diversey was a scaggy white guy, big guy with steroid biceps and a belly like a medicine ball, stringy unwashed hair down to his shoulders, no shirt but a rat-gnawed leather vest hiding his ugliest tats, stained sweatpants, flip-flops. Standing at the side of his car, door open, shouting at a flinching, cowed young woman who was neatly dressed in what looked like JCPenny seconds, clean and pressed. They made an incongruous pair but something in the girl's demeanor told Vicky right away that they were a couple. Maybe it was the way he yelled, "Get in, I said, you worthless piece of shit!" Then he slapped her.

Vicky jumped as if she'd been slapped herself, could feel the sting of it on her face. Kept staring at the scene. A tear rolled down the girlfriend's cheek; she was clearly scared and whipped, couldn't have been more than seventeen. But she did a brave thing. She shook her head no. The asshole puffed himself up. "Don't make me tell you again." He raised his arm, ham-fisted. The girl winced. They both froze like that, a *tableau*. And then he hit her once more to let her know it could come any time he wanted it to.

That was it for Vicky; she was moving, first to the corner, then starting across the street toward the scene of the crime. She didn't know what she was going to do when she got there; the guy was twice as big as she was, she knew he could ruin her face with one backhanded roundhouse, she could already feel the swollen pain on her cheekbone. But that wasn't anticipation as much as recall, because she'd been cold-cocked once before and the sense memory of that was gushing the adrenaline through her now, trying to turn her around, make her run away. She couldn't run away, though, that's not who she was, and she couldn't stand there doing nothing. Her ragged breathing was all over the place; she had to move.

So she found herself moving toward her fear, straight at the big redneck creep. And then as she passed the corner another instinct kicked in. There was a black woman holding a sleeping baby, waiting for a bus, a four-year-old boy standing at her side, hanging onto her dress. Vicky grabbed the woman's arm, firm but gentle. "Come with me. Please." The woman's first instinct was to resist, hold back. But Vicky made eye contact with her for a moment, and the woman must've seen something okay there, because she let Vicky guide her across the street toward where the abused girlfriend was now sobbing and shaking her lowered head back and forth like a baby elephant.

When the black woman saw where they were headed, to the very thing she'd been trying to ignore, she hesitated again, warning lights going off in her head. "Wait a minute, girl, where you takin' me, what you gonna do?"

"Just witness," said Vicky. It was an Amish thing, like from that old Harrison Ford flick she'd seen at the revival theater last month, where the townspeople gathered and actively witnessed the violence happening and that was somehow enough to turn the tide. Of course this wasn't a movie, it was real life. And now she was endangering the poor mother she was dragging along, as well. Vicky felt her heart thumping in her chest, her forehead got chilly damp, all her senses jacked up by the chemicals of alarm. But she kept moving.

And she witnessed. Stopped ten feet from where the creep was raising his hand to beat the sorry girl again. And just watched.

The guy saw Vicky and her reluctant accomplices. Lowered his arm an inch. "Get the fuck outta here, this ain't none of your business."

They didn't move, though. The beaten girl was quietly whimpering, the black woman at Vicky's side trembling but holding her ground; it wasn't like she hadn't seen this kind of thing before. The little boy hanging onto her dress, his eyes were open so wide it seemed like his lids were going to fly off. The baby on her shoulder stirred. And Vicky just stared as flat a stare as she could muster. Not a stare of anger or hate. Just a witness.

The guy took a step toward them, bunching his fist. The little boy grabbed Vicky's hand now, squeezed it tight. The big guy spit on the street. "The fuck you lookin' at anyway? Nothin' here but some sorry bitch gettin what she's askin' for. You askin' for it too?"

More than ever Vicky's impulse was to turn and run. But if she didn't follow through with the confrontation now, this asshole was going to beat on the girl even more. Or maybe that was a foregone conclusion no matter

For Jill - and our many lives together

Before the beginning of years
There came to the making of man
Time, with a gift of tears;
Grief, with a glass that ran;
Pleasure, with pain for leaven;
Summer, with flowers that fell;
Remembrance fallen from heaven,
And madness risen from hell;
Strength without hands to smite;
Love that endures for a breath;
Night, the shadow of light,
And life, the shadow of death.
And wrought with weeping and laughter,
And fashion'd with loathing and love,
With life before and after
And death beneath and above.

— *Charles Swinburne*

Contents

PROLOGUE

Somewhere, a dog barks.

A gaslight flickers in a fog-heavy alleyway. A weathervane, shaped like a snarling wolf, turns slowly, creaking, silhouetted over a full moon balanced near the top of the sky. And there's a knocking, a repetitive knocking, like a shutter banging in the wind.

An older man appears at the alley's maw. He's European, nineteenth century by his look. A disturbing scar runs from his left ear across his cheek down to his chin, like a twisted broken spine.

A pretty woman arrayed in yellow bruises and tattered perfumed clothes walks past him on the cobbles. She has a limp. The scar-faced man follows her.

She quickens her pace. He says something but the words are garbled, a strange and ancient language. She replies – her lips move but no sound comes out. He pulls a scalpel from his vest. It shimmers of moonlight. He stabs her in the back. Over and over. She falls, turning.

*He slips the blade into her abdomen, twists. Twists again, until the steel gets bound up in some glutted knot of tissue and he slices through that with a stroke. Blood issues from the wound, pools around the knife, overflows her belly, cascades down her sides. Eyes glazed, she dips her finger in her own blood, writes a single word on the ground. **CHAOS**.*

Somewhere, a dog barks. The moon is full. The repetitive, irregular knocking continues in the distance. The pretty woman dies.

And her body plunges into a depth of dark water, a swath of pale light illuminating other floating, dead bodies....

1

CHAPTER ONE

August 21-August 22, 2013
The Two Vics

Holding the brush with agile fingers capped by cherry-polished nails, not too long but shaped like she spent time on them, Vicky Olson applied mascara to her eyelashes up close in the deco bathroom mirror. She never really wore any makeup except the kohl-black to her lashes but she thought that touch made her eyes look bigger and wide open in a kind of pleased surprise. It was a gag that tended to be helpful in a lot of situations – jobs, boyfriends, store clerks, even the DMV if you stood in the right line. Not auditions so much; they were pretty wise to this kind of thing in that world. But in the civilian world, it was always a winner.

Not that she even thought about the issue anymore. The practical value of sex appeal to get what you wanted was so extraordinarily old hat, it was like breathing, or using a spoon to eat cereal. Just a given. And it's not like it was a new idea with her, either, like she came up with the notion. The old Spanish senoritas used to put drops from the *Datura* plant, Deadly Nightshade, into their eyes to make their pupils dilate, and it's a known fact your pupils get big like that when you see something you like. That's why they called the tincture *bella donna*, beautiful woman, since then, as now, any chick who had her eyes wide open for a guy was a hot chick to him. Sex and Deadly Nightshade, sex and death, like love and marriage, rum and Coke, all those elemental combos. Never go out of style. On the other hand, jimson weed was basically the same plant and her last boyfriend but one, Tully, used to smoke the stuff like a chimney. Didn't make him so fucking appealing.

Vicky was thirty-four and brassy cute. Hair came straight out of the bottle, *Who's-Your-Agent* blonde. Didn't take a genius to guess just by looking at her she was a good kisser. But that wasn't the whole package. She had her feet on the ground, too, there was substance to the girl. Not that she was unshakeable, but bottom line, her center was going to hold.

She finished her eyes, checked her watch – not quite late yet, grabbed her purse, pulled up her turquoise thong in back to show a hint of whale tail over the beltline, and she was outta there. Off to the salt mines. Or in this case, the no-MSG mines of the Chinese restaurant she waitressed at.

Down the stairs of her apartment building, out onto Spaulder Avenue, at the back of the half-block-big building that faced Diversey. The whole front section of the structure was an old revival movie house, which was nice if you wanted to catch a flick on the spur of the moment, not so nice when you wanted to sleep and the melodrama from the late show was bleeding through your bedroom walls. Especially those midnight horror films; man that sucked if you had to get up early.

She loved her Westside neighborhood, sort of midway between too-hip Logan Square with that fabulous Italian Ices place, and Polish Village up Milwaukee, the mecca of plum pierogis. Then just across the tracks, on California above Belmont, there was always Hot Doug's, the Encased Meat Emporium, for when you had to have calvados-infused duck sausage garnished with *foie gras*. Vicky tended to identify the various crossroads of the world, and her place among them, by the eateries that speckled the landscape.

She walked down Spaulder where her car was parked, a 2011 kickass yellow Thunderbird. This baby was her pride and joy; she was giving up shoe shopping and wine with dinner to make the payments, she'd dreamed of having one of these ever since her favorite song played on her mother's what Vicky did at this point, maybe her self-righteous posturing had done nothing more than guarantee a world of pain to this earnestly dressed young woman.

But now a door jingled in the shop his car was parked in front of. Two more ladies stood there, the sales clerk and a customer. Just stood there watching, seeing what was going on. Then the baby on the black woman's shoulder suddenly woke up, looked around. Looked at the beefy guy everyone else's eyes were riveted to.

That many people watching, just watching, even a guy like that has to turn his eyes in on himself for a second. Soon as he did, the air went out of everything. His arms dropped down to his sides, his girlfriend walked into the store. He gave Vicky a last look and it wasn't pretty. Then he got in his car, slammed the door, roared the engine and squealed off fishtailing.

Vicky turned to the mother beside her. "Thank you." They were both shaking a little. The woman nodded, walked back to the bus stop. Vicky went to her car and drove to work.

Down Diversey to Kedzie, then south, toward Humboldt Park. Replaying the whole thing in her mind, what she might have done instead. But it turned out okay, so what the fuck.

She had a mouth on her, no question. Grew up an army brat, fourth of five kids, the others all brothers, so she had to shout to get noticed and army bases weren't exactly churches to begin with. Except her mother's room, the one on the base at Ft. Riley, Kansas. That room felt kind of like a church.

Rose curtains, always closed, jasmine candles always burning, her mother in bed, dying of esophageal cancer; this was around when Vicky was like eleven. Not a pretty six months. Or rather, the room was pretty, the illness was not. Or the music was pretty – radio always tuned to her mom's favorite Oldies station – but the waxy stillness in the air was not. And the bond between them was prettiest of all, Vicky lovingly feeding the wasting woman tasteless nourishment through a tube, and brushing her hair; but the end was not. In the end, not even the jasmine could hide the smell of death. And when it came, Vicky's father pulled open the curtains to let in the sun. Vicky never really liked sunlight after that. Maybe that's why she'd pursued a life in the theater.

Never loved her dad so well after that, either. Not that it was his fault, but her mom's death happened on his watch and something about that couldn't be repaired. Or maybe it could have been, if the next thing hadn't happened. Few years later she hit her teens, and she didn't have to shout to get noticed anymore; in fact getting noticed wasn't all that big a problem. Or it was, in a different way. She got noticed by her father's colonel.

The older officer had asked her to do some filing and closed the door and before she could protest the first fondling he let it be known her father's promotion might well depend on how she acted, pressed up against this cold bank of file cabinets. So she tuned out and went home afterwards and stayed sullen for a week. But when her father finally insisted she tell him what was wrong and she told him... he didn't believe her. At least, that's what he professed, after his first stunned expression said otherwise. She actually watched the fear creep over his face, and then a moment of grief, and then anger – anger at the Colonel that had to stay buried, turning into anger at Vicky for telling such a terrible lie. She replied that if his promotion to captain was really that important to him, she'd fuck the whole general staff. He hit her.

That's the one that stung so bad, the one that came back to her left cheek whenever she got scared or angry; it was always lingering a little below the surface, like an exclamation point planted on the side of her face in invisible ink, the mark of the father who was supposed to protect her and protect her mother, and didn't protect either of them.

That was the sting on her face she'd felt earlier, when beastie boy was whaling on his girlfriend in the street. It was a physical memory Vicky could get in touch with if a role required it – if she needed to find feelings of desertion, abandonment, betrayal, violation, humiliation, despair, or over-the-top anger – but she didn't go there often, the price was too dear.

The day her father hit her she ran away. They found her, of course, that's what MPs are for. Daddy was repentant, ashamed. But she couldn't wait to split again after that, and maybe the only thing that saved her from much more dire consequences was she got involved in summer stock that July, the summer of her sixteenth year. And that was the beginning of the rest of her life.

Barely made it out of high school, spending all her time in the theater productions, before, during and after classes. Found her calling. Took it to college in the big city – that would be Chicago – and never looked back. Well… never looked back except when she wanted to plumb some chunk of childhood pain to help her find the right emotion for a role she was playing onstage; then she mined that dysfunctional family shit for all it was worth.

Now college was behind her, and a lot of other things, but she still had the acting bug in her soul even though she had to support herself with a cliché day job that she still wasn't quite late to yet, but was pushing that envelope hard in her T-Bird – cruising down Kedzie past Chicago Avenue, not far from the Black Beetle Bar, nodding to herself that yes, the Black Beetle served the best burgers on the Westside – as she slipped her mother's old comfort Beach Boys Concert CD into the CD slot, *With the radio blastin' Goes cruisin' just as fast as she can, now, And she'll have fun fun fun*….

And like that, she wasn't shook up from the encounter with the punchy asshole anymore, she was rockin' to the surfin' sound on the third coast.

But the fun was almost over.

He cruised past a rusting warehouse, *Harrison Freight and Salvage* in corrugated zinc letters across the front, but the "*l*" had fallen out of *Salvage*, and some wag had spraypainted over the "*e*" in *Freight*, so now it read *Fright and Savage*. Kept going past a sheet metal shop, locked up tight, razor wire topping the chain-link that circled it. Past a red-brick condemned factory building, four stories, pigeon shit all over the ground at the boarded-up entrance under the overhang where they liked to perch. Then what was once a scrap auto body yard, now a small jungle camp for transients, hobos, homeless vets from Viet Nam, Afghanistan and the two Iraq wars. This was all west of Kedzie, above the Eisenhower, lake side of the Conservatory.

As he made his way north a bit, up Homan past Adams, it changed some. Mostly Irish back in the day, cops and workers in the local factories. But as the businesses died, families moved on, apartments emptied out. The vacuum filled fast with bad company and drugs. The neighborhood crumbled like dry rot. Only now, in recent time, here and there you began to see buildings retaken, even gentrified, or in the process, with families staking claims.

Gliding along blocks further up the road he noticed a new funky gallery, the few pale people inside dressed in black, artists showing their colors, spilling down from Humboldt. Beyond that was a coffee house with scrounged tables, thrift store chairs, a multi-pierced guy behind the counter blowing out the espresso machine, *Arcade Fire* blasting from the Sonos speakers. Then a glad-rags shop facing the street, but its big back room did used music, mostly vinyl; you might find an original Django Reinhardt on 78 if you were up to braving the mildew in the cardboard boxes. Looking east were doorways to upstairs artist lofts, walk-down steps to the private dens of slouching eccentrics, scattered druggies and stoners. He drove past them all with an energy of purpose in his old black Chrysler, the kind that had fins and chrome and a bench front seat, early Jimi Hendrix bending strings on the tape deck, from those dynamite blues sessions that came before the hippie acid years, *ain't been home to see my baby in about ninety nine and one half days*. And he was just cruising to the music, on his way to see his baby. His name was Vic Stone.

Vic was thirty-eight. Good eyes, true heart, calloused hand. Used to have a temper but seemed to be on top of it these days. Nice fella, really. He'd always tell you he didn't have a creative bone in his body. Just liked hanging out with people who did. Artists, actors, musicians, writers. Vic his own self purely loved to build stuff. Not design it, he'd say, but put it together, start with nothing and end with a nice, solid thing. That's what he loved.

Nobody'd mistake Vic for an intellectual. Oh, he'd attended an institution of higher learning, sure – Union Park College – but only because he'd promised his mother he'd give it a shot. Chose his courses for their ease of passing and even at that spent his class time whittling miniature ships and finger puppets while his mind wandered far from the lecture. Ended up majoring in Theater Arts, where grades were handed out for hammering a fake wall together or hanging a light that cast a green shadow. How cool was that?

He'd first met Vicky back then, in school – this was almost ten years ago, now. She was in the Performance program, and Vic had crossed her path in an acting class he had to take to fulfill his degree requirement. They'd tolerated the professor's lame jokes about them sharing the same name, Vic and Vick, the two Vics; and they'd had to do a scene together, so they'd done it.

Other than that, not too much in common. She'd regarded him as a typical techie, too shallow to be bothered with exploring the depths of the human condition, and just not all that interesting to begin with. He'd thought of her as a typical actress: her favorite tool was the mirror.

The next year he'd run lights for *A Streetcar Named Desire*, Vicky as Stella. And he'd had to admit she was easy on the eyes. In fact, hot. By then she was sleeping with the director, though, so Vic had been out of the loop. After that he hadn't seen much of her. Their curricula had diverged, he had graduated, their lives had taken different arcs. He'd gotten a job in construction, mostly framing. One thing had led to another, he'd met a mason who showed him how to lay brick, which had taken him to a crew in St. Louis, where he'd met a guy in a bar who signed him on as an apprentice, forging wrought iron garden gates – until a falling anvil had broken his hand, he'd gotten laid off, no workman's comp; but his boss was a nice guy so Vic hadn't made a stink.

Meantime while all this was going on Vicky had gone to Hollywood, gotten a couple commercial gigs, bailed water with a few boyfriends in the same leaky boat. She couldn't stand what a stereotype she was becoming, though, mindlessly pursuing her M.A.W. degree (Model-Actress-Whatever) with all the other lemmings. Came to a head the day she'd read for a TV spot that involved eating a little gob of peanut butter and smiling at camera, with innuendo: "Mmm, I like it chunky." When her take was over she had gone into the bathroom to pee – and there were six previous auditioners puking into the sinks and toilets. A gaggle of gorgeous bulimics. A gaggle, was that right? Or maybe a pride, like lions. No, pride couldn't be right, more like a shame. That was it, it was a shame of bulimics, *in regurgitas* at the vomitorium. Vicky had flashed on her mother, on desperately trying to help the poor woman <u>not</u> barf, keep her food down, if you could even call that nutritious biochemical broth food. She'd had an urge to grab the nearest actress and force-feed her a whole jar of peanut butter, the chunkier the better; but had turned around, instead, and walked away from that life.

She'd still wanted to perform, though, so she'd looked around for something that actually took a measure of skill, some discipline that didn't involve counting carbs. She had began to rethink the whole move to the left coast. They had better salads, better sushi, but it was a lot like her mother's room. Looked rosy, smelled like flowers, but just below the surface lay grim tidings and the stink of death.

Further east, during the same time frame, Vic had been reconsidering his own wanderings. Kind of directionless, with a gradual accumulation of small injuries. One night in a tavern on his fifth Blatz he'd concluded there had to be a path that led to something more satisfying than that.

In the end, Vic and Vicky had converged back on Chicago, like homing pigeons loosed in distant battles, somewhat the worse for wear.

Once in Chicago again, Vic had gotten in a medium long-term hookup that ended badly – more about that later; Vicky had slept around strictly on the pleasure principle for a while and then sworn off guys altogether. Not that she was into girls – well, except that once; she'd just wanted out of the game for a while. Then a couple years ago they'd bumped into each other – literally – in the cramped torpedo room of the U505 Submarine at the Museum of Science and Industry on 57th off Lake Shore Drive. And something had just clicked. They'd spent the rest of the day doing the museum together – the rattling descent into the pretend coal mine, the trains and airplanes and ships and robots – and his excitement about all the things people make with their hands had kind of swept her off her feet. They'd ended up making out inside the giant human heart, until a guard tossed them and they went back to Vic's place, and that was the beginning of that.

They had great sex, great fun, competed for who knew the best dives to eat in, renewed common interest in the theater, especially local theater. Cheered each other's small triumphs, commiserated over setbacks, ranted about asshole impresarios. Endearments crept into conversation. Love happened. They'd even begun batting around the M word. This whole relationship thing was turning, against all odds, into good news.

Which brings us to right now. More good news is what was hurrying him through this changing near Westside neighborhood in the dog days of the sweltering Chicago summertime, with the whiff of the silvery alewives rotting on the beach faintly pungent even three miles in from the lake. Hurrying to tell Vicky.

Sweating through the back of his shirt against the torn fake leather driver's seat in the A/C-less boat of a car, he turned the corner around an alternative comic book store, a check cashing place, a blacked-out front window painted with Chinese characters – pulled up sharp to the curb, parked and got out. Walked over to the door next to the Chinese window and went in. This is where Vicky worked her day job in what she referred to as the hospitality profession. As mentioned, she was a waitress.

Chinese restaurant, nicer than anyone might have expected in this area. Banking on a rising tide. Deep red sponge finish walls, recessed lighting, neon sculpture, Philip Glass oozing softly out of the speakers in the corners, no MSG. And good central air; what a relief it was just to walk in the door, like oxygen to a pillow-smothered man. The local *artistes* ate here, but it also drew a hi-tech crowd from Humboldt Heights, even a few Logan Square yuppies and dinks.

Vic walked up to the front counter, where a middle-aged Chinese woman named Oma sat at the cash register doing a *Sudoku* on her iPad. There was a **Chicago Chamber of Commerce** calendar hanging on the wall behind her, showing a sepia tone albumin print photograph of the Water Tower from before the Fire. The date page was turned to **August 2013**, with the first twenty days Xd out, which brought it to Wednesday afternoon in Oma's world; she liked to stay on top of these things.

The here and now.

Vic pointed to the gold-leafed Buddha sitting za zen in the corner, a new addition to the decor.

"Cool Buddha."

"Totally sucks, you want my opinion." Oma's accent was pure Chicago, flat and deadpan.

"How come?"

"Too trendy."

"Nah, it's the right way to go, Oma. You want a better class of customer, you gotta dress the old girl up."

"I liked it better when we had the original place out back, fed the tool-and-die crowd."

Vic nodded in agreement, and they touched fists. Comrades of the working class, suffering the fools. Truth be told, she was a take-no-prisoners capitalist and he only worked at the fringes, and only when he had to, but they sort of bonded around the romance of labor.

"Vicky around?"

"Got off ten minutes ago, you can probably still catch her." She tipped her head toward the kitchen. "I'm sure she'd love to get caught." Vic smiled thanks, headed back.

Just a handful of people sitting at the tables and booths, lunch crowd was gone. An architect going over blueprints with some community activists, a Loop lawyer and his sizzling mistress, coupla black guys who looked more like precinct workers than anything else, a waiter pouring tea for an old Asian man. Vic turned left past the dining room, into the stainless steel kitchen. Not real busy, a few cooks, a dishwasher, a cat licking its ass, a waitress hanging up her apron – that would be Vicky.

Vic held his finger to his lips at the cooks, sidled up behind his girl, put his hands over her eyes. "Guess what," he said.

"Don't you mean 'Guess who'?"

"You know who. Guess <u>what</u>."

She slid her hand behind her, down to his crotch. "Mm, you're right, I <u>do</u> know who… at least I'm pretty sure."

The chef said something in Mandarin to the sous-chef, who laughed back in Cantonese.

Vic wasn't the kind of guy who was able to sit on good news for very long, though. So he spun her around to spill the goods. "I got the job."

She wrapped him in her arms, jokey but loving. "'Course ya did, ya big lug." Like a girl in a thirties comedy, she was thinking Carole Lombard, whose inflections she'd been studying lately. Or Myrna Loy maybe, whom she loved in *The Thin Man*; she remembered watching that on WGN the weekend she'd moved to Chicago the first time, right out of high school. If Vicky located herself in place by her proximity to commercial food sources, she located herself in time by the movies she'd seen, and what had been going on in her life when she'd seen them. So thinking Nick and Nora Charles, she gave Vick a deep, congratulatory kiss. He gave her no argument.

"But that's not all," he said. "Open auditions."

"Open Auditions is my middle name."

"Well, your two middle names."

"You were always better at math than me. But I'll swing over there right now. And hey, Baby, I can say I know the tech director."

That was the job he'd scored, tech director for the new playhouse and theater company opening something over a mile down the road, the Chi-Town Players. The sweetest kind of situation, where he got to work with people making stuff, do some construction himself, trade ideas, spend his day laughing and hammering. Day job didn't get better than that.

Kind of employment she loved was acting in little theater. No aspirations to Hollywood anymore, no dreams of celebrity, of red carpets traipsed over, or names dropped in *Daily Variety*. Just act her heart out at local productions, pour emotion onto a bare stage, while real people stared at her, rapt, from theater seats thirty feet away. So she was kind of a showgirl. Liked to flash her soul, close range. Then retreat back into the unrevealed life of a world-class waitress, pie with your coffee and service with a smile.

But she had something for Vic now, too. "Okay, close your eyes this time." He did. She opened one of the lockers in the corner, took out a large, flat white cardboard box, put it in his hands. "Now open 'em again." He did.

"What's this?"

"It's a present, you dork."

"Did you know a dork is a whale penis?"

"Gee, I hope this fits, then."

He opened the box. Inside was a black suede street jacket with burgundy satin lining and a gold zipper. He took it out of the wrapping, held it at arm's length. Kind of a knockabout style, done up in elegant evening jacket materials. Like a textile oxymoron. "What's this for?"

"You might be a whale penis, but you're my whale penis," she said. "Happy birthday."

"That's not until next month."

"Yeah, but this just went on inventory sale at Ruby's, and I saw the bitch next to me eyeing it, and they only have a three-day return policy on clearance items, so try it on fast."

He did. Fit perfectly. "It's my new favorite thing." He kissed her warmly.

The cooks applauded. Vicky bowed, her full-on stage bow.

"The thing is," said Vic, "it's not like I'm gonna get to wear it much in this stinkin' heat."

"Hey, Chicago summer, you never know when it might turn." She was right, too. There were some August days when the temperature dropped forty degrees, like ninety to fifty in a few minutes, dropped in step with the barometer, the muggy suffocating air whipped into a psychotic thunderstorm.

She waved to the cooks, went out the back door. Vic, right behind her, whispered in her ear, "Tell me exactly, what part of my anatomy is it that makes you think 'whale penis'?"

"Your blowhole."

They got outside. Behind the restaurant spread an expanse of pitted asphalt, an alley, a junk-strewn field, condemned buildings, falling-down warehouses. A dozen cars were scattered around the back entrance, some abandoned, some so rusty the steel was oxidized into brown gauze, so close to gone the sunlight through the lacy corrosion was almost translucent, the husks of the cars resembling the broken amber shells of 17-year cicadas. A few vehicles were still operational, mostly the cars of the people who worked in the little struggling businesses around the neighborhood. Vic and Vick walked toward her car.

"*Ow You're On My Hair* is playing at the Redrum Lounge tonight, wanna go?" she asked. The new lead singer was a passing friend of Vicky's from the old days.

"I don't like their new front woman, she does this Miley Cyrus twerking thing that makes me yawn, like oh well, just the usual orgasm."

"That's silly; orgasms are the same as snowflakes, no two are alike. Besides, everyone knows it was Miley's dad Billy Ray who invented twerking with *Achy Breaky Heart*...." But her flight of fancy was interrupted by a feral cat racing across the weeds and out of sight. It made her jump and pause, more shaken than was warranted.

Vic glanced at her. "Have your nightmare again last night?"

For weeks now she'd been having this recurring dream of some guy without a face, just a small hole where the mouth should be, standing at the foot of her bed and watching her. Nothing else ever happened, but it was very creepy. In any case, she shook her head – no, no nightmare last night.

"So what, then?" For a guy, he was pretty tuned in to her moods.

She brushed her hand backwards past her head, dismissing the subject. "Little dust-up on my corner this morning. Big beefy asshole had a meltdown and ended up taking it somewhere else." She shrugged, case closed.

"A beefy asshole, that's quite an image…" he began as they approached her car. But stopped short. Vicky's jaw fell open, like in a cartoon.

"Oh my God."

Her beloved, pristine yellow Thunderbird: the windshield was smashed, looked like tire iron work by the imprint. Maybe a ball bat. And someone had written WHORE on the hood in red spray paint.

Vic's voice got quiet; that's how his anger was hardwired, muted at first, then either bottled up or exploding. "Any idea who did it?"

"I don't have a clue; this is totally fucked up."

"What about the beefy asshole you were just talking about?"

"Couldn't have been him; he left before I did, he didn't see my car, I went the other direction, no way."

"You got any old boyfriends might be carrying a grudge?"

"Vic, gimme a break, we've been together over two years."

"Some grudges have long memories."

"Yeah, and I'm gonna have a _very_ long memory for this piece of work."

"What about Tully?"

"Still doing two to five at Stateville; I checked like half a year ago to make sure they weren't gonna parole him any time soon. He's not out, trust me on this."

Tully was who she'd been with just before Vic. Didn't last long; the guy welded BMW mufflers into motorized sculpture, called himself a manic depressive kinetic artist. Turned out he was just a speed freak with a brother who ran a chop shop. Tully himself tried to buy the entire stock of Sudafed off the shelf at the _Walgreens_ on Cottage Grove. When the cops came knocking they found a meth lab in his basement. He copped a plea ratting on his brother and they both got hard time, probably spent a lot of it working out their family issues.

Vic and Vicky circled her car, looking for they didn't know what. A clue of any kind. Nothing. Could it have been that creep on the street? she wondered. Like he turned around and followed her? She didn't buy that, though. She could still see him burning oil at a stoplight three blocks down Diversey when she hung a U up the cross street, not even in his field of vision. And beefy assholes are known for various things, but not intelligence.

When she and Vic came around to the front again, Vicky picked up a rock, hurled it at the spray-painted word WHORE. That was for whoever'd hurt her car, the lame gutless limp-dick bastard. Teeth clenching near tears. This day was just going from bad to totally fucked.

Vic took out his Droid and snapped pictures of the car from every angle. "Come on, I'll phone in a report to the cops and send them the photos while we get you to the audition."

"How am I supposed to audition now?"

"Just do it. They want you to come in with your best dramatic monologue; I'm thinking you're really pissed, so go with your gut."

She thought about it. "Okay, you're right; I know a Shakespeare with some good rage in it. I won't have to dive very deep to make it sing."

Two hours later Vicky was auditioning on an empty stage, playing to an empty house except for the usual suspects sitting in the shadows. The playwright, with *de rigeur* neck scarf; the director, a potent, dramatic middle-aged Jungian with a diabolically black, carefully barbered beard, widow's peak and a pony tail down to his collar; the casting director, an older guy from the Jewish Theater who seemed to know every actor in Chicago; and the gofer, a recent graduate of Roosevelt who did everything asked of her, for pittance, just so she could learn the business.

Vicky'd already done the sides from the play they were going to mount, and now she was finishing up her Shakespeare monologue from *Anthony and Cleopatra*. Resurrected her touchstone fear and anger to play it – felt the burning weight of the fist on her cheek, let it take her to that place where her forehead got damp and she wanted to scream or run but held it all in place instead; that was the brave thing, when she held fast. That's when she did wrath well.

"*Horrible villain, I'll spurn thine eyes; I'll unhair thy head, Thou shalt be whipp'd with wire, and stew'd in brine… Rogue thou hast lived too long!*" She shouted it at the end, then hung her head, heart wrenched and ratcheted.

The director crowed, pleased, from the darkness. "That was lovely, dear. Can you cry?"

She stayed still a long moment. Twisted her fury inward, impaled herself on it, like a *seppuku* dagger, felt the point of it lance some taut bag of salty grief deep inside her, spilling a river of teardrops into her heart, overflowing the brim of her eyes – so when she raised her head, a plump tear coursed slowly over the orbital ridge of her cheek.

"Bravo, well done!" The watchers in the audience had a quick whispered conference and then Sid, the casting director, called out.

"See Angelica for the paperwork, Honey, and report to wardrobe tomorrow for a fitting."

Vicky's face lit up. This was always an unexpected and always sparkling moment. "I got it?" She knew she deserved it, she just couldn't believe she'd gotten it that fast.

"You got it, Honey," said Sid.

"Thank you! Thank you!"

She bounded across the stage to the wings, where Vic was waiting with open arms. Which she jumped into.

"You were great," said Vic.

"I was fuckin' incredible. Let's celebrate."

He pointed to a rack of false walls, mostly unpainted. "I have to inventory the flats first, see what we need."

"I know exactly what I need." She kissed him so hard they fell clattering into an oversized, open trunk of theater masks.

Side by side in the pile of costumery he managed a lingering, undocking maneuver from the kiss. "Whoa, Vick…."

"Yes, Vic," she replied. "Whoa." She loved how gentle he was, knowing how volcanic he could get on occasion, if seriously provoked. Once in a bar last year she'd watched him explode all over two guys who wouldn't stop grabbing her ass, plus a third guy who ran away, all in the space of ten seconds; it was over almost before anyone had known it was happening. Except the jerks it'd happened to, of course.

His stock went way up with her that night. She started to feel like she could let down her guard a little if she could count on him to stand up for her. Made the ten miles of bad road in her rearview mirror kind of smooth out in perspective.

He smiled now, in the trunk beside her. "You know, I gotta tell you, I wasn't really sure about this relationship at first, you having the same name as me, and all."

"No, no. You had the same name as me."

"Whatever. Just because we were name mates didn't mean we were going to be soul mates."

"Namesakes. Not mates. You know, you really should have taken that English-as-a-Second-Language class again."

He moved his face closer. Studied her eyes. The boy was in love, to his ongoing shock and awe. "Mates pretty soon," he said.

"I can't wait, Baby." She brought her mouth to his, softly. Brushing lips, just a taste. Exquisite restraint.

Lying in this vaguely coffin-shaped box, surrounded by a profusion of demon, elf and clown masks, Vicky's true face emerging like a luminous, incandescent spirit – this was the moment Vic, in his deepest heart, leapt over the brink he'd been teetering at for months. "Let's tell my mother tomorrow night."

Vicky's pupils dilated like a *bella donna*. She knew what he really meant and she loved him for it and that made her even more beautiful to him. But still, even so, she said, "You sure?" Honor bound to leave him an out. "I mean, once we tell your mother, that makes it like an unreturnable gift, which makes it irrevocable, which makes it official, which makes it public, which makes it real. Then we'll fuckin' have to get married."

"In which case I guess you'll have to wear the nano-diamond ring I gave you."

"The ring you asked me not to wear until we told your mother."

"The very ring."

"Fuck the ring."

And she pulled him below the masks.

He drove her back up to her place near Avalon, off Diversey, maybe a mile from the river. Her hands were all over him in the old black Chrysler with fins and chrome and a bench front seat that Vicky took full advantage of as Muddy Waters wailed out of the speakers about a mannish boy, *Ain't that a man, I spell emmm, aaay child, ennnn.* Kind of a hot appetizer of auto erotics, with a side of raw Chicago blues.

Vic's mother had brought him up in Hyde Park, on the South Side, so he'd been kind of raised on the blues. When he was younger he listened to a lot of white kid wannabes, dropouts and hangers-on from the U of C mostly, playing some of the local lounges, trying to emulate Butterfield. But the real stuff was all around, Junior Wells and Buddy Guy and Magic Slim and B.B.King seeping from every jukebox in every bar. He used to make the trip down to Lee's Unleaded Blues on South Chicago three, four times a year, he'd been doing that since the days he had to sneak in underage, back when it was Queen Bee's.

Vicky wasn't a huge fan of this elemental Chicago sound; nor was Vic crazy about <u>her</u> musical comfort zone, the Beach Boys, the Byrds, and the Belmonts. But each appreciated that the other was just a bit retro, in different ways. It was simply one more of those little wavelengths that some couples share, one of the threads that draws them together into the patterned quilt they become if they last long enough. There was also, of course, the sex thread.

When he got to her block, Vic parked on the street. They steamed the windows for a few minutes, finally got out, Vic adjusting his pants, Vicky her top. Christ it felt good. The windows fogged up because since the time they'd been inside the playhouse, in the time it took to make evening out of the remnants of the afternoon, the weather had pivoted. It was cool, now, with a breeze, but humidity rising. Like a summer storm coming in.

Her apartment was a second floor walk-up above and behind the small revival movie house, the one that played old horror flicks every midnight. Not much traffic midweek. A necklace of light bulbs bordered the black plastic letters announcing tonight's fare: *Village of the Damned*. The original. They showed a lot of old horror here; maybe that's where her nightmare image came from, the faceless guy with the mouth-hole, maybe it was some B movie poster that slipped into her brain one night. She took Vic's arm, walked him through chilly mist refracting the glimmer of neon above the marquee, the name of the joint. *The Yesterday*. The kiosk out front was empty now, it was pretty late.

They walked around the corner, fifty feet up the side street, Spaulder, then into the foyer of the residential section of the building, where they paused for a good grope. She fumbled for her keys, he fumbled high inside her dress, between her legs; she inserted key into lock, with a small gasp at the moment of insertion. Pushed open the entry door. They made it up the one flight without tearing each other's clothes off, finally landed in the apartment with just two of their legs actually on the floor: hers were wrapped around his waist like a locking pliers, her tongue rimming his ear as he slammed the front door shut with his left foot and carried her in place all the way down the hall to her bedroom, which faced on the unlighted alley that ran along the other side of the theater.

In a minute they were on her bed in the red glow of a Japanese lantern she had hanging, for mood, in the corner. Tearing at shirts, kisses urgent, skin acute, everything so right there, so into each other, they weren't even distracted by the distant pre-Dolby screams of the horror flick downstairs and upfront, wails that sometimes kept them up, sometimes kept them amused. This time they were too absorbed in themselves to hear anything.

Also too absorbed to see the things they didn't see.

They didn't see, for example, in the smoke detector above her door, the small hole, the video camera lens.

And they didn't see the car parked down the misty alley in the street-lampless night, a shadow-faced figure sitting behind the wheel, staring at a Wi-Fi laptop. Dry-mouthed, shallow-breathed, watching the real-time moving images of Vic-Vick sex, the carmine hue that flickered from the computer monitor matching the color in the window of Vicky's bedroom, where the Japanese lantern glowed so hellfire red.

Next day the crew was in high gear onstage, building flats for the walls of the Doctor's study, gathering pig iron to the fly rail, checking circuits to lighting in the cheeks, living the jargon. Downstage right, at the front of the proscenium, the cast was milling around. First table reading, more of a get-ting-to-know-you session, really, the way these things go. Men doing their alpha male thing, either haughty, sensitive or studly, playing to their strengths; women checking lip gloss and skin tone, nerves and hearts, com-rade and foe. Everyone exposing, concealing and revealing the studied or craftless bits and pieces of themselves. Everyone flirting and fluttering with the potential energy of a new part, a new show, a new life.

At some small distance from those assembled, there was a backstage pay phone, a carryover from back in the day, before everyone had a cell. This ancient machine still took quarters, and was surrounded by a jumble of phone numbers scribbled on the wall, the usual pizza delivery places, courier services, agents, Yellow Cabs. Curiously the building was a dead zone, and nobody's cell phones got much reception, no matter who their carrier was. So the anachronistic phone on the wall got a lot more use than you'd expect. At the moment Vic was on the horn to his mother.

"I thought we might have dinner at your place tonight," he was saying.

"Why? Is there a problem?"

"There has to be a problem for me to come eat at your house?"

"You said 'we.' 'We might have dinner.'"

"Vicky's free too. We both got a job. Working on the same play together. It's a celebration dinner."

"Celebrations are my favorite thing. Come at seven, I'll make something simple but robust."

"Great, gotta go, see you at seven. Love you, bye." He hung up, breathed. Realized he'd been kind of holding his breath. Not that telling his mother he was getting married was going to be problematical, or uncomfortable, or difficult. Or anything. She was going to be fine with it.

Vic had lived alone with his mother for all his growing up years, ever since his old man had run off when Vic was too young to remember. Consequently he and Gloria had grown to depend on each other for emotional support. The kind of leaning-on that friends usually provide more than parents do children. When Vic had moved out to St. Louis to brick and mortar, Gloria had gone into a mild depression. Empty-nest type of thing. She'd pulled herself out of it after a year or so, finally, by plunging into artwork. A sort of self-therapy at first, she'd gradually found she not only liked it, she was pretty good at it. Brought her personal satisfaction as well as positive feedback, a rafter of new friends, even the occasional hefty paycheck. It was a good life. By the time Vic had returned to Chicago, she was pretty whole.

Vic had moved back in with her for a while, trying to find his feet again. But even after he got a place of his own, way up on Central Park, they'd continued to have dinners together a few times a week. Until Vicky had come along, that is. For the last year or so, most of his spare time had gone to Vicky, they were even planning to move in together as soon as the lease ran out on his efficiency apartment – so the marriage was hardly going to be a big change, so telling Gloria about it was just not going to be that big a deal. Right?

For one thing, Gloria was pretty damn fulfilled, existing happily more days in the world of her mind and spirit than on any quotidian earthly plane. So if Vic were married, or not married, or indentured to a circus – it was pretty much all one to Gloria, as long as he was good with his life. For another thing, his mother liked Vicky, and Vicky liked her. Kindred souls, living for their art. So why was Vic jittery about this dinner? Go ask Dr. Freud. Whatever the reason, it annoyed Vic with himself.

To vent this annoyance, as he hung up the phone, he snapped an order at some crew people lounging around high up on a newly built catwalk. "Give me a railing around that, I don't want anybody falling off." Al, his best guy, waved a C wrench in reply. Seeing the wrench reminded Vic there was a loose fitting he'd noticed under the stairs and he didn't want anything to be loose right now. Things were all of a sudden feeling too loose, like right around the next corner the wheels might fly off. So he took out his Droid, turned on the flashlight function, moved into the darkness to tighten things up.

Like Vicky – for whom it evoked the last time her mother was alive – Vic was a guy who felt at ease in the dark. It brought him focus, shut out all the nattering distractions. A place of peace, not fear. So now, like always, the darkness welcomed him in.

Meanwhile, stage right, four of the actors sat around a large table negotiating take-out food and newly coffee-stained scripts. The work they'd be performing was recently penned by a promising local playwright, Jonathan Exley. An allegory exploring the dark and light in every soul, the masks we wear, our double lives. Our secrets, even from ourselves. It chiefly concerned the downfall of a doctor – a powerful, increasingly demented Svengali – who manipulated the souls in his orbit until they got sucked into the abyss that was the black hole of his own spirit. Kind of a latter-day evil wizard.

The part of the Doctor was being played by Will Ratner, a somewhat long-in-the-tooth, pompous thespian and randy old goat. Will had started out at the Goodman Theater, gone on to Steppenwolf, done Chekov in the park; and with a reputation that preceded him by what was rumored to be nine inches, he'd done every aspiring starlet in every cast. And counting. His resume included television series, features, shorts, commercials, local endorsements, Broadway, off-Broadway, dinner theater, children's theater. He'd been there and gone, but never gone entirely. The man loved to act, and he loved himself so ingenuously it was usually pretty hard to get angry at him. Usually.

Beside him sat Vicky, who was playing both the leading lady and the leading lady's alter ego, a meaty part, and she was up to it. She had a little less experience than some of the others so she was going to try harder, hopefully without seeming to. But then, that's what actors do.

Otto Shoop was the young stud of the cast. Pleased to add a credit that included the great Will Ratner on the playbill, Otto was on his way up. Not a striking actor and way too superstitious in a studied kind of way, but all in all not a bad sort. He had the part of the Med Student.

Sitting next to him was Joan Webster, a character actress who'd been around the block way more times than wanted numbering. She was playing the doctor's Housekeeper, the kind of limited role she gave more to than was strictly required but that's the kind of girl she was, all pro all the time. At the moment Joan was circling some of the key dates in her day planner.

"Okay, today is Thursday, August twenty-two. I was told we faux open October fourteen, which is a Monday, which is usually dark, plus it's Columbus Day, but it's a charity event and then we work out the kinks for the public opening on the Friday after, that would be the eighteenth."

"Working out the kinks." Ratner fairly glistened with innuendo. "Tell me more about that part."

"Shit," said Otto, "I think the eighteenth is the full moon." He checked his iPhone. "October eighteenth, 2013 .... Yeah it is. Oh shit shit shit."

"So?" said Vicky, amused to be already witnessing the first of innumerable qualms, panics, funks, caveats, foibles, fables, freakouts, hissy fits, pronouncements, sulks, warnings, second thoughts and third rails the company would all be trumpeting during the course of production. Witnessing now – she guessed witnessing was her lot these days – Otto shake his head morosely. "Otto," she said, "what's up with that?"

"What's up is opening on the full moon in October is worse luck than saying the name of the Scottish play."

"Which I once had the misfortune to do the night I forgot my cod-piece, not that I need one..." said Ratner, who was clearly about to launch into one of his renowned Stories Of The Theatre.

Vicky grinned brightly to herself – here was the first fable.

But Ratner was interrupted by the entrance of Mark Dent, the self-consciously dramaturgic director with the short, tailored black beard, now with his ponytail undone, hair hanging loose to his shoulders, wearing sort of a black silk pirate shirt with puffy sleeves, and jeans. Accompanying him were Jonathan Exley, the neck-scarfed, corduroy-jacketed playwright, and teen actor Teddy Sanders. Right out of high school, Teddy had lucked into his first professional production. Kind of a utility position, multiple bit parts and walk-ons. He was totally jazzed to be meeting this skilled and expert group.

Mark, the director, made introductions around. "Everyone, this is Teddy Sanders, the new lad, he'll be playing the Stable Boy, the Street Punk, the Bus Boy, and the Newsie. Teddy, this is Otto Shoop as the Med Student, Will Ratner in the lead, Joan Webster as his maid, and in the double role of Will's Fiancée and the Urban Slut, the effervescent Vicky Olson."

"Effervescent?" said Ratner. "Did you effer see her ven she effer vasn't?" It was an old Phil Ford and Mimi Hines gag, but Ratner knew them all.

Various greetings and handshakes ensued. Vicky liked the new arrival, Teddy; she felt tender toward him, could see the stardust in his eyes, the baby-faced look of the recruit wanting his mettle tested. She remembered what that was like, the magic of entering your first troupe, of going into emotional battle onstage for the first time with hardened theater vets at your side; they sometimes tripped you up in rude rites of passage, but always watched your back. And all these feelings passed through her mind without words attached and she raised her coffee cup to him and said, "*We few, we happy few, we band of brothers, for he today that sheds his blood with me –*"

"*Shall be my brother,*" beamed Teddy. He'd seen the Shakespearian quote on the opening credits of the old Spielberg miniseries on HBO, *Band of Brothers.* He figured this actress was probably pretty impressed with him already. But then he couldn't think of anything else to say.

But it wouldn't have made any difference no matter what line of conversation he'd undertaken since nothing could long prevent Ratner from continuing a story, once started. "I was just making a case for the cod-piece as an underused prop..." the old thespian explained to Mark, to get him and all the other newcomers up to speed.

"A superfluous prop for some of us, Will," winked Otto, making the same joke Ratner had earlier. The young buck's jibe at the old goat.

Ratner smiled at the challenge. "Then you properly don't appreciate the 'physicalization of the subtext.'"

"Which is?" asked Teddy. This was great, he was already learning craft from the masters.

Mark's voice deepened just a couple cycles per second, the voice of the sensei doling out the secret knowledge to the neophyte. "When a character says one thing, but physically expresses what he really means."

"For example." Ratner opened his script to a random page, read from a random action line: "*The Doctor crosses the stage to the bedroom doorway. He smiles lovingly at his fiancée.*" And then, to Teddy: "But physicalizing the subtext, I might play it this way."

Without warning, he grabbed Vicky in the chair beside him, filled her mouth with his tongue, grabbed her left breast with gusto. She might not have reacted quite so vehemently if it hadn't been for yesterday's one-two punch of woman-slapping and car-trashing. But this was really too much, on the first day of rehearsal. So after a stunned moment she shoved him away – growing up in the middle of all those brothers, she had a pretty good arm, she could hold her own – on the backswing knocking over the coffee urn with a steaming crash that physicalized her own subtext.

Teddy nodded gratefully, taking it all in. "Huh. So that's physicalization of the subtext."

"No, sir," said Ratner theatrically. "This is physicalization of the subtext." And he stood, arms and legs spread wide, to reveal a mega hard-on pushing out the front of his pants.

Vicky rolled her eyes. "Pul-lease."

Young stud Otto raised his eyebrows at Ratner's bulge with more interest than anyone might have expected. "Oh, my."

The others laughed, shaking heads, as Vic walked up, drawn by the commotion. "Everything okay here?"

"Fine, fine," said Mark, the director, watching them all with an eye for detail, already looking for what personal traits of his players he could coax into their performances. "Will's just being an Actor." And then to Teddy, another pearl: "He's like the scorpion who stings the frog that's carrying him across the river, knowing if the frog dies they'll both drown – and so they do. But the scorpion couldn't help himself. Because that's his nature."

Teddy nodded thoughtfully, but he didn't quite get it. I mean, if the scorpion....

Vicky waved at Vic, waved him away, really. No problem, just first-day preening and posturing. Vic nodded. Actors were a breed unto themselves, they had their own doggie ass-sniffing rituals. Better just to leave them to it, he'd discovered, than to try to pull the pups apart. He walked upstage, back to fixing a broken door lock, where he could lose himself in the simple machinery of stuff.

Joan dipped chopsticks into her carton of sautéed veggies. Will, more amused with himself than anyone else was, chuckled and opened a bottle of Guinness. Jonathan the playwright, a shy man who seemed content just to be around these extravagant personalities – partly to file their chatter away for future script dialogue – dug into a bowl of turkey chili, while Otto whispered a small, grinning comment to Teddy, who laughed too loudly but didn't care. His new band of brothers had taken him in.

Vicky took a big bite of her tuna sandwich.

Took a couple chews… and spit the food out hard, her eyes wide with the sick visceral sense that comes from knowing something inside has gone very, very wrong.

Blood poured from her mouth, down her chin, thick and dizzy red.

The others gasped, or stared or stumbled back. Vicky brought her hand up to her lips, popping a pink bubble that was forming at the O of her mouth. Intruded two shaky fingers past her teeth, over her slippery tongue. Pulled out a gleaming slick razor blade.

"Oh, my God."

"Holy shit."

"Was that in your sandwich?!"

"Lie down, make her lie down...."

"Call 911, oh my God, somebody call an ambulance."

Vic heard the chaos and came running back just in time to catch Vicky as she slumped to the floor, more from the stunned shock of it all than the bleeding, which was, nonetheless, profuse.

2

CHAPTER TWO

July 4-August 6, 1976
Before The Beginning Of Years
There Came To The Making Of Man

A gunmetal haze of cordite hung over the sand, muffling the dull thud of random explosions, magnesium flares, fiery sprays across the night sky. Sleepless men huddled in scooped out depressions in the damp sand. Cowering, or taking aim, adrenalin-giddy. This wasn't the southern Normandy coast, June 6, 1944 though. It was the Southern California coast, Venice beach to be precise, July 4, 1976. The ordnance consisted of bottle rockets, cherry bombs, spinners and sparklers. The men on the beach were drunk, stoned, light-headed with Bicentennial steam, and so were the women. The whole damn country was having a two century birthday party.

Bordering the sand was the Stroll, a concrete walk that wound lazily along the beach, separating the shoreline from the long line of houses that fronted the ocean: Hollywood bungalows cheek to jowl with upscale condos, small apartment buildings, doper shacks, even a Jewish Home for the Aged. Earlier that afternoon was a frenzy of sunburned summer vacationers, brown-skinned surfers, T-shirt hawkers, muscle beachers, hustlers, roller skaters, homeless dumpster divers, a guy juggling chainsaws, African drummers, Japanese kite flyers, standup comics, jumping Frisbee dogs, hula hoopers, teeny weenie bikinis, the smell of salt spray and sweat-heavy Coppertone mingling with hashish, *Stayin' Alive* by the Bee Gees blasting from every other boom box, sunlight sparkling on the two foot swells.

The Stroll was packed that evening too, but more like a three mile rave. Music and laughter, bold flirtation, dried summer sweat, all manner of reckless dance, the barely contained belligerence that too much alcohol would release later in the evening when bars closed, gangs showed colors, sex went bad. And in a tastefully redone duplex half a dozen buildings north of the pier at Washington Boulevard, a talky shindig with mixed drinks was in full throttle.

Members of the new Yuppie demographic, who once only smoked reefer and groused about asshole landlords, now nursed martinis and commiserated over tenant problems. Eagles on the stereo were welcoming all to the Hotel California, where you can check out any time you like but you can never leave. Disco was all over the airwaves but not at this party. Beautiful people did lines on the Italian marble countertop in the bathroom, flaunting swingers cast bold glances and pheromones in all directions – this was some years before AIDS was even a word – and everyone felt pleased as punch with their no-fault, victimless indulgences. That's what it was like in California in 1976.

This place was actually the second home – the beach house – of a well-to-do Hancock Park gay couple, Joe LeMay and Alan Greene. Joe was an architecture columnist for the *Herald Examiner*, a now defunct afternoon paper. The column was titled *Form Follows Luncheon*. His life partner, Alan, was on the clinical faculty at the UCLA med school, a nephrologist with a keen mind, a philosopher's bent, a coterie of fawning students and a flare for interior design, as evidenced by the décor here. Their bicentennial guests tonight included doctors, lawyers, journalists, surfers, artists, actors – in L.A. every gathering included actors – and, of course, academics of every stripe. Guy Daniels was there.

Guy was, at that time, a forty-two year old professor of English Lit at a Cal State in the Valley, teaching Victorian fiction and Shakespeare in alternating semesters. Among the Bard's works, he usually focused on *The Tempest* or *Macbeth*, occasionally throwing in a rock-opera version of *Anthony and Cleopatra.* Then during summer session he'd do a William Butler Yeats poetry seminar that didn't require much homework either from him or from his students.

Gangly is how Guy had been described in his youth. Thin, angular, long – six four in socks – with chiseled cheeks and slender, arachnodactylic fingers that seemed more suited to origami folding than, say, ditch-digging. There was a touch of Ichabod, or some other kind of crane, in him: slightly beaked nose, all arms and legs just standing motionless but ready to take flight at the first boo, as he mused, at the head of his class, over some piece of poetry that moved him. He was, in fact, easily moved. A sensitive soul, with sensitive features. Deep eyes, expressive mouth, a shock of sandy hair always boyishly falling across his face, as if trying to shield him from the harsh ugliness of the world. From seeing it; from letting it in.

So: a man informed more by the wellsprings of interior poetry than the vagaries of external circumstance.

The current semester he was teaching no classes, only just back from sabbatical in Edinburgh, Galway and London, where he'd been doing research on Robert Louis Stevenson for a book he was intending to write over the remainder of this bicentennial summer and fall. The focus of the book was to explore his thesis that Stevenson had met Yeats in Galway in 1887, and that Yeats' occultist theories had influenced Stevenson's writing *Jekyll and Hyde,* analysis of those influences then providing a platform for Guy's disquisition on the nature of good and evil. *Daemon est Deus Inversus* was Yeats' motto: a demon is a god reflected.

Guy was rather fascinated with the shadow side of the human essence; academically fascinated, that is. Personally, he was the sweetest of people, his heart went out to everyone, no hesitation. Raised in an orphanage, he had only kind memories of the folks who'd cared for him, who'd given so selflessly of themselves to his upbringing. His adult life, consequently, had been devoted to giving back to others in like fashion. He never quite understood, at a gut level, how a person could get any joy or juice out of hurting someone else.

Of course, he'd soon enough understand that all too well.

In any case, instead of writing the sabbatical Yeats/Stevenson book – as events would come to pass – he ended up writing a journal chronicling every detail of the strange, dark journey he was about to find himself on. He wanted a record, an analytic document, for future reference, and was convinced that details mattered. Both God and the devil lived there.

So Guy's nightmare voyage began that evening of July 4, 1976, and ended… but let's not get ahead of ourselves. This is still all before the beginning, in Guy's mind; before the making of the man he was soon to become, and later to regret.

Let's say, for the sake of having to start somewhere, his expedition of discovery kicked off as he was sloshing his *Cuervo Gold* rocks/salt margarita at his host, Alan the UCLA nephrologist – who also happened to have been Guy's college roommate some twenty years earlier, and continued to be a good friend. A good friend who loved a good argument.

"That's ridiculous," Alan was saying. "You really believe good is good and bad is bad in some empirical, absolute, cosmological way?"

"Let's not get too overblown," said Guy, "I'm speaking solely of the human condition."

"About which, if I'm not mistaken, you seem to be declaring, *fecum non carborundum.*"

"I'd never say that. I can't even pronounce it. What does it mean beyond the borders of Middle Earth?"

"It's one of the basic laws of surgery. *Fecum non carborundum*, Latin for 'You Can't Shine Shit.' If a pathology is inexorably and irredeemably awful, you can't make it seem to be something it's not, just by shining it up. It is what it is. Shit."

"Exactly."

"But exactly <u>not</u> in the realm of human behavior. It's good to kill your enemy in battle. Bad to kill your mailman. So is killing good or bad? It's all relative, it's all contextual."

"No, killing is bad," Guy insisted. "Sometimes it can be tolerated, or justified by extenuating circumstances, but taking a human life is just evil."

"There is no absolute evil. There are only viewpoints."

Guy had always considered himself a thoughtful sort, who cared about ideas the same way other people in this tinsel town cared about cars or movies. With enthusiasm, affection, bold opinion. An academic's academic was Guy; so he riposted Alan's assertion of moral relativity in a scholarly fashion: "Bullshit, and I say that with the utmost respect for your intellectually and morally bankrupt conviction."

"But now you've proven my point," replied Alan. "Respect for bankruptcy of values bespeaks a belief in moral relativism that…"

"…that points like an arrow to terminal good and evil at the extreme poles of the scale."

"Poles which can only be approached asymptotically. And do scales even <u>have</u> poles?" Alan wondered. "I think not, I think scales are all about balance and relationship and the sort of contemporary ideas that imply a philosophy of moral and behavioral relativity…."

"Don't change the subject. I spent all winter in Galway and London, deep into Yeats' mysticism and Stevenson's near death illness, and I promise you *Jekyll and Hyde* is as relevant today as it was in 1886."

"Don't make promises you can't keep, buddy."

"What, you don't think the dual nature of man's soul, the free will to choose between righteousness and wickedness, resonates in the 'Me' decade?"

"Stop talking to me like I'm one of your students. Besides, you know very well that good and evil are nineteenth century place-holders. Men of Science know behavior is about serotonin, dopamine…."

"What a cop-out that is." And then, in a mocking voice meant to resemble the whine of a Felon among Men of Science: "'I couldn't help myself, Officer, I was just running low on neurochemicals.'"

Alan smiled. Raised his glass. "To neurochemicals."

And Guy, in the spirit of armistice, clinked highballs with his old friend. "To neurochemicals."

They drank, manipulating the very thing they toasted. Guy was feeling mellow. Good conversation with a dear companion, a nice buzz, a room full of pretty girls; that one in the corner looked positively Pre-Raphaelite, her russet hair tumbling all down her back. Outside, a brilliant red shower of sparks burst silently over the black water, followed some seconds later by a deep rumble.

"The fireworks are starting," someone said. "Check it out."

Alan and Guy moved outside to the patio with a dozen others as all eyes faced the Santa Monica pier, the source of the pyrotechnic display. Like electric flowers blooming in time-lapse, green, purple, white, incandescent. Alan, never one to let a train of thought pull out of the station without him, flared his fingers in imitation of the next erupting red chrysanthemum.

"See, that's what's going on in your brain all the time, these little star-bursts of serotonin-fueled neuronal activity, electrons telling you to love, or eat a French fry, or write a Shakespearian sonnet."

Guy's mind was wandering, though, as he marveled at the sheer beauty of the night. The beach full of happy souls mesmerized by the magical lights, the semi-tropical breeze over the water, good company, that peculiar tangy bouquet of brackish air and firecracker smoke drifting across the moon… but it wasn't quite just the gunpowder that made him sniff the off-shore currents like a hound picking up a scent. There was another odor mixed in with it now. What was it?

"There's nothing innately good or evil about the human soul," Alan was still rambling on, "it's neither more nor less than the wondrous, awesomely miraculous miracle of biology…."

"Do you smell that?" Guy asked.

"Smell what?"

Perfume. Guy smelled perfume. But such a scent as he'd never imagined, musky and exotic and deeply stirring. He glanced around. There was that Pre-Raphaelite woman standing nearby, was it coming from her?

"That perfume," Guy went on. "It's intense, isn't it?"

"I don't smell anything, I've got sinusitis. But that's just my point, you smell perfume because certain loci in your olfactory lobe, mediated by cate-cholaminergic neural receptors…."

Guy drifted away from Alan to walk up behind the woman in question, sniff the back of her neck. No, that wasn't it, not quite.

"It's somewhere right here," he said, looking around the gathering. "But I can't quite place it."

The woman turned around, brazenly coy, brushing her ample breast against his arm, and whispered, "I think the bedroom's open, come on, I'll show you where to place it."

He was feeling unsteady, though, as if he'd drunk too much. He turned to another girl, all punked out with tats, lip rings and safety pins, and smelled her hair. "*And in some perfumes is there more delight/Than in the breath that from my mistress reeks,"* he quoted from one of his undergraduate course sonnets.

"Fuck off, asshole." She returned some poetry of her own.

Another woman turned to him, smiled graciously, held out her wrist to his nose. He sniffed, shook his head, apologetic. She shrugged, lower lip pushed out, a gesture that seemed very French, as did her fashionable, expensive, fitted dress of taupe silk. Formal, with an undercurrent of *haute* sexuality. She was clinic-tanned, Sassoon-coiffed, Dior-accessorized except for a pair of ornate earrings that might have come from a harem in Constantinople. She spoke in a husky, Lauren Bacall voice.

"Perhaps you're appreciating an essence from someone you loved once, long ago, in a far, distant life." She handed Guy her card, which identified her as Dominique, a Certified Channeling Guide, and shook his hand. *"Enchantée."*

A huge ball of light exploded high above, sending gold streamers down to a watery end. Guy turned from Dominique, drawn to the streaks in the sky. Fixated on them as they began to twist, no longer linear, but bending into square corrugations, like the golden turrets of a medieval castle, limned in neon.

"Guy, are you okay?" said Alan. "You don't look so...."

But Guy's lips began to smack, as if lapping after the taste of some odd, elusive spice. And then the delicate fingers of his left hand started twitching and then his left arm and then the leg shook, more and more until he dropped to the deck like a flopping rag doll as party-goers stared in horror or fascination and the lights of the skyrockets burned into his brain and there was a raspy noise like someone scratching on his eardrum, an abrasive barky sound....

Somewhere, a dog barks.

A gaslight flickers above an alleyway. A weathervane, shaped like a snarling wolf, turns slowly, creaking, silhouetted over a full moon balanced near the top of the sky. And a knocking, a repetitive knocking, like a shutter banging in the wind.

An older man appears at the alley's maw. He's nineteenth century by his look. A disturbing scar runs from his left ear across his cheek down to his chin, like a twisted broken spine.

A pretty woman arrayed in yellow bruises and tattered perfumed clothes walks past him on the cobbles. She has a limp. The scar-faced man follows her.

She quickens her pace, moistens her lips which have become dry. He says something but the words are garbled, a strange and ancient language. Youyig... youyiguh... Youyiguhm... Ihuda... Youyiguhmihudan. She shakes her head, tries to reply – her lips move but no sound comes out. He pulls a scalpel from his vest. It shimmers of ivory moonlight. He stabs her in the back. Over and over. She falls, turning.

*He slips the blade into her abdomen, twists. Her lips twist, mimicking his gesture. He turns the blade again until the steel gets bound up in some glutted knot of tissue and he slices through that with a stroke, like a matador's flourish. Blood issues from the wound, pools around the knife, overflows her belly, cascades down her sides. Eyes glazed, she dips her finger in her own blood, writes a single word on the ground. **CHAOS**.*

Somewhere, a dog barks. The moon is full. The repetitive, irregular knocking continues in the distance. The pretty woman dies.

And her body suddenly plunges into a depth of dark water, a swath of pale light illuminating other floating, dead bodies... .

When Guy awoke he was in a hospital gown, in a hospital bed, under a hospital light. In a hospital, it would seem. Alan stood at the bedside wearing his doctor's lab-coat, his doctor's look of concern, his doctor's stethoscope around his neck; and a friend's caring voice.

"How are you feeling?" he asked.

"Hard to say." Disoriented, unsettled. Flashes of disturbing, violent images left him vaguely nauseated, with a fine sweat on his forehead, yellow spots floating before his eyes. A couple deep breaths, a pause and he collected himself. "What happened? You put something in my drink, right? Ludes? So you could take gay advantage of me?"

Alan offered a strained smile. "You wish. Actually, you had a seizure, Guy. Complex partial, it looked like at first, then full *grand mal* convulsions. You're in the neurosurgical unit at UCLA. It's the morning after the night before. Are you oriented times three? Know who you are, where you are, when it is?"

He flipped the answers off on his fingers. "Well, you just called me Guy, is who; told me it's UCLA, is where; mentioned prominently the morning after the night before, is when. Still 1976, I'm assuming."

"And still a smart-ass, I'm observing. Do you remember anything about what happened?"

Guy tried to bring the shape of last night full-face but his mind kept shying away from the dream-like visions of the alley, the murder, the blood. He went back in his memories to the party, tried to reconstruct the events leading up to his collapse. But when he tried to retrieve his impressions of whatever girl it was wearing that perfume – circled the memory of the smell like a hyena sniffing to discover if it was dead yet – it made him light-headed. Okay, don't go there, he thought, back off, try another image. "Last thing I can hang onto is the lights from the fireworks getting wavy and then they got all choppy, like jagged squiggles, or the teeth in a big gear...." He couldn't place it.

"Like the turret of a castle maybe?" Alan prompted.

"Yes! How did you know?"

"You kept obsessing about somebody's perfume, too. Lights shaped like turrets dancing through your field of vision – in medical jargon we call them 'scintillating scotomata.' And the smell of perfume is a common herald as well. Together they're called 'auras,' they can signal the start of an epileptic event. So be warned, buddy, if they come again, you better lie down before you get hurt – you'll be on the verge of another convulsion."

But this is surely a mistake, Guy thought. A lab error. Doctors screw things up all the time; this must be somebody else's illness, it didn't belong to Guy. He'd been healthy all his life. None of it made any sense. Right? "I can't have epilepsy," he insisted. It was out of the question.

"Not epilepsy *per se*, not exactly." Alan began to pace, balancing on that point-wide line between comforting friendship and medical detachment. "We've been doing tests all night, while you were out of it. Since you have no next of kin, I signed the authorization myself, I hope that was all right. CAT scan, EEG, ultrasound, nothing too invasive yet."

"What do you mean 'yet,' White Man?" Guy tried to smile but his lip just quivered uncontrollably, like it was having a little seizure of its own.

"There's no good way to say this, Guy – but imaging indicates the seizures were caused by a mass lesion."

"Talk English."

"A brain tumor, most likely. Looks like you're going to need surgery."

He felt corpse-cold and shivering as they wheeled him into the operating
theater. Because they'd shaved his head bare, he thought at first. But it was
more than that, of course. He was cold in his heart, and his soul is what shivered. Knowing he was about to undergo brain surgery was bad enough; the
idea of having to go through it while he was awake nearly undid him.

The neurosurgeon had explained that was the most precise method of
mapping the extent of the tumor – determining how deeply into his brain
they could cut away by asking him to perform certain tasks as they probed.
If he couldn't move his little finger on command, it meant the surgeon was
dissecting too close to the vital brain structures which controlled that motor
function. Arteriograms had suggested the cancer was invading near optic
pathways – the doctor didn't want to induce blindness by slicing too much
away, so he needed Guy to tell him about any visual impairments that developed as the operation progressed. All in all, a grim proposition.

So they wheeled him into the O.R., cranked his bed up to a sitting 45
degree angle. There were a lot of people in the room, it was like a strange,
muted party, as if perhaps Kafka were putting on his own bizarre bicentennial celebration. There was the attending neurosurgeon, the senior resident,
the junior resident, the anaesthesiologist, a scrub nurse, a circulating nurse,
a third year and a fourth year medical student, the stereotactic technician, a
post-grad research Fellow waiting to abscond with a sample of tumor tissue
to ultracentrifuge for further analysis of the mitochondrial layer. Even Alan
was here observing, a couple steps removed, like the second tier at a busy
bar – not as the patient's old friend, but as the patient's internist.

"I'm just goin' to put some Versed in your IV," said the anaesthesiologist,
whose accent suggested somewhere south of the Virginias. "It's goin' to put
you to sleep. Then we'll wake y'all up a little futher on down the line. Now I
want you to count backwards at a comfortable speed, startin' with one hundred." He injected the solution, and as Guy was wondering how fast a comfortable speed was, and if he should amuse them by counting in French – or

if they would, instead of being amused, use his choice of language as a diagnostic indicator – he lost consciousness.

The R-One injected local anaesthetic into the bare skin and sub-dermal tissues, starting above Guy's left ear, moving circumferentially; the R-Two made a long, transverse incision from over the brow to behind the occiput and peeled the scalp back like carpet, or sod. Next he trephined a hole in the skull and inserted a bone saw that emitted a whining noise, like a dentist's drill, the sawing accompanied by that same kind of cool water spray, to dissipate the frictional heat. It didn't much diminish the smell of burning bone, though, and one of the medical students gagged. When the resident was done drilling and sawing, he lifted off a large melon-rind slice of skull, like a geometric piece from a child's jigsaw puzzle, leaving the *dura mater*, the fibrous, papery covering of the cerebral tissue – which he proceeded to snip away and peel back, as well. Revealing Guy's brain.

Grayish, vaguely pink, glistening, highlighted by the slightest arterial pulsing – and with a plum-sized, caseous white, irregular mass covering several sulci and gyri, plunging deep.

"Shit," said Alan.

"All right, bring him up," the attending neurosurgeon told the Carolina anaesthesiologist.

The gas man injected a little Narcan into the IV. Guy's eyes fluttered awake. He wrinkled his nose at an odd odor, a kind of smoldering, and he mentioned it to the assembled group because he was afraid it was an aura, that it meant he was about to have another seizure.

"Don't worry," said the attending. "It's just a little charred bone. You'll get used to that."

That's when Guy caught a glimpse of himself in the reflection of the glass cabinets along the wall. He would've jumped off the table but he was tied down everywhere. Cloth straps held his thighs, arms and chest to the gurney; his cranium was clamped in place by stereotactic steel prongs that gripped him at the temples, held his head motionless. And the top of his skull was, of course, missing. He wanted to throw up.

"Mr. Daniels, you're in the operating room, everything is going fine. I know it's all a little strange but I want you to lift your left index finger if you understand me. Can you do that?"

Guy lifted his left index finger off the gurney.

"Excellent. Now from time to time I'm going to ask you to move something. If you can, do it. All right?"

"All right," he whispered. His voice sounded distant to himself, disembodied, as if he were someone else. He could hear his heartbeat. The attending surgeon nodded to his assistant. "Retract the temporal lobe, if you would." And to his scrub nurse: "Knife, please."

She slapped the scalpel into the neurosurgeon's palm and he began to cut. Guy averted his eyes from his reflection in the glass, he didn't want to watch, it was too horrific.

And yet there were so many more disturbing images yet to come in his troubled life.

"Suction... can you feel any of this, Mr. Daniels?"

"No," he whispered.

"Good. Now if there's anything you want me to be aware of, you just tell me. Pain, smells, lights, memories, numbness, tingling, anything. And if you can't tell me using words, for some reason, raise your left index finger. We have a medical student standing here, her whole job is to watch your finger and tell me when you have something to communicate. Anything at all, you lift your finger. Are we on the same page with that?"

He lifted his finger. But then it began to twitch in some secret, private Morse code. And then his entire hand started shaking with a wild tremor, dazzling corrugated lights sparkling at the edges of his visual field, and an overpowering perfume that nobody else in the crowd was aware of, that completely expunged the smoky odor of his own burning skull, engulfing him and filling all the corners of the operating suite, all the corners of the entire universe, and Guy could hear clearly that familiar raspy, barky sound....

Somewhere, a dog barks.

A gaslight flickers above an alleyway. A weathervane, shaped like a snarling wolf with rust-red teeth, turns slowly, creaking, silhouetted over a full moon balanced near the top of the sky. And a knocking, a repetitive knocking, like a shutter banging in the wind.

An older man appears at the alley's maw. He's nineteenth century by his look. A disturbing scar runs from his left ear across his cheek down to his chin, like a twisted broken spine.

A pretty woman arrayed in yellow bruises and tattered perfumed clothes walks past him on the cobbles. She has a limp. The scar-faced man flares his nostrils and follows her.

She quickens her pace, moistens her lips which have become dry with fear, with foreboding. He says something but the words are garbled, a strange and ancient language. Youyig... youyiguh... Youyiguhm... Ihuda... Guhmihudan... Youyiguhmihudan. Youyiguhmihudan...

She shakes her head, tries to reply, looking back at him – her lips move but no sound comes out, as if she's choking for air but too despairing to gasp. He pulls a scalpel from his vest. It shimmers of ivory moonlight. He stabs her in the back. Over and over. She falls, turning.

He slips the blade into her abdomen, twists. Her lips twist, as if mimicking his gesture. He pinches her lip hard, to still it, and twists the blade in her belly again until the beveled steel gets bound up in some glutted knot of tissue and he slices through that with a stroke, like a matador's flourish. Blood issues from the wound, pools around the knife, overflows her belly, cascades down her sides. Eyes glazed, she dips her finger in her own blood, writes not one word on the ground, but two. **RED CHAOS.**

Somewhere, a dog barks. The moon is full. The repetitive, irregular knocking continues in the distance. The pretty woman dies.

And her body plunges into a depth of dark water, a swath of pale light illuminating other floating, dead bodies....

Guy awoke once again in a hospital bed, his head wrapped in thick Kerlix bandages. The surgeon had already been in to check the incision and to tell him the news. But his thought processes had been sluggish, unwieldy, and he'd gone back to sleep. Now he found himself on his side, with something on his mind, something disturbing, even dire, but he couldn't think of what, as he lay there staring out the windowpane.

Framed by the window, it seemed the entire world meant to awe him with its splendor. The way the leaves trembled in the California breeze, orange and crimson bougainvillea petals, the chrome curve of a Porsche

Turbo Carrera at cruising speed, the cool sunlight and moving shadow, distant laughter, an eighteen-wheeler truck honking like an animal of the veldt – it all seemed overwhelmingly poignant to him now. The signatures of life. He felt so close to it all of a sudden, and so far away. His emotion overflowed. A tear brimmed his lower lid, stung the corner of his eye, like heartache squeezed into a painful drop.

There was a knock in the doorway and he turned to find Alan standing there, looking doctorial.

"Hey. How's it going?" Alan asked.

"The surgeon said he had to leave some tumor behind." That was it, that's what was on his mind, the troubling thing he couldn't remember, not just on his mind but on his brain. Now he remembered it, rushing back to consciousness, a night-train without brakes hitting Central Station. The cancer.

Alan nodded. "Glioblastoma, it's called. Grade III or IV, there's some disagreement among the pathologists. It went in too deep near vital structures. If they'd removed any more of it, it would've left you blind. Or worse."

"Yeah, this is a lot better."

"Hey, surgery wasn't the last resort. We've got you scheduled for six weeks of radiation therapy now, they have a new experimental regimen and there's every reason to believe…."

"I got the impression long-term survival wasn't part of the picture." That was the other troubling thing. Surgeons used these words – prognosis, five-year survival, promising new protocols – like they meant something. Guy knew better. Nothing meant anything now.

"Look, if we're aggressive with radiation, and if we follow it up with chemo, we could extend your life expectancy at least twelve, eighteen months and maybe longer if…." Alan stopped himself when he saw the emptiness of his words reflected in Guy's face.

"So what do you think?" Guy tried to make light of it, though he felt so hollow. "Get my house in order or binge for a year?"

"Hey, nobody gets out of here alive." Alan returned the banter. But it was glib philosophy coming from someone not facing a death sentence.

Guy summarized: "*Fecum non carborundum.*"

Alan couldn't really find a handy retort to that. Guy let the silence linger. Alan tried one last empty aphorism. "You just can't lose hope, Guy."

But Guy was brought to mind of a Philip Larkin poem he'd always liked, titled *Next, Please*, he read it often to his summer poetry class. He recited from memory: "*Only one ship is seeking us, a black-Sailed unfamiliar, towing at her back a huge and birdless silence. In her wake No waters breed or break.*"

Alan could only nod, and kissed his friend on the forehead. And wished there were some regulation against letting men with poetry in their eternal souls getting cancer in their internal organs.

Alan acted as Guy's intermittent chauffeur the rest of the day – wheel-chairing him to X ray, to electroencephalography. That night Guy had another small series of convulsions and the resident on call gave him enough Valium IV to stop the clonic movements, and upped his Dilantin.

Alan came by in the morning, read the chart, talked to the night staff, called the attending, reassured Guy: these anti-seizure medication dosages were very idiosyncratic, everyone had their own maintenance level, and once they figured out Guy's, he'd likely be seizure-free. Not to worry.

But there was actually something else on Guy's mind, something even more bizarre and deeper down than epilepsy and he didn't want to deal with it; yet when would he, if he didn't now, and his death was fast approaching? Still, he wasn't sure how to broach the subject. He might as well have told Alan he'd seen God; that would have met with less skepticism. But he had to say something, and in the end, okay, so what if his old friend thought he was getting a bit flaky? That was the least of Guy's problems. "Something else weird is going on," he said.

"You mean besides somebody opening up your skull and taking out a brain tumor while you were awake? Can't be any weirder than that."

Guy shook his head, though. "I've been… seeing things. When I had the seizure at the party, and then again during surgery, and then last night, too."

"Seeing what kind of things?"

"A dog, a full moon, a scar-faced old man stabbing a woman to death. His scar was like this." And he traced a ragged line from his left ear across his cheek and down to his chin. Then he forced himself to say the most impor-tant part. "But the thing is, the images were like *déjà vu*. You know when you see something feels like it happened before? Only it feels like this <u>did</u> happen before. Like it really happened." There. He'd said it.

But Alan was confused. "What happened?"

Guy bit his lip. "A murder. A long time ago. And I was there. In a past life. I was the killer." He paused as elements of the dream flashed through his mind. "Victorian Europe, I think. I'm not sure what country. England, maybe, or somewhere like Romania, it seemed like the man was talking a foreign language, only it wasn't any language I know so maybe he was just talking in tongues. Or he was an alien from alpha centauri." He shook his head, baffled to hear himself saying these things out loud.

Alan wanted to make sure he was hearing this right. Nomenclature was important to doctors, that's how they wrapped their minds around ideas. "You think you've been having reincarnation dreams."

"It sounds insane, I know; I never believed in that crap, I <u>don't</u> believe in it, part of me thinks I must be going crazy."

"You're not crazy, you're just a little upside down; people have been sticking their fingers in your brains, for God's sake."

Guy nodded slowly, certain his old friend must be right. And yet.... "It's just, the feeling was so powerful, I was imbued with the sense I was watching a past life, I was <u>living</u> a past life, I felt the chaos in my soul, like I was there...."

"Of course there's chaos in your soul, Guy, look what you're going through. And a murderous feeling? I were you, I'd want to kill someone, too."

"But the details...."

"Sound like a scene out of *Jekyll and Hyde* to me. You've been researching Stevenson for months. Aren't those Victorian murder images already floating around 'your fevered brain?'"

Guy was partly relieved at Alan's resistance, was reassured the way a child might be reassured at hearing a beloved catechism. But there was another part of him that felt wounded by the scoffing tone in Alan's voice. It made him want to back out of the conversation, curl up under the covers. "But then you weren't there, were you?" He smiled sadly at the doctor. "You can't really know what I saw, or sensed. Hell, we learned that in Solipsism 101."

Alan saw the hurt in his friend's eye and backed off. God, what was he thinking? Here Guy was dealing with his own imminent mortality and Alan was trying to engage him in an academic debate. "Okay. You're right. I don't know what you're going through. And we have plenty of time to talk about your dreams. But right now let's concentrate on fighting this tumor, starting the radiation treatments, taking the anti-seizure meds...."

Maybe it came from wanting to lash out at Alan, the bearer of all these terrible tidings – rage, rage against the dying of the light – or maybe Guy was just an academic's academic, always following a line of thought wherever it might lead. In either case he felt compelled to keep formulating his admittedly outlandish notion. "But if I keep taking those meds, I might not have another seizure. And then I wouldn't get any more clues about my past life – or whatever it is that's really going on."

Alan pulled up a chair, sat at the bedside, brought his face close to the man whose life he wanted to prolong as much as humanly possible. "Listen to me. You've invented a cliché reincarnation fantasy as a defense mechanism, a denial of your mortality. Like it doesn't matter if you have a brain tumor and die, your eternal soul will migrate forever. But Guy – this is the life you have to deal with now. Let's focus on that, let's not lose sight of battling the cancer."

Guy got a little agitated as another idea came to him, a deepening of the premise of past lives, a foundation of the notion, the impossible notion, that he had, in fact, experienced a glimpse of one of those pasts. "What if I'm being punished with this tumor? Punished for the murder I did in that earlier life?" The thought began working itself out, all on its own. It made a kind of sense, there was a justice to it, it had an appealing internal logic. If the visions were real, there had to be a reason for them, and a connection to who he was now.

The suggestion only angered Alan, though. "Oh, so now you deserve the cancer, it's your punishment? What kind of New Age junk science blame-the-victim bullshit is that?"

But the logic carried more weight the more Guy thought about it. Okay, maybe he didn't have to believe it, maybe it was only a metaphor, but there was no reason not to follow the line of reasoning as an intellectual exercise. At least that. "In fact," he posited, "maybe if I figure out who I killed back then, and atone for it, or repair the consequences, my tumor will go away. Maybe I can fix this life by attending to the last one."

He sounded so hopeful, and so hopeless, Alan didn't have the heart to push. So he just clasped the long frail fingers of Guy's hand in his own, like the dear old friend he was, and gave back a loving smile.

Most of the month of July 1976 merged into a series of disconnected images for Guy, like a single long night of lucid dreaming.

Phlebotomists stabbed needles into his arms, sucking up ruby blood to test for antibodies, for enzymes and metabolites, for medication levels, for organ function. Medical students at various levels of training asked him the same questions over and over and over, as if they were interrogating a captured spy, trying to catch him in a deception. He began to feel like that's exactly what he was, a secret agent conducting espionage on a society he no longer belonged to. The world of the living. The country of here and now.

It was a land where he found himself stumbling. Once, getting lost in the bowels of the hospital after making a series of wrong turns on his way to the Nuclear Medicine clinic, he wandered in a restricted back door to the morgue, immediately stopping short: directly in front of him was a dead woman's body, lying naked on a steel table.

Her countenance was beautiful, serene. Hard to tell her age, maybe thirty or forty, not a worry on her face. But the entire front of her body was flayed open from neckbone to pubis, ribs cut away to expose the heart and lungs, intestines shoved to one side of the abdomen to reveal an empty space where the liver had been, and the brown glistening liver sitting on a stainless steel scale beside the body, the scale registering the liver's weight in kilograms, as if ready to be wrapped in white butcher paper and sold for dinner.

And that was all a shock, but it wasn't the biggest shock to Guy. What arrested him most was the cadaver's left hand. The back of it was dissected open, showing in fine detail the internal anatomy, the white tendons in their gristly sheaths, fused seamlessly to dozens of little red muscle bundles, woven through yellow globules of fat, purpling strings of blood vessels, gray knobs of bone, all the elaborate intricacies of the human hand... and her fingernails were still beautifully manicured, painted red and shaped an oval quarter inch long, meticulously done by someone who obviously cared a great deal about how she looked.

Now she just looked graphically, emphatically, dead. This was her here and now. All our conceits and hopes and silly modesties – this is what it was reduced to in the end. And this is where Guy was headed, whether he was handsome, or smart, or moral, or proud of his fingernails. This was his irrevocable future.

He backed out of the room in a thin chilly sweat and here's the thought that came to mind: Wouldn't it be right and proper if that meat on the table was not the end of the story?

When he finally made his way to Radiation Therapy, technicians painted a red target on his scalp – they called it a port – and lined it up carefully with the cross-hairs of the radiation gun. Guy lay very still as they shot his brain full of gamma rays every day, focused on the remains of the tumor, five times a week. It was a bit like carpet bombing the guerilla cancer cells into submission. It gave Guy hellish headaches, made him dizzy and exhausted, made him throw up so hard he tore muscles in his back. He wondered if it was just collateral damage from the bombing raids, or if something more subtle was going on – if this was, in fact, all part of the extreme interrogation technique of his surgical captors.

But he was able to tolerate the medical torture by focusing on something more compelling. Between radiation sessions, he read everything he could get his hands on that might help him divine the code of his seizure visions. He backed off a bit from the reincarnation model at first. If this was to be an academic inquiry, it should start out broad, delving into the whole expansive universe of the meaning of visions. He read about the vision quests of Indian *brujos*, scanned the writings of Castenada, studied the rites-of-passage dreams common to many of the more primitive religions. He investigated the role of hallucinogens in and out of laboratory settings, primarily LSD, peyote and mescaline. He made library calls for books chronicling Aboriginal walkabout tales, as well as the visions of seers, of witches, of telepaths, empaths, psychopaths.

But when all was said and done, he kept getting drawn back to where he'd started this maze. He didn't want to go there, he resisted that path for both intellectual and emotional reasons – until something he read struck

him one night, a zen koan: *The obstacle is the path.* So he decided to stop
resisting what now seemed inevitable. To look much more closely into the
concept of reincarnation.

He read texts and case studies, like the biography of Bridey Murphy, or
news accounts of Shanti Devi, the young Indian girl who seemed to know so
much about a distant village she'd never been to. Hinduism. Tibetan Bud-
dhism. Parapsychology. He pursued scientific tracts, as well. He found a
monograph in a biopsychology journal entitled "Inherited Memory," that
made some interesting points about the generational passage of genetic
information. Anything he could find in literature, poetry, religion, philosophy or science, anything that delved into the realm of the rebirth of the
soul – that's what became his sole focus of inquiry.

The distillation of all these library research efforts resulted in what might
be called the Cliff's Notes on Guy's understanding of reincarnation. This
understanding rested primarily on the Hindu paradigm, which, whether
totally correct or not, seemed to provide the most complete spiritual and
intellectual framework. The broad strokes went something like this:

It was as if there existed a great, mystic engine, a Great Wheel, that
installed old souls into physical bodies at the moment those bodies were
born into our earthly reality. The now soul-embodied living beings grew
and aged, learned and loved, gave and suffered pain. And when they finally
died, the engine extracted the souls from their corpses, like nut-meats from
the shell, and carried those eternal spirits into some karmic way station,
where they stayed until they were ready to inhabit a bright new future body
in the land of the living.

And the people we knew in each life, we were either drawn to or repulsed
by according to our experiences with them in previous lives – that is,
according to the karma we'd either burned off or stored up. Karma, that's
the Hindu reap-what-you-sow, what-goes-around-comes-around energy we
spend each physical life dealing with. We reap past accumulations of it, or
sow future pay-offs, both good and bad.

Ways to remember your last life, according to Hinduism: be open to
your strong likes and dislikes, embrace them, explore them until they shine
a light on the once-upon-a-time they came from; meditate back to those
infant months after you first drew breath, when the shock of being born

again thrust your last-life memories deep into your soul; know yourself, visualize who you truly are, to understand where you came from, where you are going; stay close to God.

He woke out of a deep sleep one night, just in time to have another seizure, another vision, this one so horrific, so powerfully sensate, he could smell the iron-tangy blood flowing from the limping woman's wound, feel her intestines twitch under his hand as he twisted the scalpel. It left him stunned in the morning and he couldn't stop throwing up. The doctors increased his Dilantin, to suppress the seizures completely. And so the dreams stopped.

The ringing in his ears – tinnitus his doctors called it, as if naming it controlled it – developed a more sonorous echo, less a ringing than a gonging. And along with the ringing he developed a left-sided hemiparesis causing him to favor that leg, giving him a slight limp – like the limping woman in his dream – which he theorized was physical evidence tying his two lives together.

"You can see, I've got a limp now," he told Alan. "Just like the murder victim in my dreams. Not that I think I'm the victim – I feel much more identified with the killer – but the limp is what connects me physically to the dream. To that previous life."

Alan paused to compose a response. "You don't think it's possible you've developed a limp because, hateful as this thought is, the cancer is spreading? Or even, in the best of worlds, because of some psychogenic cause related to your <u>wanting</u> there to be a physical connection to your dream, some 'proof' you lived a past life as a murderer who killed a woman with a limp, making <u>your</u> limp a particularly appropriate 'punishment' for having killed that woman?"

Guy said no, that was unlikely. Alan arranged for Guy to see a staff psychiatrist, Dr. Hoffman.

"Alan tells me you think you're being punished for some long ago transgression," said Hoffman, looking professionally concerned.

"That's how it feels. About 1880, judging by the clothes the killer is wearing in my dream."

"Why would you be punished for something that happened before you were born?"

"Maybe it was my same eternal soul inside that person."

The psychiatrist nodded, non-judgmental. "Why do you think you can suddenly see into a past life?"

"I don't know, that's a good question. I've thought about it a lot. It might be due to a diminution of other senses that the tumor destroyed, and that diminution is what's allowed me to appreciate this softer voice inside me. Or maybe it's the tumor itself. I mean it's a <u>brain</u> tumor, right? It's made up of brain cells. Brain cells are what create consciousness, so why shouldn't a brain tumor be conscious, as well?"

"You think your brain tumor is conscious."

"Maybe. Random nerve connections, able to think differently. Maybe it can sense past lives, maybe there's a wavelength for those images."

"Images of crimes in past lives. So the tumor is both the punishment for the bad thing you did, and the visionary organ by which you can see it. Is there anything you think you ought to be punished for in your <u>own</u> childhood? Your own 'past life,' as it were?"

Guy just stared at the shrink. Something about the pompous way he'd said "your own past life" was the final tipping point for Guy. It was no longer a question now, it had become an unshakable certitude in that moment, focused into perfect clarity by the lens of this therapist's skepticism. And Guy knew, as certainly as he'd ever known anything, that if he didn't follow the trail of his previous life now, he was dead.

That night when the nurse came in with his Dilantin dose, he put the fat pill in his mouth, swigged it down with a gulp of water. And when she left the room he took the pill out of his mouth, crushed it on the bed-stand with his dinner spoon, brushed the powder onto the floor. He did this with every dose for the next two days, and he could almost feel his blood levels of Dilantin dropping to nil.

On the evening of the third day Guy lay staring out the window at the auto and street lights twinkling in the vivid city night. No longer the poignant beauty of the daytime scene; there was a blackened, grainy quality to it, now, like old sixteen millimeter film jumping on bad sprockets. And the sounds all echoed and all the air was cruel. He felt raw, naked, vulnerable as a baby lying on the fast lane of the Santa Monica Freeway in the glimmering midnight. He was sure of it: tonight was showtime.

He rolled on his side so he wouldn't swallow his tongue, and propped the pillows all around him, as a cushion – didn't want to hurt his head when he started banging the bedrails convulsively, after all. He stared at the spectrum of the night; the wavelengths glittered as through a prism, scattered wild by a new crystal layer of reality, yellow clusters of street lamps hanging over the cityscape like stars in an upside down sky.

He smelled the perfume, the sensual musky aura of his altered state. He watched the red and white car lights moving along the distant roadways elongate into parallel lines and then the lines bent into crenellated turrets, etched in neon, crackling with that hoarse raspy bark across the inner membranes of his mind's ear....

Somewhere, a dog barks.

A gaslight flickers above an alleyway. A weathervane, shaped like a snarling wolf with rust-red teeth, turns slowly, creaking, silhouetted over a full moon balanced near the top of the sky. And a repetitive knocking, like a shutter banging in the wind.

An older man appears at the alley's maw. He's nineteenth century by his look. A disturbing scar runs from his left ear across his cheek down to his chin, like a twisted broken spine.

A pretty woman arrayed in purple bruises and tattered perfumed clothes walks past him on the cobbles. She has a limp. The scar-faced man flares his nostrils, as if aroused by the perfume, and follows her.

She quickens her pace, moistens her lips which have become dry with fear, with foreboding. He says something but the words are garbled, a strange and ancient language. Youyig... youyiguh... Youyiguhm... Ihuda... Guhmihudan... Youyiguhmihudan. Youyiguhmihudan... Youyiguhmihudan....

She shakes her head, she doesn't understand, she tries to reply, looking back at him as she keeps walking – her lips move but no sound comes out, as if she's too despairing to gasp, too terrified to get any air through her windpipe. He pulls a scalpel from his vest. It shimmers of ivory moonlight. He stabs her in the back. She falls, turning.

He slips the blade into her abdomen, twists. Her lips twist, as if mimicking his gesture. He pinches her lip hard, to still it, and turns the blade in her belly again until the beveled steel gets bound up in some glutted knot of tissue and he slices through that with a stroke, like a matador's flourish, and reaches his hand into the gash and comes out holding some slithery stump of organ. Blood gushes from the wound, pools around the knife, overflows her belly, cascades down her sides. Eyes glazed, she dips her finger in her own blood, writes two words on the ground. **RED CHAOS.**

*And then she writes something else. The numbers **2426.***

Somewhere, a dog barks. The moon is full. The repetitive, irregular knocking continues in the distance. The pretty woman dies.

A shovel is digging a grave. The knocking continues. The shovel rolls the pretty woman's body into the grave.

But her body plunges into a depth of dark water, a swath of pale light illuminating other floating, dead bodies.

And now, the tolling of bells....

He sat bolt upright in his hospital bed, the tolling of the bells loud in his ears. He thought, at first, it was another kind of tinnitus caused by the radiation treatments – but no, this was a far deeper sound, more resonant in tone and memory, more discordant as well. More bone-jarring. Bells he'd heard often, as recently as this past year. And he suddenly knew, as surely as if he were standing in the shadow of the thing, exactly where the tintinnabulation of these bells came from, where and when and what it was.

"St. Nicholas," he said to the dark room.

He slowly got to his feet. Silently dressed. Packed up his personal items in the drawer and the closet, left no trace he was ever here. Because now he knew what he had to do for the rest of his life. To save his mortal soul from the crushing karmic responsibility of killing that poor girl.

He had to go to Galway.

3

CHAPTER THREE

August 22, 2013
What Beast of the Soul

There was the aborted table-reading and there was the sharp surprise in the tuna sandwich. And now an hour after the razor had hit the soft tissue a solicitous nurse was directing Vic into the exam room of the E.R. at Sacred Heart Hospital on Franklin, where Vicky had just gotten sutured up with 6-0 Ethilon thread at the vermillion border of her lip, and dissolvable Vicryl on the inside, where the laceration ran down to the gutter of her lower gum. Sliced up her tongue, too, but the distracted doctor left that one unstitched, said it would most likely heal on its own if she stayed off solid foods for a couple days. Her mouth was puffy, red, molested. She looked pale and shaken, very Not Vicky. Vic walked up, hugged her with every sinew he had. She held onto him like a kid reunited with her favorite stuffed bear.

"You okay?"

"I guess." She touched her lip, ginger. It felt fat and numb. "You think it'll leave a big scar?"

"Hope so. Then nobody else will want you and you'll have to stay with me forever."

"Very fuckin' funny." So some of her brass was already returning, like color to her cheeks.

"I'm serious about staying with me, though. I don't want you going home tonight. We'll head straight to my place; I'll call my mother, tell her we can't make it for dinner."

Her face rouged with anger. "I'm going right back to rehearsal and I'm going to your mother's tonight and I am not about to start cowering in a corner just because some asshole thinks he can…."

"Don't worry, ma'am, we'll get the asshole."

They turned to see this Medicare aged guy standing in the doorway. Unfashionable tweed sport coat, flat Westside Chicago accent, hairline receded almost to the max, a comb-over waiting to happen and a face like a fallen soufflé. But still, far as you could tell, he didn't look like anybody's fool. He was holding up his badge.

"Detective Olivetti," he said. "I just have a few questions."

"Yeah, so do I," said Vic. "Like who the hell did this?" He gestured at Vicky's mouth. She looked appropriately aggrieved, though she kind of liked Vic taking charge as her spokesman and defender.

Olivetti shrugged at Vicky. "My bet, same guy who axed your car yesterday afternoon."

"Which I reported last night, which is, okay, technically less than 24 hours, but still, nobody ever got back to me about it."

"Okay, well, it's a big city, we're a little backed up, non-injury automotive vandalism isn't the top priority it used to be."

"It's gone a little farther than misdemeanor vandalism, don't you think?" said Vic.

"Which is why I'm here now." Olivetti wished the boyfriend wasn't around, trying to act all macho, but what are you gonna do? He kept his attention focused on the girl. "When this razor thing got called in a couple hours ago, your yesterday complaint popped up on the computer too. So my best guess, it's startin' to look like someone's targeting you."

"That's crackerjack detective work," said Vic. He usually didn't go in for sarcasm, but the attack on Vicky had him bent. Made him feel kind of ineffectual, too, like he was falling down on his job, his job in this case being to protect and care for his woman. So he took it out on the cop.

He didn't want to let himself get too angry, though, he'd been down that road and back. Learned some anger management techniques from a therapist his mother knew, strategies to prevent an explosion that might end up doing real damage to somebody, which he'd been known to do on occasion. Humor was one of those techniques – hence the sarcasm – and another tool was visualization. Make the object of your wrath the visual, physical representation of your attitude toward him. So when Vic called Olivetti a crackerjack detective, he saw the guy as a giant, overflowing box of Cracker Jacks standing before them. And he couldn't help but smile.

Olivetti'd seen this kind of passive-aggressive behavior before, this derision by a victim's loved one. The companion felt helpless, so apparently there was nothing to do but belittle the cop who was trying to help. It didn't much faze Olivetti anymore. So it didn't take all that much effort not to talk back. Long as it didn't go on and on. Just relate to the victim for the time being. "How's the lip doin' now?"

"It feels fat. Does it look fat?"

Right, she was an actress. Not too much drama queen, he hoped. He smiled sympathetically. "Looks great. Now you won't need collagen, right?"

She didn't think she liked this guy. Here he was making jokes about her vanity, like that was the biggest problem in the room. She didn't make much effort to hide her feelings, either, gave him one of those ha-ha smiles.

All the times in his life he'd helped ungrateful people, you'd think it'd just wash over him by now. Still atoning for all the wounded kids he hadn't saved back when he was a medic in Viet Nam, that's what the CPD shrink had told him once, while he was on 30 day suspension for that thing that had happened when he was hitting the bottle too much for a while. It was all horseshit, of course, but the shrink had gotten him into a program and back on the job, so maybe the guy'd had something on the ball after all.

Anyway, that was a while ago. And Olivetti still couldn't help taking care of people, whether they wanted it or not. And then feeling pissed off when they weren't grateful enough.

He touched her puffed up lip. "What you wanna do is, you wanna keep that iced up real good for a couple days, and here's a trick they won't mention – sleep sitting up, you know, with lots of pillows. That way it won't get even puffier overnight, the swelling'll drain down from your face." They looked at him curiously a moment and he shrugged. "I used to have a little medical experience."

Vic nodded, kind of a man-to-man thanks. The medical advice softened Vicky's attitude, too. Now that they were all old pals, Olivetti pulled out a plastic evidence bag with the razor in it. Held it up to Vicky. "Ever see this before you tried to eat it? The lab guys tell me it's a Triple O Cutt-Ex matt blade."

Vic and Vicky both shook their heads. But merely the sight of the razor made Vicky queasy again, made her lose some of her natural bravado, made her vision dim; she had to fight the urge to pass out. Told herself: I will not faint, godammit, not in front of this cynical balding flatfoot.

Vic got frustrated all over again. "Anybody on the set or the sandwich place could've slipped that razor in her food. I mean this is the 21st century, don't you guys know how to run a DNA on it?"

Olivetti counted silently to three before answering. "Yeah, we know how to run DNA, but first we'll probably have to talk to all those people you just mentioned, so it'd be nice if you two could narrow it down a little first." Olivetti wouldn't have minded taking Vic to the station, teach him some manners. But he was also realizing how shaken Vicky was, only barely holding it together. So he put his hand on her shoulder. "You look like a nice kid," he said gently. "Who wouldn't like you?"

The question knocked the air out of her. Snuck through all her defenses. Her eyes welled up. "I have no idea."

The sight of her like that brought Vic back down to earth, too. He just wanted to help. And then, casting about for any explanation that might lead somewhere, he remembered something. "That guy," he said.

She shook her head, knowing exactly who he was referring to. "I told you, couldn't have been him."

"Who?" said Olivetti.

Vicky rolled her eyes. Vic explained, "Some creep was beating on his girlfriend in the street yesterday, Vicky broke it up, and the guy wasn't real happy about it."

Olivetti to Vicky: "You know this guy?"

"Never saw him before, he burned rubber getting outta there, he didn't know me from Adam, he never saw where I went after he left; he couldn't have followed me, and nobody around there knows where I work, or even who I am, so please don't waste any time following that hot trail."

Olivetti nodded agreeably, like he was taking it under advisement.

Vic ventured another theory. "I thought maybe one of her old boyfriends, too, but she said no way."

"How about your old girlfriends?" Olivetti finally gave Vic his full attention, the guy seemed to want it so much. Guy looked like he might be stringin' a few babes along.

Vic just shrugged. "I dated around before Vicky. Nothing serious, mostly. Last steady girlfriend I had was years ago. Kendra Daly."

"You know where she's at now?"

The question caught Vic off-guard. He hadn't thought about Kendra in quite a while and it wasn't a great memory. "She was in an accident. Hit and run." He let it lay there a long moment, but Olivetti didn't pick it up, he just waited for the silence to play itself out, silence often being the best interrogator. And finally Vic finished his thought. "She's dead."

Joan, the character actress, was standing at the pay phone backstage, running her finger over the wall of scrawled phone numbers, names, emails, limericks. Found what she was looking for; she should have known it by heart by now, but she had a terrible head for numbers, they just flew in one ear and out the other. Dropped in her quarters, waited for the dial tone, punched in the numerals. Got her favorite take-out place; wasn't fast-food, it was just good.

"Hi, Oma, it's Joan from the Chi-Town Playhouse, yeah, time for dinner already, I'd like to order one Mu Shu Pork...."

Ratner, the old goat, insinuated himself behind her, grabbed her hips, boinked his pelvis into her ample backside. "Someone say pork?" That's the kind of dedicated romantic lead he was.

She started to take a swing at him with the phone receiver when Mark's sonorous directorial voice boomed out from the audience. "Let's go, places everyone! Act One, Scene Two, before I die of old age!"

Joan glared needles at Ratner, who merely gave her a courtly bow. "Milady," he said.

"Eat me," she glowered.

"After rehearsal, darling. Right now, the show must go on." He strode out to the stage.

Grabbed his script off a chair. Took his position in front of a wall being painted *trompe l'oeuil* bookshelves in a library. Stood there a beat, finding the moment, getting in character though not yet in costume.

A long beat later Otto burst onstage from the opposite wing. He was holding his script open, too. Nobody was off-book yet, everybody was running lines in the hallways.

Ratner was a professional, though, instantly inhabiting the part of the concerned Doctor, furrowing his brow at Otto, who was doing his best to look like a rattled medical student named Doyle.

"Mister Doyle," said Ratner with a certain studied curiosity, "you look as if you'd seen a ghost."

"I think I have, Doctor," replied Otto. "And remarkable as it may sound… he looked just like you."

"They say everyone has a double."

"And everyone has a shadow," Otto/Doyle added quickly, then lowered his voice in theatric reluctance: "But shadows don't glide off to make their own dark mischief in the middle of the night."

"Oh, but shadows do, Mister Doyle, shadows do."

This was a recurring theme in the play, the notion of our shadow selves, our darkness within and how it teases itself out, how we project it into the world like a shadow of the hell in our hearts. How we fear hell for our transgressions. Never understanding our transgressions are precisely what *create* hell, hell on earth, hells of our own conception and construction, personalized and precious.

While Will and Otto kept up their patter, Vicky stood backstage waiting to make her entrance. She'd insisted Vic bring her back here from the E.R., she didn't want to be a crybaby about the whole razor thing. Although it was nice that everyone made a big fuss over her when she did show up. She got lots of commiseration and indignation and stories of other cast members' oral catastrophes. Joan had locked braces with her boyfriend, age thirteen, resulting in lacerated gums and shredded pride. Teddy, at a school picnic, had lifted a can of Coke off the grass and taken a sip, only to get his tongue stung by a bee that had crawled inside and drunk itself silly. His tongue had swelled up to twice normal size and hurt like fuck, Teddy assured them all. Otto had a fight story, punched in the mouth, but he got his revenge because his front tooth cut the knuckle of the puncher and the cut was so badly infected by Otto's saliva, the man had to be hospitalized and nearly lost his hand. Ratner's tale, of course, had to do with injury from a defective battery-operated vibrating device, sustained while he was giving oral pleasure to a young lady who... but he was shouted down before he could finish.

So they all patted her or hugged her and went back to work. But she was having trouble staying focused. Among other things, she hadn't eaten all day, and now her mouth was too sore to chew. So Vic, the sweetheart, had made a run out to her favorite Cuban restaurant, *Habaneros*, even though it was all the way in Lincoln Park, and picked up a takeout quart of their *mojo de ajo*, this fabulous garlic soup that always made her feel better.

But even after the garlic soup she couldn't keep her mind from lurching around from thought to thought. Like who would do this to her? She knew it wasn't an old boyfriend, that made no sense. Well, maybe Tully made sense, he'd been crazy enough in the old days; but Tully was serving time and anyway that was so long ago she couldn't believe their fling still had any howl for him.

That's when she noticed someone out of the corner of her eye, watching her from the shadows. Her heart skipped, flashing that this was her nightmare man come to life, the faceless watcher with the small round hole for a mouth. And then she thought no, it's the offending slug who'd been tormenting her. She whirled around, to pin him – but it was only Teddy, the new kid, the teen actor, simultaneously trying to study her ass and hide a big crush. He waved sheepishly, soon as she nailed him with her gaze.

She got annoyed with herself for being so jumpy. So she tried to put him at ease, make it seem like she was turning to ask him a question. "My hair all up?" she said.

He seemed surprised that she was talking to him. "What?"

"I'm the fiancée in this scene and the fiancée is wound up tight as a nun's ass. I can't have any loose hair."

"Got kind of a little flyaway thing happening over here," he said. He held up a paper clip. "Paper clips, you can't have too many. I carry 'em everywhere, they're like an all-purpose lifehack." He tucked in a loose strand at the back of her neck, fixed it in place with his clip. He had a gentle touch.

She glanced over her shoulder at him with a smile she couldn't stop from looking flirtatious. It was just hardwired into her. "Thanks."

"Lookin' good," Teddy nodded, touching her stitched lip. "But isn't this taking the 'stiff upper lip' thing kinda far? I mean, you didn't have to come back this afternoon."

But she stiffened when he touched her – she really really really did not want to be touched right now. Especially right there, where she'd been violated. So she brought her hand up to Teddy's mouth, paused, and poked <u>his</u> lip, to show him what it felt like. To have your space invaded and jabbed at like that. There you are, darling, she thought sarcastically – and swiveled around, entering stage left.

Never noticing that Vic had been watching this whole interaction from high in the rafters. It was one of the safe, dark places he liked to sit sometimes and watch all the theatrical activity bubbling below him. Just now he'd been watching and wondering about the meaning of Teddy ogling Vicky's legs, then fondling the hair at the back of her neck and then touching her lip. Where the hell did he get off touching any damn part of Vicky? Vic didn't like it; didn't like it at all. And then Vicky had turned around and touched <u>Teddy's</u> lip with that little sparkle she flashed at men sometimes.

Vic felt his teeth clench, then let his jaw hang loose for five seconds, then deep breathed from the diaphragm – those were a couple tricks his anger management teacher had shown him. And they seemed to be working pretty good, he didn't really get in rages anymore the way he used to. And he wasn't now, either. Anyway, it was stupid to even worry about, this business between Vicky and the kid was simply more actor bonding, Vic supposed. He just didn't care for it all that much.

Meanwhile Vicky was walking up to Ratner's character onstage with a hint of aggressive impatience, finally speaking up with her entrance line. "There you are, darling. The guests are arriving, and…"

"…and you felt somehow compelled to interrupt my train of thought with one of your frivolous…"

She slapped him. Hard. And here's the thing: that wasn't in the script. It just came out of her. Kind of an explosion, from all the other crap that had been building. The unfaced nightmare man, the spraypainted WHORE on her battered car, the sandwiched razor blade, the less-than-sympathetic E.R. doc, the painful stitches, swollen tongue, the plodding detective, the kid poking her lip – and whap! Ratner got the brunt. There was an astonished silence, then he pulled himself together in a hurry. He was, after all, an actor first and foremost. So he stayed in character, in the moment, in the lime-light, and didn't break stride.

"Perhaps we can continue this conversation later, my dear," he said stiffly, speaking as the Doctor.

Joan entered, curtsied. "Sir, the Spanish ambassador and his wife are waiting."

"Yes, well," said Ratner. "We'd best go see them, then."

He held out his arm to Vicky. She took it and accompanied him back-stage, as Joan and Otto continued the scene in the library, discussing how oddly the Doctor had been acting of late – a scene that worked even better in the wake of Ratner's way-too-mild response to Vicky's ad-libbed wallop.

In the wings, Vicky turned to Ratner with an apologetic blush. "Will, I'm so sorry, I don't know what I was thinking of."

Mark hopped up onstage from his director's chair, into the wings. Dark, brooding intensity, his ponytail bobbing with excitement. He took Vicky's hands in his hands, held her eyes in his gaze, her spirit in his thrall. "That was brilliant."

"Vicky was simply following her intuition, which is, of course, what an actor must do," said Will. He was beginning to own the slap. In future sto-ries, he'd tell people the slap was <u>his</u> idea. Or that he'd whispered something personally, offensively sexual, to <u>make</u> her slap him.

Vic came over. "I guess that's why I'll never be an actor. I don't have an ounce of intuition in me. I don't even believe in it."

"Oh, but you must, sir." Ratner was expounding now. "Intuition is an ancient and sacred sense we've nearly lost, one of the greatest losses of the so-called civilized world. But we can find it if we listen carefully to our instincts, if we stay open." He lowered his voice, as if to impart an acting pearl, not for everyone. "And you never know what beast of the soul it will bring."

The evening was another notch cooler than the night before, another inkling of the change of season. Like a premonition of autumn; an intuition, Ratner might say. In the chill, Vic took Vicky to his mother's for dinner.

Gloria had a decrepit, two-story brown shingled house in Hyde Park, on Blackstone near 56th. Smaller than most in that area. But there was a big back yard and a double-size garage she used for storing easels, tools, paints and found objects she expected might come in handy for some project some day.

Vic got off the Drive at 53rd, then cruised up Dorchester until he turned up his mother's block. Parked his Chrysler in the driveway. They got out, he took Vicky's arm, they walked up to the front steps.

"I look okay?" he asked. He was wearing the black suede jacket she'd given him. It was like the weather had turned just so he could wear her present.

"Yeah, you look great. Don't be nervous."

He eyeballed her up and down. She'd put on a white cotton knit shift, simple but sleek. Hair up, hoop earrings, strappy heels. "You're too gorgeous for me."

"I know." She gave his butt a squeeze. "Let's go, Baby."

As they walked up the front steps, he said, "I happened to notice this morning, my lease runs out in a couple months; I'm thinkin' I should just move in with you now. You know, be easier with the play and all."

She smiled as they reached the landing. The door opened and Gloria stood there beaming: a handsome, middle-aged woman with white hair askew, oil paint smudged on her cheek, jeans and a torn pullover. She stood him back at arm's length, rubbed her fingers over the soft black suede and burgundy satin of his jacket. "This is nice, Victor. Where'd you get it?"

"Vicky gave it to me."

"Trying to class you up? Won't work."

"Tell me about it," said Vicky.

The women hugged.

"Come on, you're not going to stand outside all night, are you?" Gloria ushered her son into the house, Vicky right behind him.

The place was what some people might call shabby. Unashamedly artsy-fartsy, Gloria would say. Her paintings hung all over the walls, frame to frame with the work of various friends. Other items – sketches, recycled canvas, studies, lithographs – sat in piles on tables, on chairs, in corners on the floor. Kind of a joyous mess.

Vic didn't see anything resembling dinner preparations. "Are we early?"

"No, I'm late, as usual. Couldn't get that new epoxy to dry fast enough on the assemblage I'm doing." She noticed the stitches on Vicky's swollen lip. "What happened to your lip, sweetie?"

"Just a little accident, it's not worth talking about." She didn't want to give it any more air time, so she changed the subject. "Need any help in the kitchen, Gloria?"

"Yeah, buy me a stove that works, set the table, mix me a Wild Turkey rocks and break out the wine in the cupboard for yourself; I'm going to get dressed." And she was on her way up the narrow steps to the bedroom upstairs.

Wine and bourbon fueled a working class meal of lamb stew and black bread. The pre-industrial feel was matched by the lighting – all candles, subtly scented – and there was a kind of jolly bohemian atmosphere about the whole deal. French gypsy tango music from the '30s played quietly on the stereo, vinyl spinning. The art that lined the walls included everything from figurative oils to movie posters to Chinese calligraphy to the guts of an old tube radio spray-painted purple. Gloria herself had transformed into an artwork of sorts, wearing an elegant Argentine ball gown accessorized with a Disneyland tiara in her hair. But still paint smudged on her face.

She was regaling them with chatter Vic had heard many times. "Art isn't the stuff, art is the spirit <u>inside</u> the stuff."

Vicky nodded. "Well, stuff is just matter, and physicists talk about matter being nothing but another kind of energy, right? So… oh!" Vicky stopped mid-sentence, staring at Vic. The way he was sitting, wine glass tipped, the dancing lights reflecting in his curved goblet, the gentle fragrance of the rose-scented candles, the gypsy fiddle underscoring it all… it was like she'd been here before, witnessing this very moment.

"'Oh' what?" said Vic.

"I just had a *déjà vu*," she said.

"I don't think *déjà vu* exists," said Vic.

"You can't say it doesn't exist. People have it. You can say you don't get it, if you want."

"Okay, I don't get it. It's not logical and you can't measure it or hammer it."

"Life isn't logical or holdable or measurable, though, Victor," said Gloria. "It's miraculous and inconceivable and *sui generis* and *outré*."

Vicky raised her glass. "To what she said."

They lifted their glasses and drank. Vic gazed at Vicky the way lovers do and decided this was the moment. He turned to Gloria. "Mom – we're getting married."

Gloria, for all her urban sophistication and devil-may-care facade, was unprepared for the news. Waited a beat too long. "That is terrific. God bless you." She wagged her finger at Vic. "See, Victor? I told you it was lucky she had the same name as you."

"Actually you said it was bad luck but who's counting?"

"Good luck, bad luck, it's all the same thing. Once you understand that, you've got it made." And then, to Vicky: "Now stand up and let me give you a proper hug."

She rose to embrace Vicky, but in the process knocked a glass of the red all over the girl's white dress. "Oh, God, I'm so sorry, sweetie."

"No, no, it's fine."

"You'll need lots of salt to absorb it. I'll get the box." But as she turned toward the kitchen, she whacked her knee on the corner of the table, sank back to her chair with a groan. One of those situations that just keeps getting worse the harder everyone tries.

"Stay," said Vicky. "I can find the salt."

She headed for the kitchen, leaving Vic and Gloria alone.

"You're not happy about this, are you?" asked Vic.

"It's not Vicky. It's not even a real problem. It's just… I remember what you went through after Kendra died. I don't want to see you torn up like that again."

He'd in fact become darkly depressed, holed up in his room. That notched up to drinking heavily, big chip on his shoulder, there were a couple bar fights that could have ended badly. He nearly beat one guy to disability. It wasn't long after that he got a new job, new attitude, got back on track. Met Vicky.

Vic took Gloria's hand now. "Mom, listen to me. I love Vicky and the weird amazing thing is, she loves me back. I want to be with her the rest of my life. And nothing's going to happen to her. I'm not going to lose her."

"Losing someone isn't the only danger in getting too close, you know."

"Meaning what?"

She wanted to tell him that sometimes getting too close could be dangerous all by itself. The closeness made you vulnerable and that's when all kinds of wicked things happened, she could tell him… but she couldn't. So she just smiled sadly, put her palm on his cheek. And then Vicky returned, and the moment was over.

Vic rose to pull out Vicky's chair for her. Watching her walk up to him, she was so beautiful, so part of him already, he was sure everything was going to be all right.

Vic dropped her off at her place when the evening was over. He had to spend the night at his old apartment one last time because he had to meet his landlord first thing in the morning to go over everything. But Vicky was so tipsy and tired when she got home, she just had time to undress before she passed out on the bed.

Half an hour later the stalker let himself into Vicky's place by the back door with a lock pick and silently crossed to the bedroom. He stood at the foot of the bed, just staring at her for a few minutes – naked, sleeping the deep sleep of the pleasantly drunk.

He imagined all the things he could do to her. He could kill her before she even woke up. He didn't want to do that, though. Not now, not yet.

He took out a dropper bottle and walked to the head of the bed. Carefully dripped a few drops of chloral hydrate into Vicky's mouth. She smacked her lips and rolled away – almost woke up from the taste – but settled back down quickly enough so that the next few drops he squeezed between her lips went down without protest. Soon she was in a deep, drugged sleep.

The watcher took down his pants and rubbed himself on Vicky's foot. Up her leg. He straddled her, fondled her. Grabbed her hand and wrapped it around himself, wrapped his own hand around hers, rubbed their hands up and down, to his groaning release. Rubbed the results all over her face.

Then he took a lipstick out of her purse and painted big clown lips all around her mouth. Painted her breasts with it, too, and her palms, and the soles of her feet. She didn't move a muscle.

Finally he pissed into a half-full bottle of Merlot standing on the bedside table. Then he got dressed, stuffed a small wad of laundry down the toilet and left by the back door, laughing all the way to his car, imagining the show he'd see live-streaming on his computer when she woke up in the morning.

4

CHAPTER FOUR

August 8-September 6, 1976
Pleasure, With Pain For Leaven;
Summer, With Flowers That Fell

Guy landed at Dublin airport two days later. It was evening by the time he caught a bus into the city, so he changed his money, found a small hotel south of the Liffey and sat in the Temple Bar drinking Guinness to a fiddle and squeezebox duo until it was time to catch the night bus to Galway. He boarded the bus, exhausted, and fell asleep immediately. When he was jostled awake in the morning, he found himself in Dingle – over 150 miles south down the coast from Galway. He'd taken the wrong bus.

Dingle was a little seaside town. He walked around enough to establish most of the shops were either pubs or hair salons and ended up in *An Droichhead Beag,* a Gaelic bar on lower Main Street where he ate beef and Guinness stew until he dozed off. He awoke to an older gent playing on the Uillean pipes. When the song was over, Guy asked the man if it was *Donkey Rider* he'd been playing and the fellow said, "Could well ha' been, lad."

He walked back to the station in time to catch a bus going north. There were sheep everywhere, and green rolling hills edged by low stone walls covered in moss. A most pretty country, as Guy remembered. The bus passed

Bunratty Castle and ended up in Doolin that evening in a dense, chilly mist. Also as Guy remembered.

He ate at O'Connor's Pub, a steamy family place, and slept in the station that night. Caught a bus to Galway the next morning, ditched his suitcase at the hotel next to the station, and walked. Past Eyre Square, left on William Street, all familiar territory from the segment of his sabbatical research semester he'd spent on Yeats. William Street became Shop Street at Lynch Castle, twisting and cobblestoned, flooded with the end-of-summer tourist crowd bustling all around him.

He remembered loving Galway. The craft shops and stalls, the street musicians, the pubs, the booksellers – they evoked a time gone by that didn't exist in America anymore, if it ever did. Not to mention people speaking Gaelic, which sounded to Guy like Arabic with a Norwegian accent. Of course there were boom boxes here, too, and they slammed him back into 1976 in a hurry: Strains of ABBA singing *Mamma Mia*, Donna Summer's breathy *Love to Love You, Baby*, or Wild Cherry doing *Play That Funky Music White Boy* drifted out of half the diners, grocers and parks. In 1976 pop music was American even on this side of the pond.

He started to cross Abbeygate Street, looking left for cars – when a horn screamed at him from the right and someone's hand yanked him back onto the curb just in time to save him from the swerving minibus.

"You all right, Yank?" asked the shaggy coiffed Rod Stewart wannabe with a guitar slung over his back, yellow brown teeth from a lifetime of cigarettes and tea.

Guy nodded, shaken. "Yeah. Thanks. I always forget about how you Brits drive on the wrong side of the road here."

"Right. Just don't call these Irish sods Brits, or you'll wish you'd been hit by a lorrie instead."

The Brit walked down Abbeygate and Guy proceeded along Shop Street into a growing throng of locals, tourists, hippies, Christian proselytizers preaching Gospel, sheep farmers, buskers and drunkards, past news agents, betting parlors and woolens stores to a Commons with an open air market that backed onto a string of pubs and fronted on the Church of St. Nicholas, a great medieval stone structure of naves and spires, dedicated to the patron saint of sailors. Guy stared at the church as if he were waiting for something. But nothing came.

What now? he wondered.

He'd heard the bells of St. Nicholas in his last seizure, so his previous life must have happened here, within earshot of where he was standing. They were characteristic bells, some of them cracked and out of tune back in the day, so Guy was certain this was the locale in his seizure dream. But Galway was a warren of lanes and the sound of the bells could carry for miles on the wind. So where to look? What to gloss over, what to notice? How to know when he found something?

The choices were overwhelming, the damp thick August air suffocating. Guy had the urge to return to his hotel and lie down, try to think it through. But that was just fear talking and he really had nothing to be afraid of. After all, what was the worst that could happen to a man already dying of brain cancer? Get into a dicey situation and die of something else? Big deal. He walked across the street to *Taaffe's* pub, ordered a pint, sat at an outside table and watched the church while he ordered his thoughts, as a duo played fiddle and bodhran inside the tavern.

He was being careful. He was on his anti-seizure meds again, for one thing. He didn't think it would be a good idea to start inadvertently convulsing in a foreign city, in traffic, on a riverbank, out alone at night. That would be counterproductive. So he was doing everything his doctors had told him to do, striving to keep the machinery of his body intact long enough to translate the encoded images of his spirit.

For another thing, he'd cashed in all his savings so he wouldn't get caught short; he'd have enough money to last, by all expectations, the rest of his life. That was only about a year, of course, but if his quest was successful, and if he rectified the wrongs of his past, who knows? With any luck at all he could buy himself more time. But no matter what the outcome, this was no moment for timidity. It was a moment for bold moves.

He was ready to take on Galway. It was a middling sized town, yes, but it was finite. A man who walked, who just started walking, and walked every day, down every street, up every alley, around every mews, might cover every inch of pavement. Might see a clue, an indicator. And if not, might start over and see something he'd missed the first time. So: there was nothing to do but start.

He started with the church itself. Explored all the nooks and crannies, read all the plaques. Built in 1320, it had always been the church of sailors in this port town. Christopher Columbus had worshipped here in 1477, doubtless contemplating his leap of faith to the New World. Oliver Cromwell's army had looted it in 1650, turning it into a stables for his army during the Siege of Galway, part of the British colonization of Ireland. None of this helped Guy, though; nor did the church records he was able to peruse. It was time to examine the city.

He picked a direction more or less at random. And he limped into the haze.

He criss-crossed streets in the city centre, assiduously scanning the buildings, especially the older ones. No apartment, shop, office complex or museum escaped his piercing scrutiny. He walked along the River Corrib, watching the swans float on the calm sections, sensing the power of the plunging whitewater where it rushed under the bridges. Salmon Weir Bridge, past Wolfe Tone Bridge to Galway Bay. The docks, the Claddagh fishing village, its dark night shadows and blind alleys unsettling, but ultimately without incident.

Sometimes he'd go into an aging red brick library, wander through the musty stacks, or go over the microfiche of old newspapers, letting his gaze wander, half-focused, until it landed on some article of potential interest. He never knew what he was looking for exactly; ever hopeful he'd know it when he saw it. A memory. A feeling. A sign.

Days passed thus. His limp was sometimes better, sometimes a little worse. When it really gave him trouble he found he liked to sit in old pubs, nurse a pint, scribble the conundrums of his life in his journal. He'd written out all the details of the seizure dream he could remember – the full moon, the wolf weathervane, the killing – but lately he'd begun sketching his memories, as well: the scar-faced older man, whose shadows seemed to emerge from within him; the pretty young woman he'd murdered, her expression stunned at her collision with death. The faces, the knife strokes, the shovel digging the grave, the bodies floating in water, like specimens in a jar.

The drawings had emotional power but they never quite captured either the kinetic dark energy of the dream state, or the precise physical character-istics Guy had seen in his mind. Still, he kept at it – doing the drawings over and over, embroidering the detail each time, finding nuances, shading glances. He'd taken a few life-drawing classes years before and he wasn't half bad for an amateur. Of course he'd lost some of his skills, but he was highly motivated now to get them back. To draw things the way he truly saw them. The way they were, once upon a time.

It was while he was drinking his second black and tan at the *Tig Coili* not far from St. Nick's that something struck him. He was doing a pencil drawing of the woman, the murder victim, as she lay dying, her life running out on the cobblestones. She'd written **RED CHAOS** in blood on the pave-ment in a kind of desperate scrawl. But now, for the first time, Guy remem-bered another detail he'd forgotten until that moment. He remembered that she'd written something else, something he'd only glimpsed during his last seizure episode. She'd written the numbers **2426**.

He wrote the numerals on his sketch pad and stared at them. Tapped them with his finger. Stood up and walked over to the barman.

"Excuse me. Where can I find a map of Galway? A map with street num-bers?"

From City Hall, it turned out. It also turned out not many places had the address 2426. He exhausted the few that did in an afternoon. Maybe he needed to look for a permutation of 2426. Such as 242/6, meaning apart-ment 6 at the address 242. Or possibly 24-26, a duplex, both houses inclu-sive. So he compiled a list of all the possibilities and set off.

The Latin Quarter, the Claddagh, all around the Lough, even out to Salt-hill. There was a hotel numbered 2426, a house, a tobacconist, an empty lot, a print shop, a grocer, another house, an apartment building, and on and on. Nothing looked familiar. Nothing rang a bell from his nightmare.

Even so he spent hours at each place, going inside if he could, tracking down its history in the library or hall of records when possible, talking to neighbors and tenants and sweet old ladies at the Historical Society. Nothing revealed itself.

A couple weeks passed this way, with Guy waking, walking, talking, writing and drawing, all in a kind of vaporous immersion. He slept badly, shaved intermittently, ate irregularly. He thought of it as his *Take It To the Limit* period, since the Quaalude addict in the hostel room next to his played nothing but the Eagles' *One of These Nights* tape on his boom box, and mostly just that track.

Summer insinuated itself into September without Guy being fully aware of the fact. The weather outside turned drizzly; the weather within him much the same. Evenings chilled with fog, leaves became jaundiced, fell, browned, got trampled and matted on the ground. Guy was lost, deeply lost.

By the end of the first week in September the rains passed, the air got crisp. Guy was losing weight, his eyes looked a little hollow. He spent his days hobbling aimlessly or drawing in his journal; people took him for an artist, or a leftover hippie, or a down-on-his-luck mendicant, or a cancer patient on the dole, which was, of course, closest to the truth of the matter.

He lame-gaited and peered and concentrated and zoned out in this way until the afternoon he wandered along a row of downscale shops selling antiques, mostly forgeries, strictly tourist, and happened to glance in a window.

And there was the wolf weathervane. Against all odds, just like the one in his dream. A small sound escaped his lips, like the startled cry of a lost child seeing its mother, as if the cry itself were racing to get home.

Guy hurried inside, took the weathervane from the display to inspect it closely, his heart racing with anticipation. It was a foot long, a snarling wolf cut out of some kind of metal alloy, something with copper, by the dull glint of turquoise that mottled its length. The beast's mouth settled wide in a howl, its tail came to a nasty point. Guy ran his delicate fingers over the corroded surface, caressing the snout of the wild thing, trembling over its crooked, rusted teeth. This was it, he was certain, nothing else looked just like this, he almost held it to his heart, it was like discovering the grail, he found himself close to sobbing.

"Fancy that, do you, lad?" the shopkeeper said, coming up behind him.

Guy jumped, and cut his finger on the thin edge of the wolf. A drop of blood welled up like a little bubble. Guy wiped it on his pants. "Yes, I was curious, actually."

"Twelve pounds; a bit steep I know, but hand-tooled, a real nineteenth century antique, that is, to be sure."

"Where did you get it?"

"Interesting story, that. I got three of 'em from a party said she found 'em cleaning up an old gardener's shed, said she thinks there's more in the cellar, too, been there Lord knows how long."

"Where, though?" Guy interrupted impatiently. "Can you tell me where exactly it came from?"

The shopkeeper smiled cagily. "Could do, lad, but then you might buy one direct from the source."

"I'll buy every damn one you have!" Guy shouted. "Just give me the address!"

The shopkeeper sold him every damn one. And the address for five bob extra. It was 2426 Old Mews Road, Kinvarra.

It was actually a bit outside of Kinvarra, about 30 miles south of Galway, along the coast. Guy rented a car, and driving on the wrong side nearly had accidents twice, one very nearly serious. Driving seated on the right seat of the car while cruising the left side of the road, he couldn't judge distances to the soft shoulder, and kept scraping the left side of the car on hedges and fences. Eventually he got the hang of it, meandering all around the area for a while until he finally found the proper turn-off and curved gently up a long, narrow countryside road through verdant, small hills and the prettiest yellow wildflower. The usual low, mossy stone walls wound up and down the greenscape like ancient serpents. Finally a tiny hamlet emerged, hardly a dozen cottages, followed by more open spaces, until at last he came to a scattering of estates, some circled by walls that enclosed gardens, lawns, out-buildings, a few highly manicured, others more long gone to seed.

And then the largest estate of all, its rambling acreage surrounding a tree-enclosed structure set back some distance from the road. He parked down the lane, walked until he came upon what looked like the front gateway; tried it, but it was locked.

He set off, in his asymmetric gait, along a high stone wall that went on for fifty or sixty yards, then rounded a corner, where it turned into a tall, wrought-iron fence, cemented in place. Guy peered through the ironworks like a child staring through the gates of the old haunted house at the edge of town.

The grounds were smothered in overgrown gardens. Weeping willow, out of control ivy, climbing trumpet vine with wine-red blossoms littering the ground, great swaths of shaggy grass and briar all vied for control of the landscape.

Toward the back of the property Guy could see a small, paint-peeled gardener's cottage. And turning slowly atop the roof of the cottage: a wolf weathervane.

The hair on the back of his neck stood up, adrenalin-prickly. This was the place. The very place of his vision. He could hardly believe it, he could hardly stand it, his impulse was to run until he was far, far away. But he had to go closer. Didn't he? Had to enter this estate, this world? To seek his destiny?

He stood there a long moment, his heart thumping, forgetting to breathe, then gasping paroxysmally. He brought his face up close, sniffed the aging bars. They smelled like iron. This was no vision, no altered plane of existence. It was real iron, the stuff of this earth.

A distant church bell clanged. The stuff of the earth, the toll of the bell. Saved by the bell. Guy remembered that in 17th-century England, when grave robbers disinterred corpses to sell to anatomists, they sometimes found fingernail scratchings on the inside of the coffin lid. People, it seemed, were occasionally being buried alive. After that the recently deceased were sometimes laid to rest with a long string inside the casket, connected to a bell outside, so if they woke up in suffocating blackness and mortal terror, they could pull the string and be… saved by the bell.

Guy's entire life, his daily existence up until this moment – that, he now realized, was his coffin. He'd been suffocating in darkness and scratching at the lid for years; as good as dead. And now here was his wake-up call, pealing from the church tower, ringing him into new life. Saving him by the bell.

Guy planted his paresthetic foot firmly on a smithied iron leaf, climbed the two meter fence and dropped to the ground on the other side.

Quietly he made his way to the small cottage all the way at the back. Fifty yards to his left the main estate loomed, like Mandalay, overlooking the grounds. One of those grand Victorians, four stories, five steeples, seven gables, innumerable widow's walks from which the British lord who'd taken over this tract of the Emerald Isle could survey his little piece of the Empire. Guy stayed in the farther shadows of the tangled overgrowth to avoid casual observation from that direction. But halfway to the cottage, not far from a cluster of massive ferns… he smelled a certain something.

He paused. He sniffed the air. What was it? Something familiar, something musty, something perfumed….

It was the perfume of his seizure. It was the aura, the herald of the next convulsion, one of the cardinal signs rising up now despite his having taken all his Dilantin. Or had he forgotten to take it? No, he was sure of it, every dose; but there it was, getting stronger now, the musky perfume. Any moment might come the corrugated lights, signaling an imminent event. Guy took Alan's warning seriously: if he was out in the world when this happened, find a soft place to lie on his side so he wouldn't fall, wouldn't hit his head, wouldn't gag on the secretions in his mouth once the seizure was full upon him.

His pulsebeat quickened, he looked around anxiously. The ground was soft and damp surrounding the ferns. He ran over to the biggest one, lay down under a large frond, positioned himself on his side and waited for the seizure to come. The aromatic scent was almost overpowering. He closed his eyes, expecting the turret-shaped lights to appear any moment, to flash across his visual field, to bring the twitching and twisting corrugations.

"Might I ask why you're lying down in my garden, then?" a woman's voice said in a lilting Irish accent.

Guy opened his eyes with trepidation. A lady's feet stood before him, wearing designer sandals. He tilted his head up a flowing, flowered Laura Ashley dress, to the face of a twenty-something young woman with black hair in a thick braid and a gaze in her liquid blue eyes that arrested him, drew him like an eddy teasing a leaf to its center.

Guy's nostrils flared. "That perfume," he said with stunned realization. "You're wearing it."

"You wouldn't want me to drink it now, would you?" She smiled with great good humor. But there was an intensity to her as well, a curiosity and an intelligence, as if she were looking deep into his marrow, as if she recognized something or someone there, but wasn't quite sure what.

He sat up unsteadily. "I'm sorry, I could have sworn I was about to have a seizure."

"Yes, I'm told I often make men swoon."

"No, I mean I have epilepsy."

"I'm sorry, then, I didn't mean to joke." The smile melted off her face.

"No, that's all right."

"Of course many great men of letters have had epilepsy, to be sure, to be sure," she said. "Lewis Carroll, Charles Dickens, Poe, Dante, Dostoyevsky. So perhaps you're also an extraordinary writer. Although, I must say – admiring the fern, as you seemed to be – I'd rather hoped you were here to take the gardener's job."

"What job is that?"

"Reshaping the yard. The pay is poor but we offer free quarters in the gardener's cottage over there and the garden's yours to mold – not that we have any mold in the garden," she added quickly, as an afterthought. And then, as another afterthought, she smiled brightly once more and extended her hand. "My name's Claire Deloup, with a silent P, to distinguish it from Claire de Lune, the enchanted wood nymph who only danced in the silvery moonlight to the accompaniment, one presumes, of the Debussy melody named after herself."

He pulled himself up with her hand, standing hesitantly. "Guy Daniels. And I don't dance, I'm afraid."

They studied each other closely as they continued holding hands for a moment longer than the situation warranted. She had an open face, with a wanting about it. Corvid black hair, upturned Irish nose, lips about to smile, Atlantic blue eyes, fathomless and romantic and occasionally glistered by something like lightning low on the horizon.

She was stirred by Guy's own deep gaze, sensitive mouth, that shock of sandy hair falling across his face as if he were trying to hide, but he couldn't really hide from her, though he tried concealing his embarrassment by unhanding her hand and retreating to one of the commoner banalities.

"How do you do?" he said with a small dip of his head.

"Quite well, thanks." Her eyes twinkled and she curtsied, to tease him just a bit, then continued: "But you look thirsty for something. Come on, this way then, we'll just go to the kitchen, it's right 'round back."

As she led him toward the back of the mansion he pointed to the small out-building. "I was noticing that weathervane from the street."

"Beautiful work, isn't it? It was made for my husband's family; his name's Deloup, of course, which means 'of the wolf,' in French." She affectionately rubbed her minimally bulging belly. "And here's my little wolf cub." She was hardly showing but always subliminally aware of this miracle growing inside her.

She took him past the only really cared-for section of garden on the lot, a small luxuriant area of rose, lily and marigold under the rear window – and from there, in the back door to a wonderful old kitchen with copper sinks, butler's pantries, even a wood-burning stove. She filled a glass with tap water and handed it to him.

"Thanks."

"Not at all," said Claire. "I can remember what it was like to be a starving actress."

"Is that what I look like?"

"Well, the starving part, anyway."

"I think I may've neglected to eat today."

"Here, let me fix you…."

"No, really, that wasn't a subtle hint for you to feed me."

"Well… it wasn't subtle, anyway."

They smiled at each other. It felt so easy between them, as easy as if they'd been friends a long time already.

She took two jars down from a cupboard, along with a loaf of bread, and began spreading. "I was born in Galway, but moved to the States and lived in Ohio until I was six," she explained, "so peanut butter and jelly is still comfort food to me."

"I got much comfort eating bangers and beans the time I spent in England on my dissertation."

"Really? What did you do it on?"

"*Man's Dual Nature In Nineteenth Century Literature.* I focused mainly on Stevenson's *Jekyll and Hyde,* and the influences Yeats had on it."

"I didn't know Yeats and Stevenson were acquainted."

"It's my pet theory." He took a bite of the comfort food. And again, they shared a tender smile. "Why'd you leave Ohio?" he asked.

"My father was in the diplomatic corps. After a bit of bouncing around he got stationed at the embassy in Dublin. And there we stayed."

"They still live there?"

"They died in a car accident when I was eighteen, I'm afraid. My brother, too, he was with them."

"I'm sorry. I guess we're both orphans, then."

"Orphans of the storm." It occurred to her in that moment that she wanted not to let him go. "So if you're not here about the job, why were you in my garden?"

"I was looking at your weathervane. I think I've been dreaming about it."

"Weathervane dreams. Quite revealing."

"How, pray tell?"

"Well, weather is a female characteristic, don't you know – storms, turbulent emotion, wild nature – and vanes tell direction. So since a person is all the parts of his dreams, in these dreams you are clearly seeking the direction of your feminine self."

"My inner woman. I guess that makes you and me girlfriends."

"Good. I could use a girlfriend." The melancholy within her rose even closer to the surface, like tears from the depth of those Galway eyes. She hadn't planned on sharing so much of herself so she took a moment to put her feelings away and offer a social smile. "Come on, then. I'll show you the house."

They walked down the grand hall; once grand, anyway, now a little tattered around the edges. The Ottoman Empire carpet was worn through in spots, the original William Morris wallpaper curling back at the top corners and chewed on by earwigs. Stained-glass sconces, once gaslit, were now electric but hardly less feeble. A long row of dusty aged oil paintings lined the dim hallway. Guy gestured to this family gallery.

"Dukes of yore?"

"My husband's ancestors. Lords of the manor for two centuries."

"I love portraiture – actually I did quick sketches in college...." But he stopped in front of one of the paintings and caught his breath, the hairs on his arms tingling.

The picture before him was a formal, 1850s portrait of a young nobleman – a nobleman who happened to look remarkably like the old scar-faced man in Guy's epileptic vision. Except this young Victorian gentleman had no scar on his cheek. And he looked thirty years younger than the scarified murderer Guy had dreamed of – as if this youthful fellow in the painting were *before*, and Guy's hideous nightmare killer were *after* – but what horrifying sequence of life events had befallen the man in the portrait to bring him to such an act of brutal homicide, Guy couldn't even venture to guess, and all this was racing through his mind at the speed of thought.

Claire backstepped to where he was frozen before the picture. "Something wrong, is it?" she asked.

"That man. Who is he?"

"Ah, now you've picked out the black sheep of the lot," she laughed. "That's my husband's great-great-grandfather, Earl. A scoundrel by all accounts." Then she lowered her voice with a confidential sparkle in her eye. "He's even rumored to have killed someone in a fit of pique."

Guy knew that. He'd seen it happen, often, when Earl was thirty years older than he'd been when he'd stood for this painting. But Guy also knew it wasn't a fit of pique, it was a cold and pathological act, close-up and personal as a serrated knife penetrating tender flesh. He was still dizzy with trying to assimilate all this information, though, when Claire's husband approached from behind him.

Eric Deloup, to the manor born, was handsome, if dissolute. He smiled with a mechanical ease at his wife, over Guy's shoulder. "Hello, my dear," he said.

Guy turned – and in that moment had an even more jarring dislocation. Because Eric looked a lot like the man in the oil painting, his great-great-grandfather, Earl.

"Eric, I'd like you to meet Guy Daniels. Guy, my husband, Eric."

"My pleasure," said Eric. His voice had a suave, educated arrogance, tinged with an echo of cruelty and infused with 300 years of British aristocracy.

Guy was riveted by Eric's appearance, though. He couldn't speak, he couldn't take his eyes away, couldn't stem an almost physical sense of repugnance – it was a case of hate at first sight – until, by sheer dint of will, he broke his own uncomfortable silence.

"Please, pardon my staring. I was struck by your resemblance to this portrait."

"Genes will out but I'm honored by the comparison nonetheless," Eric said graciously. "Earl was a great man – a builder, a philanthropist, and a patron of the arts."

"Don't forget 'violent offender,'" Claire stage whispered.

Eric smiled graciously at her little joke. But there was an undercurrent of strain to his manner; he didn't like his lineage insulted, he didn't like Claire, or anybody, taking those kinds of liberties. Claire realized instantly she'd gone too far.

Eric swiveled his gaze back on Guy. "And to what do I owe the honor of your presence in my home?" There seemed to be a subtext to nearly everything he said. This particular question was cordial on the surface, but the words "owe," "honor," "your presence," and "my home" were layered with aggressive innuendo. "Owe" established obligations between them, one already in the other's debt; "honor" had a sarcastic tone, as if they both knew such a value was at best quaint; "your presence" almost implied an affront to the master of the estate; and "my home" left no doubt as to who was top dog here. It was a minefield question.

Guy was at a crossroads and he knew it. The direction he had to go was both clear and obscure. But though he couldn't quite see the exact path he needed to take out of the woods, he knew he'd met the wolf. So he held on tight and with grace under pressure brazenly committed to the only next step he would allow himself to take. "I've come to see about the gardener's job, actually. I hope it's still available."

He glanced at Claire, who was simultaneously surprised and pleased. She had a choice now, too. Yet before she'd even consciously decided, she found herself keeping Guy's secret – the truth being that he hadn't really come about the job – conspiring with him to find a way to keep him around. She turned to Eric. "I was just going to tell you, darling. Guy's landscaping ideas are brilliant, I think he'd be perfect. But of course it's up to you." She said it ingratiatingly, the tone some women take to allow their men to believe what they want to believe about who's really in control.

Eric looked between the two of them. Just an inkling flitted through his mind: was something going on here? He tended to be a jealous man but he knew this was a failing and therefore guarded against the feeling when it arose. So he dismissed it, but like all jealous men, catalogued it for future reference.

He smiled beneficently at Claire. "If you think Guy is perfect, then he's our man." The two men took each other's measure. Then Eric, the perfect host, continued, to Guy, the new gardener, "Of course you'll stay for dinner."

That night Eric sat at the head of a large formal table in the large formal dining room, making small talk with Claire, seated down-table and to his right. The room had twenty-foot ceilings, eighteen-foot leaded windows, fully draped with red velvet. A chandelier hung high over the marble floor, its crystal teardrops tinkling in the draft, sending a long echo down the hallway. A fireplace nearly filled one wall, burning bright with cedar logs, yet still insufficient to the task of warming a room as frosty as its owner.

Eric did have a wintry way about him. Like the hard January ground, you didn't feel encouraged to try digging very deep; it was flinty work and uncertain yield. On the other hand, his features were quite captivating and he spoke well, so that people often gravitated to him at gatherings, then didn't realize until the evening was over, and they were waiting for theirs cars to be brought around, that they were drawing their jackets more tightly about themselves.

Guy entered, favoring his game leg on the long walk to the dining table at the center of the room. Eric stood, as the mannered gentleman he was, on formality. "You are welcome," he said, and indicated the down-table seat on his left flank.

"Thank you," said Guy, sitting, exchanging a polite nod with Claire.

"Why do you limp?" Eric asked rather abruptly.

"Eric, really." Claire was mortified by the lack of tact.

"I don't mean to be rude, just curious and disinclined to notice an elephant in the room without mentioning it."

Claire, to Guy: "You must forgive my laddie, he's forgotten all...."

"But first you must allow me to guess," Eric ran right over her apology, "since I fancy myself an observant fellow and something of a naturalist. I'm going to say congenital hip dysplasia because that's what my cousin Bruno had and he walked quite like you."

Guy smiled and responded with a story. "When Jacob was coming out of the wilderness to reconcile with his brother Esau, he stopped at a gorge to rest, where he was visited by an angel with whom he wrestled all night. An angel in the King James version, but more recent scholarly translations suggest it was actually God Himself who came down to wrestle. At daybreak neither had won the battle, this is all in the neighborhood of Genesis 32:24-31, at which point God 'touched the hollow of Jacob's thigh, and the hollow of Jacob's thigh was out of joint.' And then God said, 'Your name shall no longer be Jacob, but Israel, which means he who struggles with God.' So Jacob – evermore known as Israel – knew he'd been touched by the hand of God."

"Am I to understand you believe you've been touched by God, who gave you this limp?"

"Well, not literally. Metaphorically I like to think I struggle with my own idea of God, which might be my soul, or my spiritual center, or my moral compass – so maybe my hip dysfunction is a somatic expression of that metaphysical conflict."

"Sounds like physicalization of the subtext, to me," Claire chimed in. "You know what I'm getting on about, then, that Method Acting notion of expressing your inner demons through physical manifestation?"

"Demons or gods, yes."

Eric took a sip from his wine glass, then raised the glass high. "To the new Master of Landscape and Philosophy." The men tipped their wine glasses.

"I'm afraid I'm both overqualified and underqualified for this gardening assignment," said Guy. "But I'll do my best."

"I'll give you the grand tour tomorrow," said Claire. "I've got some thoughts, of course; I've always wanted a hedge labyrinth."

"That's because your mind is so puzzling, my dear."

"Intuitive, I'm sure you're meanin'," she corrected. And then, to Guy: "I was an actress once. Actresses depend on intuition."

"Actresses depend on benefactors, of which I was a prime exemplar."

"Really, Eric."

"There's no need to be shy about our archetypes in front of the gardener, darling." Then, as if in afterthought, he turned to Guy. "Oh, dear, you're not going to be the archetypal gardener, I hope – out with Lady Chatterly in the bushes."

"<u>Really</u>, Eric." She hoped he wasn't getting into one of his volatile moods.

Guy tried to steer the conversation off the shoals. "Lady Chatterly carried on with the gameskeeper, if I'm not mistaken."

"Yes, well, I'm sure she's done some of that, too." He threw Claire a razor smile. She turned her head, hurt – but now laced with fear. Again trying to defuse whatever was simmering, Guy filled in the silence with congeniality.

"I'm afraid my archetype is less the manly ruffian than the effete intellectual trying to find meaningful work with his hands."

"But you mentioned you were a sketch artist once," said Claire. "Surely that's hand work."

"Yes," laughed Guy, "but still effete."

"Real-world labor," agreed Eric. "Nothing like it." He puffed himself up before continuing. "I left Oxford in order to devote my efforts to an education in the manly trades, skills that every gentleman of generations past would have learned, certainly in your country – wheel-wrighting, tinkering, farming – so I could get a real appreciation of what it took to assume hands-on management of my family's affairs."

"And what affairs might those be?"

"Real estate, community development, construction...." And then, in a tone that was meant to sound self-deprecating while actually inviting protestation: "Quite boring work, I suppose, when you come right down to it."

Claire took the opportunity to redeem herself. "Don't let Eric demur, he's got the soul of an artist. He owns several galleries and a small symphony orchestra in Dublin. Great-great-grandfather Earl had nothing on Eric."

The compliment had its desired effect. Eric cast his wife a loving look and she basked in the glow of it like a child swaddled in praise. Only now did Guy realize that Eric had been steaming all this time, ever since that first encounter in the grand hall. All the cutting remarks to Claire at dinner had been in return for her inadvertent insult earlier in the day, that remark about great-great-grandfather Earl's criminal behavior.

"How did you two meet?" Guy asked. He wanted to learn everything he could about these two people, Eric's ancestors, this mansion that had once housed a murderer.

"I saw Claire do Miranda in a production of *The Tempest* at a small playhouse near Edinburgh, during the Festival – and fell instantly in love."

"It starts out with vengeance and retribution but by the end it's really about redemption and the improvement of one's character." She bestowed upon her husband a pointed, if droll, gaze. He bowed his head to her superior character. "In any case," she continued, "Eric bought our little Edinburgh company, moved us across the water to Dublin, built us a theater – yes, the madman actually built a playhouse, where he continued producing *The Tempest*, and proposing until I said yes."

"She loves being my puppet, she just won't admit it in mixed company."

Alice, a plain, down-trodden, middle-aged Scottish woman of the working classes, entered carrying a tray of soups, lobster bisque by the smell and color, and began serving as Claire continued the story of her courtship by Eric.

"But he didn't just buy the theater. He bought a newspaper and reviewed every performance I did, every review more glorious than the last. Truly, it was hard to resist."

As Alice set down a bowl of the creamy orange soup in front of Guy, she spilled a large dollop on his lap, leaving a deep stain. "Och, I'm so sorry, sir."

Eric spoke in a seething quiet. "You clumsy bitch."

Guy was immediately embarrassed. "No, no, it's fine, really."

"It's not fine, it's pathetic." Eric turned his glower on the mortified maid. "You're pathetic, Alice. Wouldn't you agree with that assessment?"

"Yes, sir," said Alice, eyes down. "Very much so." Then, to Guy: "If you'd lea' your trousers with me before you go, sir, I'll wash them."

"No, that's completely unnecessary," Guy protested.

"If she doesn't have them clean by morning, I'll take it out of her pay or her skin," Eric said darkly.

"But I can just…."

"It's not a problem, Guy," Claire interrupted. There was a pleading tone in her voice, begging Guy to let it drop. "If you'd like to borrow a pair of Eric's pants while Alice cleans yours, I'm sure the two of you are close enough to the same size."

There was a long silence.

Eric spoke to Alice in a voice that could freeze good brandy. "What are you just standing there for?"

Alice backed out of the room, head bowed. Claire looked flushed with shame. The dead air expanded to fill the room.

Eric sipped his soup to get his anger under control, then shrugged the ill will off his shoulders as if it were unwanted cat dander. "Sorry about that."

But it was unclear if he was apologizing for himself or Alice. And in some distant room, Guy thought he could hear the muffled sobs of the maid, choked as a twisted memory.

5

CHAPTER FIVE

August 25-October 16, 2013
Love Dies

Next morning when Vicky woke up it wasn't pretty. She felt horribly hungover and had no idea how her face and hands had gotten lipsticked and when she got up she tracked the red gloss across the floor until she slipped and fell on her ass. Then she got sick and threw up in the toilet, and when she flushed, it backed up all over the floor. She just sat in the shower for half an hour, washing herself clean and trying to remember how she could have gotten so drunk it led to this. She threw towels and dirty laundry down on the filthy bathroom floor, poured bleach over it all and left for work.

And then, weirdly, everything turned around. As soon as she arrived, Vic got down on his knees and proposed in front of everybody and slipped the nano-diamond ring on her finger. She squealed and said yes and practically humped him right there. Then she showed the ring around the set, getting the usual responses. Oohs and squeals from the ladies, fair market appraisals from the gents. After that, there was nothing to do but work on the play.

Teddy was amazed to see Vicky cry during one of her speeches to Joan, then dry up in a flash. "Dude, how do you do that? Cry on command? I mean like actors, how do they, I mean how do we do it?"

"It's just practice. Start with small things. Don't you have anything you can think of that gives you any kind of physical, visceral response?"

"Only when I get horny."

"Yeah, well like I said, start with small things." She walked out the door.

He followed close on her heels, making jokes, whispering amusements into her ear as they went back to the stage, making her laugh, and once to pat him on the cheek.

That's the part Vic saw, the laughter and the tender touch, and it pinched his heart. No reason to get a bug up his ass, he told himself, it was just part of working together all day with people, jokes and flirting and sliding scales of intimacy were necessary and inevitable. It's just… he and Vicky were engaged now, people had to respect that. He felt a familiar spasm of anger behind his eyes, looked around for Vicky so she could tell him to stop over-reacting. But she was nowhere to be seen.

In fact she'd gone to get the stitches out of her mouth and on the way back decided she still looked pretty fine, in fact it was kind of an interesting scar, she thought it gave her character. She flicked stares at it in the rear-view mirror, driving her yellow T-Bird, now back from the shop and repainted cherry red to cover the graffiti and wipe away the creepy associations of that odd series of assaults, the car vandalism, the razor blade. These things tended to happen in threes anyway, so there wasn't much to worry about now. Except she was still a little rattled by all that bizarre lipsticking when she woke up. Could she have been sleepwalking? Vic said he'd seen her do that once; after she'd taken an Ambien, he'd found her sitting on the floor, looking like a zombie, staring into the open refrigerator. According to her doctor, such things happened sometimes on Ambien. But she didn't think she'd taken any Ambien last night.

She did think she'd had her nightmare again last night, though, a variant of the recurring one where the guy without a face, just a little hole where his mouth should be, was standing at the foot of her bed. In last night's version Blankface had begun making an inhuman sound, like a soul in despair. And then he'd cut off her lips with a scissors and stapled them around the hole in his non-face, so his face-hole looked more like a freaky patched-together mouth. Leaving her bare bloody teeth gaping out, an appalling grin, no mouth to close around it. And then she'd awakened to find her face smeared with lipstick. The more she thought about it the more she thought she must have done it to herself, acting out the nightmare like an automaton.

No two ways about it, she had to start getting more sleep.

Rehearsals moved past Labor Day and through another sticky spell in September, terrarium-hot, finally into October. Summer was done, the earliest autumn leaves just starting to redden and crisp up. The Chi-Town troupers went through the usual trysts, snits and reconciliations that go along with mounting a play. People did what they could be expected to do. Conceits bloated, attractions smoldered or sparked, nerves got frayed, lines got learned and personalized. There were short tempers, long nights.

The sets got built with a little extra *sturm & drang* thrown in due to the set designer's AIDS flaring up. Vic was tagged to replace the poor soul. He protested, told them he wasn't a creative guy, just a hands-on guy (and Vicky thought, You got that right). But they told him he was a creative guy now. By the harvest moon he was wearing two hats. Techie all day, designer half the night.

So all the time Vicky spent rehearsing, waitressing, and nightmaring, Vic spent most of his hours designing and set-building. It was a wonder they managed to find any time for each other at all. But somehow they did; somehow even managed to collapse into some great sleepy sex at the end of an exhausting day.

The woman walked down the frozen dinner section of the *Food 4 Less* on Damen Avenue, putting a stack of Wolfgang Puck four-cheese pizzas into her cart. The stalker paused behind a pyramid display of Cheerios on sale. Imagined her stripped of clothing, her skin taut from the refrigerated air wafting up from the wall-length, open-topped freezer compartment. Imagined lifting her by the hair and stuffing her in her cart. Stabbing her with an icicle. That would be good, like an ice knife, then tearing open the flesh with his teeth, tasting that slick salty wet, pulling her guts out and stretching them full length in the freezer, making her watch her own intestines frost up. Cold bitch that she was.

Imagined her without clothes; then without skin. What would it be like to skin somebody alive? And lick the muscle? Was there a tang to the adrenaline of fear and pain that the muscle cells would be bathed in? Would the juice run down his chin like brandy? He had to pause, his breath catching at the thought. She walked up the aisle.

Trembling, he followed. Followed her into the brisk evening, people strolling about on the leaf-turning avenue in the cool dusk. Sometimes she was obscured as she walked through a crowd waiting for a bus. But her scent was never obscured. The stalker could follow her scent like a bloodhound. Like fresh meat to a hungry animal.

She strolled into a small city park a few blocks away. Opened her bag, started broadcasting bread crumbs to the pigeons. The stalker moved around in a wide circle, found a good watching place not far behind her, in the cover of some oleander bushes. Shady, leafy, lovely watching the clueless prey from cover, biding time for the moment to pounce, owning the moment, owning the prey… but wait. Something was wrong. Look at her. There was no screaming fear smell, she looked too happy. Too oblivious to all the pain she'd caused, all the retribution that awaited her. Bitch needed a reminder.

Dispersing the last of the crumbs to the pigeons, the woman thought she heard someone behind her. But as she felt that faintest hint of unease, the catch in the throat that signaled the world was tilting just a little, she started to turn… and got pushed down hard to the ground. A strong hand held the back of her head, jamming her face into the earth, dirt in her mouth gritty and damp. She choked, struggled, tried to twist her head back and forth. Then, curiously, met no resistance. And now nobody was gripping her head anymore, nobody sitting on her back. Was he standing above her with a gun? Or worse: a knife?

Footsteps disappeared into the bushes. She turned in time to see the assailant was gone. But now she saw her dress was on fire.

She beat at it with frantic hands, threw some loose soil on the small blaze, finally put it out. A little skin on her legs was singed, some minor blistering; nothing more. But her heart was racing, she felt sick, felt like throwing up. Looked toward the bushes where the attacker had fled. It was nearly full dark now, though. The shadow was gone. But then, she knew, shadows never completely disappeared.

Detective Olivetti entered the Chinese restaurant, showed Oma his badge. "Ask you a few questions?"

"You mean like do we use MSG?"

"Yeah, that's a good one. Now tell me about Vicky Olson."

"I've known her a few years, since she started working for us. At the old place first, and then when we set up here. She's a good worker. The customers like her."

"So who doesn't like her?"

"All I can think is, she used to run with a wild crowd. Before she met Vic."

"Any of her gentleman friends get jealous when she moved on?"

"Gentleman friends, that's pretty funny. There was one seriously bad apple, he sort of took it the wrong way when she went off with Vic. Guy named Tully."

"Yeah, his name's come up before. He took it the wrong way how?"

"The story I heard, he went to where he thought Vic lived, knocked on the door and beat the living crap out of the poor joker who answered. Turned out Vic lived next door. Tully was a meth head, though, so what do you expect. They busted him later that day, he's still in prison, far as I know."

Olivetti smiled. "Guess I'll check into that."

Nighttime October 15, Vic and Vicky went for a walk in Jackson Park, just off Lake Michigan. Thick with what looked like mutant trees scrawling moonlight shadows around the delicate lagoon of a Japanese garden. Deserted at this hour. A wooden bridge spanned the pond; rising wind off the lake rustled the arid leaves that had dropped, scraping the gravel path. You could see the Museum from here, used to be called the Palais des Beaux Arts, all classical columns and karyatids. This park went on for acres, one of the green serene oases in the city, it seemed timeless, motionless. Manicured in some places, primeval in others. A shelter for lovers, dealers and other secret sharers.

They'd been quiet for a while, walking slowly, listening to the hush. The play was nearly ready, everybody'd been working righteous overtime, this was a rare peaceful hour for them. Vic absently tied long blades of grass into sailors' knots – he liked doing mindless manipulations with his hands, it helped him work out the chatter in his brain. Vicky calmed her mind by exercising the facial muscles of specific, exaggerated raw emotions. Anger. Grief. Surprise. Pity. Gaiety. Anybody saw her, they'd think she was off her meds or maybe the opposite, chugging too much Haldol. They probably made quite a sight, if anybody'd been watching – the two of them walking side by side, knotting weeds, making weird faces. If anybody'd been watching.

When Vicky finally contorted her features into Suspicion, it brought on a rush of memory-sense that somehow reminded her of Gloria.

"I don't think your mother trusts me. Last time we talked on the phone she was all like 'How do you have any time for Victor these days, it must be such a strain for you, you're not having second thoughts, are you, sweetie?' Like Angela Lansbury in *The Manchurian Candidate*, when she's sounding so solicitous to her son Raymond about his well-being but you can really tell she's totally a manipulative evil bitch." Pause. Went a little too far. "Not that your mother...."

"That's okay, you're tired. Plus fiancées are always iffy about mother-in-laws."

"Mothers-in-law." She held up the back of her hand to her face, admired the moon-glint on her cute little diamond. "Like at our dinner with her last month, whenever it was, when I was in the kitchen getting salt I heard you accuse her of not liking me."

"Then you also must've eavesdropped enough to hear she just doesn't want you to break my heart."

"Hey." She stopped, faced him with a warning: "I am gonna break your heart every fuckin' day for the rest of your sweet life."

She grabbed him by the head, pulled his face to hers. Kissed him hard. Winced, drew back, touched her lip. Though the stitches had been out for weeks, there was still an almost imperceptible swelling, a stubborn tenderness. Traumatic neuritis, the doctor called it, could take a few months to resolve. He had her on vitamin B6 supplements.

Vic brought his fingers gently up to the soft edge of her lip, traced the delicate line all the way around her mouth. "You okay? You seem way too tired, all the sleep you're not getting, rehearsals all day, waitressing every off-hour, I feel like you're slipping away, here."

"Not likely."

"No? I see you spending the little energy you got on that stoner, Teddy, like flirting with him is the best thing you got going; maybe I'm being paranoid, but I just want that out on the table."

She looked at him like he was insane. "Are you fuckin' nuts? Teddy? Kid still walks with training wheels, and you're jealous? That is so <u>sweet</u>!"

She sucked his index finger with those savvy lips of hers, lots of eye contact. Then yanked his finger out, pulled his mouth back to that same spot. More lust. Traumatic neuritis or no; pain be damned.

He pushed her against a tree, moved his hands up her dress. She slid hers down below his belt, one hand in front, one in back. Small sounds gurgled out of their throats. Like a duet of erotic urges half-contained, letting off vocal steam… except at some point they both realized neither one of them was making all those little voice-box noises.

Vicky paused. "You hear that, Baby?"

He listened. There it was again. Maybe twenty feet away, beyond a rustling cluster of dim shapes. An inhuman sound, like a soul in despair, like the echo of someone buried alive, a kind of gurgled scrabbling. Vicky shivered – wait, was she dreaming this, was this the part where the faceless man cut off her lips? She felt at her mouth – her lips were still there. No, this was real. But it was messing with her mind. She drew close to Vic and they walked slowly toward the keening, toward the muffled wail that might've been rising from beneath the chilly earth.

They neared the moans. Vic paused. Looked behind him. Was someone there, too? Or was that just a branch settling in the breeze, or a nocturnal gardener on his appointed rounds? Or was he only getting jumpy?

Maniac silhouettes reeled in the moonlight.

"Maybe we should just get the fuck out of here," said Vicky.

The whimpering got louder, though. Impossible to walk away from if you're the least bit curious. Vic took out his Droid, turned on the flashlight function and stepped into the overgrowth. Vicky was so close behind, her hand was on his back.

She was actually the first one to see it, cowering under a thicket. A small, mongrel puppy. Relief washed over her like a happy flood.

"Aww, look at the poor thing." She picked it up, cuddled it. Her first impulse was to protect the foundling.

"Does it have a collar?" Vic, the male of the species, was out of the gate more focused on identification. He checked. No collar, no ID. The puppy shivered, tried to burrow into Vicky.

"It's freezing," she said. "Some asshole just dumped it here and took off."

Vic looked around the empty park and shouted. "Anybody looking for a dog?"

Silence.

"We found your puppy!" he yelled again.

"We gotta take it home, Vic."

"We can't take care of a dog now. I'm working eighteen hours a day tech-directing and set-designing, you've got rehearsal all the time, not to mention your day job, not to mention opening night is around the corner."

"Vic, look at the thing, it needs us; it's gonna die out here. I'm taking it home. Come on, it's a sign."

"Of what?"

"Our love, you jerk."

She gave him the Evil Eye. No way he was gonna win this argument. So he just capitulated to his manifest destiny. Put his arm around her, walked her back to the car, her arms engulfing the small mammal as gray cumuli passed over the moon, bringing a dark chill to the off-shore scud that pushed the mist around the lovers like a cloak.

Vicky's apartment, two a.m. Standing in the shower, Vic behind her, reaching around, lathered up, sliding his rough slippery hands over the softest places.

Then the bedroom floor, she put on his black suede jacket and nothing else, the burgundy satin lining soft and shivery against her skin as she strad-dled him, holding his wrists, pinning him there.

And then on the overstuffed chair he grabbed her arms, held them to her sides, swung her onto the bed, twisting in the sheets, her cheek up against the cold hard wall, he kept pushing her closer, almost to the edge, just hanging there for it seemed like ever. And then over the edge, both of them, couldn't stop, as the puppy snuffled nearby in its cardboard box and the heavy vapors outside condensed into a soft drizzle.

Until at last they all settled, quiet – and, briefly, at peace.

Vicky's apartment, three a.m. The mongrel was sleeping sound on newspapers spread over the bottom of a big cardboard box in the corner of the bedroom. Fifteen feet away, Vic and Vicky slept even harder in the aftermath of driven sex. Quite still, twined in each other's legs, hair, sheets, breath, her perfume, his fingers wrapping her arm, her head on his chest. Silent dark, like a late night benediction in the Church of Two Souls.

It was raining outside, the continuous patter emphasizing the almost painterly motionlessness within the room, making it seem even more like a cocoon, shielding them from the elements rattling the window.

But there were some elements that would not be kept at bay.

There was a distant screaming; it wouldn't end. Vic was running barefoot down a maze of cold streets, a kind of throbbing lope over shards and splintered glass; he could hear the screams but couldn't find where they were coming from, and it was scaring him shitless. Sounds of revulsion, bottomless pain. At some point he knew he was in a dream and he tried to just go back to sleep; but then he vaguely understood, in that dream-heavy way, that the wails were real and he was just incorporating them into his night terror, like the night terrors he used to have when he was a kid, *pavor nocturnis* the doctors called it. They didn't know what to do about it either.

He tried to concentrate now. Street noises. Were the shrieks coming from the boulevard? No. Must be voices from the movie theater downstairs at the front of the building, they were midnight showing *Black Sunday*, he'd seen that one, about a vampire woman they closed into a coffin with nails pointing inward and she screeched as the lid came down, it was almost an animal yowl as the barbed spikes impaled her body. But the midnight movie was long over by now, wasn't it? Wasn't it the middle of the night already? Vic's eyes popped open.

There was a stillness to the world. He peered around the room. The rain had stopped, it was a brittle clear black fall night outside the window. Nothing here seemed out of place, nothing tipped, nothing tumbled. There was simply... a shudder in the air. And it crawled under his skin.

He extricated himself gingerly from the bunched up sheets, didn't want to wake Vicky; she needed every second of sleep she could get and she had an early call to boot. Grabbed his cell phone off the nightstand, turned on its flashlight app. Got out of bed, shined the beam around. Windows closed, no scratches on the latches. Drawers shut, clothes strewn on the floor where they'd been left in the hurry of love. But he still had the disquieting echo of that dying-vampire scream in his head, that animal shriek.

He looked across the room at the puppy's cardboard box. Padded over to it. Looked inside.

It was empty. He knelt down, checked the edges. No gaps in the cardboard the dog could have crawled through. The walls of the box too high to jump. But now he noticed something scrawled on a newspaper page covering the bottom of the box. Something he didn't remember being there before. Something written in big block letters with a Magic Marker in red ink: **LOVE DIES**.

He grabbed the defaced page, looked around the darkened room again. Listened with all his being, with every sense. No breathing, aside from Vicky's. He pulled on his pants, lying in a heap on the rug. Grabbed a baseball bat from under the bed where he insisted Vicky keep it. Tip-toed out the bedroom door.

Down the hall to the living room. Nobody here. He checked the front door. Locked. Listened to the apartment. Wait – was that a creak at the back of the place? He strode barefoot to the kitchen. Quiet, empty. But the back door was wide open.

He hurried out to the rear porch, gripping his bat, looking everywhere at once. Vacant alley, unlit buildings. His feet felt cold and his dream suddenly came back to him in a rush, shards of glass cutting into his soles. He hurried back into the kitchen.

The window beside the open door was covered by a gauzy half-curtain, swaying now in an after-rain breeze. Vic pulled the curtain aside. There was a perfectly circular hole in the window, size of a dinner plate, obviously made by a glass cutter. Within arm's reach of the door lock.

He walked back to the open door, crumpled the newspaper page with **LOVE DIES** written on it, peered up and down the long alley. Still too dark to see. He put on his shoes and walked out into the night, to try to pick up the intruder's trail.

It was even darker in a warehouse basement half an hour later, where the stalker moved through a maze of concrete rooms and corridors navigated so often they no longer needed light. Like the inevitable world of a recurring dream. But this was no imaginary place. The stalker moved swiftly, dodged every dangling pipe, stepped over every pothole. Passed easily around a corroded boiler, avoiding piles of old machine parts, twisted like body parts in a mass grave. And maybe a few body parts in the pile, as well: the smell would have generated a gag reflex in most people, redolent of maggot-scoured fish heads or some other fleshly decay, commingled with basement mildew and a mix of undefined rancid oils. A charnel house bouquet.

At last there came a turning that glowed a little, frayed wires feeding a bare 15 watt bulb hanging from mold-slick crossbeams. This opened on a large storage room, scattered with oversized crates and rot-damaged furniture, resembling in shadow the broken spines of ancient creatures from some mythic hell. Some sections of the floor were cement, some flat stone, others just hardpack dirt. The figure walked past an open cistern, mostly sunk below ground level, with a two foot steel lip rising above the concrete floor that anchored it in place. Filled with a thousand gallons of fetid water, sinking who knows to what depths, a few dead rats floating just below the surface, a slow drip into the vat from a rusted pipe in the ceiling, guaranteeing it would always be full.

Against one wall was a rolltop desk, an easy chair, a hospital gurney, an old but high candle-power lamp. And horribly, sickeningly out of place: a tray of gleaming, modern, stainless steel surgical instruments.

Past the gurney was a rough-hewn slat door, closing off the next room. The door was padlocked, but there was space between the slats, through which a curious person might see an obscure shape in the chamber beyond. As the stalker approached, a low growl came from this shape on the other side of the door. A frightening sound, of primitive urges and unknowable appetites.

The stalker brought gloved hands up to the slatted door, holding the mongrel puppy just taken from Vicky's apartment. Clutched the small dog in one hand, picked up an ornate vial off the desk with the other. A beautiful vial, gold filigree over lavender glass. Opened it, sprinkled liquid from the vial all over the puppy. The puppy whimpered, licked the gloved hand of its malevolent abductor.

There was a kind of window, a smaller door actually, built into the top of the slatted door. The stalker opened this port now. The beast inside growled louder. The stalker tossed the puppy through the window into the room beyond. Then watched the beastial creature in there maul the little dog in a wild flurry of yelping and thudding and bone-cracking puppy screams.

And the psycho smiled.

"I'm late for rehearsal, gotta run." Vicky careened into the kitchen, throwing things into her purse, brushing her hair. Vic, sitting at the table sipping coffee, handed her a full mug as she breezed by. "Thanks, you're a godsend...." But she paused at the back door; looked around, perplexed. "Wait, where's the puppy? He's not in the box, isn't he here with you?"

"I'm afraid he must've got out last night."

"Got out? What do you mean got out, how could he get out?"

"Climbed over the top of his box, I guess. Climbed on that chair up to the counter and then out the open back window is all I can figure."

He'd pushed open the sash window, so the portion with the hole cut in it was now sitting higher, behind the bunched-up curtains. Wouldn't have taken much scrutiny, but she was running too late to look too close and he didn't want to swamp her with news this bad this early.

Her face fell. "That's fucked up."

"He'll be okay, I'm sure."

She threw him a look that said Yeah, right, kissed him on the forehead, had a big gulp of coffee and ran out the back door.

Vic contemplated the break-in, pondered his options and finally called the precinct to report it. But Olivetti wasn't there. So Vic left a brief message with a guy named Shaw, the man's voice oozing indifference.

Then he closed the kitchen window with the hole cut in it, leaving it the way he'd found it in the middle of the night. Locked up Vicky's place, went down to his car, which was parked on Spaulder. Sat there a minute. His nightmare of running on glass shards, those screams, the open back door… he realized now that the wails he was hearing in his dream must have been the puppy yelping. He didn't like to think about that. So he sat here behind the wheel of his parked Chrysler Imperial, making an origami bird out of a parking ticket stub while Jimi Hendrix wailed *Voodoo Chile Blues* out of the speakers, *Night I was born, Lord, the moon stood a fire red.*

He put his car in gear, hung a left on Diversey, going east past the movie house. Glanced for no particular reason up the alley that ran along the other side of the building – and swerved over to the right-hand curb with a screech of rubber. Quickly landed in a Loading Zone Only spot, closed his door softly, jogged across the street. Walked casually past the alley, going back the other way.

There was a car parked up Vicky's alley. A white POS Toyota Corolla, primer over the driver side front fender. Parked under the wooden stairway that led up to Vicky's back door. And there was a guy at the top of the stairs. Reaching through the hole in her back window.

Vic moved up the alley flat against the wall of the opposite building, fast and quiet toward the stairs. The guy at the top didn't see him, his back was to the street, as he tried to reach around to get at the inside door lock. Ten feet from the steps Vic raced over and bounded up, two at a time. The clatter got the guy's attention. He pulled his arm out of the fenestration and turned around just as Vic made it up to the landing and slammed him against the door.

"Tully."

The guy was thirty-something. Used-up low-browed face poking out of a dirty gray hoodie. Mean looking sonofabitch with a hardtime story, lot of blood over the dam, some of his flesh and soul with it. "Who the fuck are you?" he demanded.

Vic grabbed him by the hood. "The guy who's taking you in, you piece of shit."

He started to yank Tully backwards by the hood but the piece of shit used the momentum to spin himself around and land a solid punch into Vic's neck. Both men tumbled ass over elbow down the stairs, Tully ending on top. He stood, kicked Vic hard in the gut, kicked him a second time, ran the ten feet for his car, opened the front door.

Vic scrambled over, slammed the door on Tully's hand. Tully yowled, tottered away. Vic pushed him and he fell against the trunk. Grabbed Tully's sweatshirt at the waist, pulled it over his head. Punched him in the face, through the soft cotton of the inverted sweatshirt. Punched him again. Punched him again. Punched him again.

Soon as Olivetti got downstairs he saw the commotion. And what do you know. It was the boyfriend, Vic, dragging in a guy whose face looked like an overripe plum with a mouth. Vic dumped him at the front desk, but spoke to Olivetti.

"There's your stalker," he said. "Vicky's boyfriend for over a year, freakin' meth head, he got two to five, I thought two minimum; guess he did less than that, though, came back out of stir, wrote **WHORE** on her car, put razors in her food, broke into her place last night, I caught him trying to break in again this morning. His name's Mike Tully. You're welcome."

An hour later Tully was at Cook County under medical supervision and police guard. Vic was at the set telling Vicky the good news-bad news. Vicky dropped her jaw.

"It was <u>Tully</u>?! You're shitting me!"

"No, he's out on good behavior, I figure, which for him is knocking politely before he breaks and enters."

"That fucking bastard, how could he do this?!"

"Love dies. That's what I found scrawled on some papers last night. I didn't tell you because I didn't want to worry you but the guy has some kind of sick fixation."

"Love dies." Tears came up quickly, and he held her. Tully's love was balled into hate and her own love for Vic had been so perfunctory lately it was nearly in a vegetative state. She held him tighter. "I love you," she whispered.

"You got me," he answered.

She couldn't stop crying. She didn't want to depend on him, didn't want to depend on love at all, as a matter of fact. What had it ever gotten her but hurt? And now here he was being dependable and stalwart, and she felt herself wanting to melt into him, be taken by him, and it made her crazy with fear and gratitude, flailing and drowning in the great Sea of Losing Control. So in the end all she could do was give it up and let herself sink into the embracing waves and stutter out a single, muted, "Thank you."

Couple hours after that, Olivetti phoned the set, asked Vic to meet him over at Vicky's place.

"My place too, now. I mean, we moved in together. But sure, I can meet you there. You want to see if Tully left any prints inside?"

"Well, that's the thing. Tully's not your boy."

Vic waited for clarification. None came. "What do you mean? The guy who's been after Vicky? Of course he is."

"Tully's been locked down at Stateville Correctional outside Joliet for two years. I shoulda called earlier to find that out, sorry. He was just released yesterday afternoon. There's no way he could've done any of the shit that's happened to your fiancée."

"There's gotta be some mistake."

"He went from the prison to the bus yesterday, spent a big chunk of last night on the bus; we got a ticket-taker, a driver and three passengers all put him there. Got to the Greyhound station on Randolph at 5:30 this morning, got a car from a buddy, buddy says Tully drove off around eight this morning, that's just a little before you did your number on him."

Vic was stunned. "But I saw him with his arm through the window, trying to open the door."

"Yeah, that probably won't thrill his parole officer, but what Tully says is he just wanted to see the girl again, say he was sorry, probably hoped he was gonna get laid, he knocked on her door, no answer, there was a hole in the window, he thought he'd let himself in and leave a note. He realizes now that was a major fuckin' error in judgment."

Vic didn't say anything.

"You still there?" said Olivetti into his phone.

"Yeah. This isn't making a lot of sense to me. But I'll meet you there in ten."

Vic stood in Vicky's kitchen watching Detective Olivetti pull aside the curtain to examine the cut-out back window.

"So if it wasn't Tully doing the stalking, who was it?"

"Whoever it was, looks like he's done this before," said Olivetti, pointing to the circular hole in the window.

"What makes you say that?"

"Man uses a glass cutter, makes a perfect hand-window within reach of the door lock, he knows what he's doin'." Vic nodded. Olivetti eyeballed the room. "How's she dealing?"

"I just told her on the set about catching Tully; she was pretty relieved. Now I don't know. She left in a rush for rehearsal this morning. If she thinks somebody's still out there, she'll freak. I mean, I'll tell her, she just doesn't need to know this second."

"Got any new ideas who the real perp is?"

"No, but can't you get some prints off the glass?"

"Doubtful," explained the detective. "Guy uses a glass cutter, he's probably using gloves, too. But I'll send somebody over, we'll give it a try, you never know."

"What if Tully was hiring somebody else to do it all, like a proxy stalker or something?"

"Not impossible, but I gotta tell you, I talked to Tully and I believe the guy. I also gotta say, I'm leaning more towards another particular theory."

"Which is?"

"There's a connection between your old girlfriend's death and these assaults on your new fiancée."

"Why would you think that?"

"Anybody with a grudge against you has a potential motive to hurt both Vicky and your last girl. You know, as a way to get to you."

"I told you, I never really had any girlfriends serious enough to push it this far."

Olivetti paused. "Doesn't have to be a girlfriend. A workplace rival, maybe some asswipe thought you cut him off in traffic, somebody you pissed off in an internet chat room – you know, there's crazies out there these days." People who whale on their fiancée's ex-boyfriends, for example.

Vic thought a long moment. "Nobody comes to mind. And neither one of us does chat rooms."

Olivetti nodded. "Yeah, that counter girl at the Chinese restaurant said Vicky was bad with computers."

Vic was taken aback. "You were talking to Oma?"

"I talked to a bunch of people, at the theater, the restaurant, in the neighborhood, tryin' to get a feel for who's in your lives that might be doin' this. You know it's gotta be somebody you know."

"I don't see who."

Time to push a little. "I read Kendra's file – that was your old girlfriend, actually a couple people said fiancée."

"I know who Kendra was."

"Whatever. Girlfriend, fiancée, lotta times that kinda thing's a judgment call. Anyway, witnesses at the scene said the car that hit Kendra was a red Chevy. You see a car like that around the neighborhood lately? Or you know anyone who had a red car?"

He shrugged. "Vicky has a red car, a new T-Bird, but she just painted it like that a couple weeks ago, used to be yellow." But saying it made something click for him, some catch in his mind.

"Yeah, that doesn't help much, I'm talkin' about a car's been around a few years."

Vic wished he could be alone to think. Too much information coming at him all at once, it made him want to do something with his hands, to settle it all down. He started peeling the label off an empty beer bottle while he brooded.

Olivetti had no problem waiting. He always liked to let the pressure of silence be his best interrogator.

Finally Vic shook his head no. "Sorry. Nothing rings a bell. But wait, I forgot to show you this." He turned to get a large scrap of paper balled up on the floor. He unfolded it, keeping his head turned away from the detective. He didn't want Olivetti to see what was on his face.

But Olivetti could tell he was holding something back. Olivetti knew this guy was part of it somehow.

Vic handed him the uncrumpled newspaper. "Here, I forgot to give this to you when we got here. I found it on the bottom of the puppy box last night when I got up."

Olivetti finished straightening out the newsprint and glanced at the Magic Marker scrawled on it. **LOVE DIES**. "Ain't that the truth."

"It's block letters, so you probably can't do handwriting analysis, but maybe the ink's traceable?"

"Looks like a standard Magic Marker. But I'll give it to the lab, you never know." He stared at Vic, gestured to the hand-printed letters. "Mean anything to you?"

"'Love dies'? I thought it pointed right to Tully, but I guess not. I guess it just means whoever the fuck-wit is who's doing this just had a few disappointments in life."

"Yeah, just like me."

"Except you still have your looks."

Olivetti smiled at Vic for the first time. "Keep your eyes open for a red car."

As soon as Olivetti left, Vic drove to his mother's house. East to Lake Shore Drive, then a straight shot south to Hyde Park. The Lake was visible on his left pretty much the whole way, gunmetal gray today, with whitecaps frothing the peak of every low wave. He glided by all his favorite landmarks without noticing them – Buckingham Fountain, the Field Museum of Natural History, the Aquarium, the Planetarium. His mind was locked on his mission.

He was pretty sure his mother would be gone now, this was the day her friend Doris picked her up to go do the art museums. He got off the Drive at 55th, went south on Blackstone, pulled into her driveway, walked to the front window, peered inside. It had an empty look about it. He knocked, no answer. Walked down the driveway to the two-car garage, unlocked it with the spare he kept on his ring, lifted the door. Let himself in.

It was big, cluttered. Arts and crafts junk filled every available surface, crammed around an old green two-door Impala nosed up against the far wall. There were tubes of oil paint and acrylic, canvas stretchers, easels, brushes, pen nibs, turpentine cans, glue guns, butcher paper, feathers, modeling clay wrapped in plastic, chalks, gesso, jelly jars full of sequins, buttons, beads and butterfly wings. In other words, an artist's garage.

Vic walked around a big pile of newspapers beside an ancient oil stain, to the right front fender of the car, accidentally knocking into a jar full of clothespins, all of it clattering to the cement. He stood there a minute, rattled by the noise, listening for interlopers. Anybody coming? No, he was alone here, he could do what he came to do.

He crouched down, took out his Droid, turned the flashlight on the car. Thought about what he'd said to Olivetti, about Vicky repainting her car after it got vandalized. Thought about the flicker of another memory that set off. Okay, enough thinking. Time to act. So with the toothy edge of his brass house key, he scraped a short, deep scratch in his mother's car, barely above the undercarriage, on the skirt, near the bumper.

Beneath the scratch in the green finish, there was an undercoat of dark red paint.

This was the half-memory, the nagging feeling he couldn't hold down, the thing he was trying to hide from Detective Olivetti. This Chevy used to be red. But he didn't know where to go from here.

"Victor, is that you?"

It was Gloria, standing in the driveway, her shock of white hair looking almost electrified. Startled Vic so much, he fell back on his butt. Tried to smile. "Hi, Mom."

"I thought I heard something. What are you doing here?"

"I just stopped by to borrow your hot glue gun, the one on the set broke. I thought you'd gone off with Doris already." He stood up, dusted himself off.

"She's late, as usual." She regarded him curiously. He'd never been a very good liar, at least not to her. "What are you really up to?"

He wanted to protect her. Whatever she'd been doing – if she'd been doing anything, that is – was at least partly on Vic's head, he felt. It was a guilt he carried in that deep place we all carry something – in his case an unshakable belief that his father had run away all those years ago because of him. That he was the cause of the break-up of the marriage, of his mother's aloneness in the world. And that's why she acted a little odd sometimes, or acted out. All Vic's fault.

So he projected his guilt onto Gloria now, letting his emotional spillage divert attention from his true suspicions about her painted-over car. "I was just wondering," he said, "I mean, now that you've had a chance to think about it – are you really okay with me marrying Vicky?"

She put her hand lovingly on his cheek. "As long as you're safe and happy, Victor. That's all I ever wanted."

But what price, he wondered, would they all pay for that motherly cliché?

"I just wish," she continued, "I could be sure marrying Vicky is what you want. That you're not rushing headlong down a road that's going to be terribly painful at the end. Painful for everybody."

He glanced at the scratch on the Chevy bumper, red as blood, cold as iron, loud as a silent accusation.

6

CHAPTER SIX

September 6-October 9, 1976
Remembrance Fallen From Heaven,
And Madness Risen From Hell

Guy exited the rear entrance after dinner, wearing an old pair of Eric's corduroy pants, while back in the maid's quarters Alice toiled diligently over the soup stain on Guy's slacks. He shuffled across the yard toward the gardener's cottage, perplexed by this strange turn his life had taken. Perplexed, mystified, fascinated, energized… and, yes, obsessed. That was, finally, the only word for it. What else but obsession could have led him to fly to a foreign country, where he'd wandered the pubs and streets until managing to initiate a covert surveillance operation on his own previous existence? Well, obsession it was, then. So be it.

The evening air was cool and humid, autumnal fog beginning to curl around the edges of the house. The moon was even brighter than usual, its light diffracted through the mist. And in that silvery luminescence, the silhouettes of the surrounding vegetation – the vinery, the oak and willow branches, the tracery of climbing roses – seemed to come alive, to vibrate with souls of their own, to lean in toward Guy, to whisper their foliate secrets. *Ssshhhhhh*, they sussurated in the moving air. *Ssshhhhh, don't tell.*

Guy turned slowly, taking it all in, trying to understand. Overwhelmed, he sat down.

Sat down right in the mulchy garden and dug his spidery fingers into the cool earth, bringing up handfuls of dirt, inhaling the leafy scent. He rubbed his palms together. It felt good. It made Guy feel connected to the planet, somehow more real, more distinct from all the ethereal machinations of his mind, the philosophies and dark puzzles that had been tormenting him since the 4th of July, Independence Day – which was amusing, since it was the day he'd begun to understand his complete lack of independence, his absolute connection to everyone else and to the metaphysical planes of this world. He peered at the soil he was holding. Surely this was no mind game; just good, solid earth, to hold in his hands, to touch, to smell, to crumble in his fingers.

He looked at his hands. Pale, frail, they'd previously been used in large measure for annotating book pages. But in the funny way life sometimes turns an unexpected corner, it occurred to Guy this gardener's job could well be exactly what he needed, a steadying influence, something coupling him to the physical nature of his being. If he was, truly, a spirit incarnated into a temporal body, shouldn't he take hold of that physicality in every way it was linked to this world of matter? Embrace the corporeal, touch it, shout it, claim it, own it?

He felt more deeply satisfied than he'd been in months. This is what being in the moment was all about: existing in the very instant of each life. It was about sensing with all his senses, smelling the heavy mist, seeing the moonlight-silhouetted pattern of a torn spider web strung between decussating branches, hearing the skitter of mice racing over the dead fallen leaves, feeling the earth, holding and molding it in his hands. He looked at his hands again, flexed them, opened them, squinted at the clay he'd squeezed into an amorphous lump. It occurred to him he'd never made anything with his hands before.

He had a strong urge to make something with his hands.

Two hours later the near-full moon was higher over the mizzled main house as Claire peered into the front window of the gardener's cottage. Original glass, it was rippling with age, thicker at the bottom, distorting slightly the dimly lit interior. She held a traditional ceramic blue-and-white lidded Wedgewood bowl in one hand, knocked on the window with the other. The front door opened. Claire jumped.

"Hello," she said. "I hope I'm not disturbing you this late."

Guy smiled. "No, I was just reading."

"Reading what?"

He held up the book in his hand, his finger marking the page he was on. The title was *Reincarnation and the Interpretation of Dreams.*

Claire's curiosity was piqued. "Moving on from the dual nature of the human spirit to its multiple nature, then, are you?"

"It's a recent interest of mine." And gesturing her inside: "Please, come in."

She did so. The cottage was small but tidy. A wooden table, two country chairs, a farmhouse armoire, a single bed behind a torn, yellowed *shoji* screen. Small bathroom and kitchenette, looked like they'd been added on maybe fifty years earlier, at the far side of the cottage, with a five gallon wall-mounted electric heater for the water. A lamp spilled light over a white Princess phone and Guy's sketchbook, which was open to a dark pencil drawing of a Victorian alleyway. A number of books stood upright between two rough-hewn wooden bookends on the table. Claire put her bowl down beside them.

"I've never seen those bookends before."

"I just made them," said Guy, quite pleased. "Found some scrapwood out back and tools in the shed. I've never really done woodwork before but I had an impulse."

"Excellent impulse," she said, though in fact the craftsmanship was less than first-rate. "Never done woodwork, never done gardening – you're having quite a sea change, then, aren't you."

"I think I'm starting over."

Glancing between the bookends, she noticed most of the texts were about past life experiences. The two exceptions were copies of *The Tempest* and *Macbeth*, both dog-eared and oft-read. She lifted the first book, let it fall open to the page it wanted to, and found herself in Act II, Scene 1, some of Antonio's lines highlighted. "'*What's past is prologue...*'" she read, then put the book down and tilted her head curiously at Guy. "Just what is it about reincarnation that interests you?"

"It seems like one of those ideas that are supported by our everyday experience but we routinely deny."

"I don't know what experiences you could possibly mean. Shopping? Eating a rosemary-infused rack of lamb? Reincarnation's not even on my radar."

He stood near the door, watching her explore the room. "Haven't you ever met a person you've never seen before but you instantaneously feel drawn to them, or feel like you've known them forever? Like a, like a deeply imbedded remembrance?"

She turned to face him. They looked a long moment at each other; and yes, she knew that feeling. "That does happen now and again," she said. "Pheromones is the explanation that makes sense to me. Subconscious, aromatic, biochemical attractions."

"That's what Western science would say, of course. A reductionist view, distilling all natural phenomena down to the lowest denominator of chemistry and physics. The Hindus or the Tibetans would embrace more overriding principles."

"Like reincarnation." She nodded. "Two people met in a past life, that's why they recognize each other now."

"It's not just recognition, though. It's karma. When two people are actively drawn to each other, to resolve some issue between them that generated karmic debt in the previous life."

"And karmic debt would be…?"

"Like any debt, it's something you owe. You do something bad, you owe something good to make up for it. But maybe you don't get to pay it back until your next life. That's what's called burning off bad karma."

"And the energy of that conflagration generates <u>good</u> karma you can carry with you to subsequent incarnations?"

"Exactly. It's a balancing act. Every time we appear in a new physical existence we're being given a chance to fix something that got broken last time. That's how we burn off bad karma."

"We who?"

"We… anybody, I guess."

But it was clear to both of them they were the only two people in the room. "You've given this quite some thought, I can see," she said quietly.

He didn't want to frighten her away his first night, didn't want to sound like a complete raver; so he tried to minimize. "What can I say? I'm an academic. I've always pretty much lived in my head."

"You were speaking with your heart, though, I could feel that clear enough."

And he could feel she was looking right through him to his core. It felt too close, too fast. He needed to back off a little, to explain away his zeal with a non-reason. "If by 'heart' you mean sincerity, then yes, I've always had strong opinions about whatever I was studying," he said.

"Even in your last life?" She smiled gently.

"Hey, that was then, this is now, right?" He shook his head, a lock of hair falling across his face.

She could sense his retreat, his need to hide some vulnerability; so she turned away, changed the subject, gestured around the simple room. "And speaking of now – are you comfortable here?"

"Cozy as a hobbit."

She indicated the bowl she'd put on the table. "Can I interest you in some hearty bean soup?"

He took the lid off the soup bowl, inhaled the aroma, the steam, the warmth of human comfort. "Smells heavenly."

"My own recipe."

"I'll try not to spill it on my pants," he said, referencing her husband's tirade at dinner.

"I'm sorry about Eric's temper. He has a problem with maids in general, and Alice in particular."

"Why doesn't he just let her go, then? It would be so much easier on both of them."

She took a moment, weighing how much to say. "Alice was Eric's high school teacher fifteen years ago. She failed him in some class and I'm afraid he never forgot the humiliation. Five years ago he got her fired from her job, then he hired her himself."

"If he always treats her as badly as he did tonight, why doesn't she just quit?"

Again Claire hesitated. "Six years ago, her husband was in a traffic accident; someone hit him, he's in a wheelchair, they have lots of bills for specialists, and extras... and Eric pays Alice quite well, actually. She's not really in a position to quit."

Guy was stunned. "That's cold."

The word was like a trigger, reminding Claire just how winter cheerless her own life was – which made her shiver once.

"Somebody walk over your grave?" he asked.

She tried to explain the shudder away on the weather. "This is the chilliest I can remember it getting this early in the fall." She nodded at the gibbous moon, visible through his window beyond the congealing fog. "See, there, and it's not even harvest moon yet."

He decided not to push her on her husband's issues any further for the time being so he went with her tack. "Harvest moon, that's the full moon in September, right?"

"Quite. Preceding the full moon in October – the hunter's moon."

"Why hunter?"

"It's the first full moon after the fields are harvested – so it's easy to see your prey."

Guy had a flashback, an image from his seizure dream, of the older scar-faced man stalking his pretty prey and stabbing her in the back with a full moon low in the sky above them, outlining the half-barren branches of a dying, fire-blackened tree.

"Are you all right?" Claire asked. Guy's face had turned on a dime; it was distant, scattered, everywhere but here.

Something was coming together for him, though. "Hunter's moon – is that when Eric's great-great-grandfather, Earl, hunted his prey?"

She wasn't sure what he was asking, but the topic made her stomach twist in on itself. "I don't think Eric wants me blathering on about the skeletons in his family's closet." She was unconsciously rubbing her upper arm in a state of visceral distress.

Guy noticed her wince, and had another intuition. He lifted her sleeve. Over her biceps was a bad bruise, wrapping the arm like tendrils, outlined in little discolored puffs. They almost looked like... finger marks.

"He hits you."

She tried to sound casual, but it just came out weary. "He doesn't mean to, really. He's very kind and then I'll just do something aggravating and he'll explode."

"You're describing typical abusive behavior. Jekyll and Hyde territory. He won't get better, Claire, he'll only keep hurting you worse and worse."

She shook her head. "You don't know that."

"Leave him. Just leave him." It was an elementally simple equation to Guy.

She shook her head slowly, though, and held back tears and held her belly. "I have my baby to think of now."

"Even more reason to go." He was keeping his own emotions in check. He'd only known this woman less than a day, but already felt the strongest of ties, almost like a blood bond. "You don't have to take that kind of –"

"Please!" She raised her voice, then brought it down again. "Sometimes it's just… a game, you know? 'Bit of the bounce and tickle.' It starts out as role-playing, to spice things up for kicks." She raised her other sleeve. There was a ligation mark.

He took a mental step back. "Sex play, you're saying."

"Sometimes it just gets a bit out of control." She sounded embarrassed. "The thing is, it doesn't always just happen during sex anymore. It's not like he ever means to have these episodes, he never intends to get so violent, he feels terrible about it afterwards. And he is getting better, really; his doctor says there may even be a genetic factor, like a, like a gene for rage."

"Stop making excuses for him."

"There's a history of violence in his family, you know his great-great-grandfather killed that man…." But she stopped there, not at all clear on how to finish her thought, or where it was going, or how it could lead anywhere but down. She felt lost.

Her comment caught Guy off guard, though – pulling him, against his will, down his own slippery path. "Wait – you said 'killed that man.' It wasn't a woman he killed?" In his dream it was a woman, it was always the pretty woman in the tattered dress.

"A man." She shook her head. "Earl's neighbor, they fought publicly and often. Supposedly one night the man turned his dog loose on Earl. Next day the fellow just disappeared, vanished, and so did his dog. Of course everyone assumed Earl had...."

Guy's agitation increased. "Did the dog bite Earl on the cheek? Did it leave a scar?" he pressed.

"I've no idea."

"But there could have been a scar. One that looked like this, don't you think? This could be from a dog bite."

He flipped through the pages of his sketchbook until he came to a detailed close-up of the killer in his dream, the man with the scar that ran from his left ear across his cheek and down to his chin.

She studied the drawing. It certainly looked like an older version of the portrait of Eric's ancestor Earl in her hallway, an older Earl, but with a scar on his face. "I suppose it could be a dog bite." She glanced at his reincarnation book lying open on the table. The text was full of underlinings, margin notes, exclamation points. She looked back at Guy, searching his face, and deeper. She did feel a connection to him, an intimacy she couldn't understand, hadn't wanted to examine too closely. But now she pushed: "Why did you take this job? Why did you really come here?"

"I was following a nightmare." He looked at her, imploring. "Why did you let me stay?"

"I told you." She smiled sadly. "I needed a girlfriend."

A tear welled up in her eye. He hugged her, a comforting embrace. Her softness, her feminine warmth against his lanky body, seemed to fill him, surround him, complement him. The vaguest hint of her fragrance wrapped them both in a subtle chrysalis.

She pulled away, to dab her eyes with a handkerchief she extracted from her dress pocket – inadvertently pulling a small vial out as well, which fell to the floor. Guy picked it up.

It was beautiful. Gold filigree over lavender glass. "What's this?" he asked, anticipating the answer.

"My perfume. Eric special-orders it for me."

He sniffed the tiny cork. "Can I keep it?"

She shrugged. "I have a boxful of them, he orders them in quantity from a private lavender perfumist near St. Paul de Vence. What do you want it for?"

"It's the scent of my seizures."

She took a step closer to him. "Would you like me to put some on?" Her voice was coming from a little lower in her throat.

"Are you trying to make me swoon?" he said, recalling the joke she'd made to him on their first meeting, trying to make light of the matter. But they were standing very close now, and it wasn't light at all, it was electric, and a little dangerous, like just before a violent storm.

The seven-eighths moon was visible above her shoulder. The yellowing globe, the way they were standing, the backlit shape of her body through her diaphanous dress, the hint of perfume – it all felt so evocative of his dreams. They leaned closer. Their lips touched. They didn't advance, didn't pull back, just lingered there, mouths brushing lightly, exquisitely tender, just short of passion… until she stepped away, flustered.

"I'd better go."

He nodded assent, he was just as disconcerted as she was. "I could call you," he offered. "I mean, if you just wanted to talk."

She pulled his open notebook to the edge of the table, wrote the numbers **77** in the margin. "We have a house phone system – this is my private line. I mean, if you wanted to talk."

They both smiled with the odd poignancy of being outside themselves, looking in. She went to the door, opened it, paused, glanced back. Something here seemed like a beginning for Claire, as if the swell of his sea-change could carry her along on its rising tide. It was a secret feeling and she held it close. It felt as if time had stopped.

He seemed to read her mind. "*Thus though we cannot make our sun…*"

"*…stand still, Yet we will make him run.*" she finished the couplet, riding the same poetic wavelength, and shut the door behind her.

She scurried across the wide lawn, toward the mansion, but didn't see, silhouetted in a second story window, the figure of Eric. Watching her.

Eric continued to watch her as she came upstairs. She smiled thinly, walked past him into her dressing room. He watched her get undressed, watched her put on her nightgown.

It made her uncomfortable, almost like he was violating her with his gaze, like some tawdry *voyeur* as opposed to her loving husband. "What are you looking at, Eric?"

"You, my dear, beautiful you."

She didn't want his covetous, penetrating eyes, though; she wanted to be alone with her thoughts, she wanted privacy. She walked back into the bedroom, past a wall-sized medieval tapestry of hunters, their hounds tearing into a wild boar. Walked to the four-poster, turned down the goose-feather covers. "I'm to bed early tonight, boy-o."

"I thought you might come to the south of France with me tomorrow." It was more a statement of fact than a request.

It caught her off guard. "What?"

"Just a silly business trip, really, but I thought we might turn it into something more pleasant."

She was flustered. "I'll have to check my calendar."

"Nothing we can't rearrange, I'm sure."

"But I don't fancy leaving just now, Eric."

"You used to love the Riviera. I've been dying to take you back to that little restaurant, *Le Portique*." Petulance crept into his tone.

"I don't know, maybe I'm just tired."

"Of me," he said, distinctly more sinister than petulant.

"No, of course not."

"Then why not come to France? I'll go to my meetings while you sprawl in the sun, if you're so bloody tired. What's keeping you here?"

She couldn't think what to say and she couldn't say what she felt. And if she could, she wasn't about to say it to Eric.

His suspicion fed on itself. "Don't tell me you still have one of your old lovers sniffing around? One of those actors who...."

"Eric, please," she said quietly, distastefully.

"No categorical denial? That's it, then, isn't it? You've taken a lover. In fact, I wouldn't be surprised if one of them sired this pretender fetus you're carrying."

She slapped him. He let her, remained motionless save for a slow smile. "If you don't hit any harder than that, I'll start to think you don't love me anymore."

She began to raise her hand again, then stopped. They remained frozen like that a moment, frozen as a portrait of their true relationship. She kept her voice level, wound tight. "I'm not having an affair, and this child is yours, Eric. You are the father."

He shrugged apologetically. "Of course I am, darling. I don't mean to be so hurtful. Forgive me?"

He took her in his arms, control masquerading as remorse. She let herself be embraced and then caressed, as his hands roamed first over her breasts, and then between her legs, more roughly. But she remained passive, her gaze adrift – floating inward, to avoid the awareness of his physical touch, and then when that touch became too intrusive to ignore, she found herself glancing around the room, looking for some anchor. That's when she fixed on her private phone, sitting on the vanity in her dressing room; the private line, 77, like a lifeline, and at the other end of it was Guy. It was Guy, waiting for her.

"Of course I'll go with you, darling." Her voice sounded flat. "Forgive me, I was just tired."

And when she returned from France, Guy would be here.

With Eric and Claire gone for a few days, Guy plunged into his new job, devoting himself to the physical labor. There was a purging aspect to it. He tore out great clumps of dead weeds, cut back gnarled bushes to stubs, dug up and turned over wide swaths of packed earth for planting. Somehow his limp even seemed to improve with all the hard gardening. He played with a scythe on the dry, tall grass and used a hedge clippers to endeavor a topiary shape on some wild privet. What the topiary meant exactly to represent was up to some interpretation. A juvenile rhinoceros in heat, Claire later guessed; a quivering rabbit, Guy suggested. It was a projection of the viewer's inner gardener, in any case: a Rohrshach bush, then.

And furthering his transformation from the man who lived in his head to the man who actively inhabited his body, he dabbled with his rudimentary woodworking skills, making first a doorstop, then a brace to hold open one of his windows whose internal counterweight had long ago succumbed to weather. Guy was becoming a tiller of the soil, a manipulator of wood, a shaper of growing things, a willful walker on the corporeal world.

He worked, he sweated. His muscles ached. The palms of his hands blistered, and when the blisters flattened, their skin turned numb, like the calluses they'd become if he continued toiling in this manner. He ate dinners in the kitchen with Alice, the maid; simple fare, usually meat pies and beer. One night he asked her about the master of the house.

"How long have you known Mr. Deloup?"

"Och, since he was a wee child. I knew his father, too."

"Could I ask… what do you know about these family rumors? The great-great-grandfather killing his neighbor, and so on?"

"There were more o' rumors than just the killing of the neighbor, I can tell you that."

"What kind of stories?"

"These are the people I work for. I'll no' speak against them."

He tried something he wasn't sure about. "But you'll act against them if you can get something out of it. You sold those family weathervanes to that antique shop, didn't you?"

She was taken by surprise. "I never… I did no'…."

"You took them from the gardener's cottage and sold them. The shop owner told me." The antique dealer hadn't said exactly who – but it was a reasonable guess Claire hadn't pawned the artifacts for money.

Alice looked ashamed. "They were in a box o' doodads nobody even knew were there. I needed the money plain and simple. You won't tell him, will you?" Fear crept into her voice now.

Guy shook his head. "I have no reason to say anything. But I thought Eric paid you well here. You couldn't have gotten all that much for a few old weathervanes."

"It's not anything I'm proud of. There's just times he makes me feel so bad… sometimes I find little ways to get back. No' that it really ever evens things out. It just makes me feel a touch less beaten. I beg you not to tell him, though. I can promise you it won't happen again." She couldn't look at him. She didn't want to look at herself.

He took a different tack, though, away from Alice altogether. "She's not happy here either, is she?"

They both knew who he was talking about, and Alice became protective of Claire. "She's a bonnie lass with a grand house, who little needs the pity of her groundskeeper," she shot back. Then, without waiting for his reply, she stood up to clear the dishes. "You want my advice, Mr. Daniels, you'll steer clear o' the whole mess."

Whereupon she kept her back to him at the sink, and that ended the matter.

Claire and Eric returned from the Continent the next day. Eric seemed relaxed, his business concluded successfully, while a number of wrapped boxes indicated Claire had come away a triumphant consumer.

She was thrilled to see Guy had made such energetic inroads into the garden and they took most of that day walking every foot of the property's seven acres as she pointed out where she wanted a Japanese bridge over the pond, where an herb and vegetable patch would be lovely, where an oak grove might thrive, or roses flourish, lilies rise to the challenge of too much shade behind the perfectly situated gazebo at the edge of the croquet lawn.

They spoke little of consequence: the state of French manners, English poetry and American movies, interspersed with favorite music and pet peeves of contemporary language usage. (Claire's: "I could care less," when what was meant was "I couldn't care less." Guy's: use of "literally" to mean "figuratively." As in: "It was raining so hard, I was literally drenched to the bone.") By the time they reached an ivy-covered lattice near the farthest stone wall of the estate it was evening and they were literally hoarse from talking so much.

She leaned back against the lattice, eyes closed, a picture of equanimity, poised on the equinox. "How nice you've come to be my gardener," she said.

"I could garden here for years and never finish," he replied, almost as if it were a trial balloon, with an undercurrent of yearning.

"All right," she said simply, and as if it were settled.

She opened her eyes, took a step toward him – but her long hair caught in the lattice and held her there. "Ow." She laughed.

He stepped forward to untangle her tresses from the cross-hatching of thin lattice strips and ivy, bringing his arms up around the top of her head, his chest touching hers, their faces so close. He stopped there. Their eyes bore into each other, played with each other, recalled deep, olden, incomprehensible feelings. She brought her arms up behind her, gripped the vines above her head with her fingers. "Are we going to have an affair?" she whispered.

"I thought we already were."

He brought his lips down to her neck, kissed her tender flesh, it was like slow electricity and her eyes closed again as if she were falling and flaming and bursting all at once; and a car door slammed in the distance and just like that it was all over, she was back in her tar-baby life and took three steps away from Guy, tearing hair on the lattice.

"That was Eric's car," she said. "I can't do this, I don't know what I was thinking."

He just stood there, nodding, trying to dampen his hatred of Eric, a hate that seemed to grow a little more every day, like a cellular memory and the cells just kept dividing. But he wouldn't burden Claire with all that. "Listen. You're married, you're pregnant. We don't have to do… anything. I just want to be around you. Talk about books. Walk in the garden. We can do that, can't we?"

She wiped her sleeve across her eye, and smiled back. "We can do that."

Some weeks passed. Guy dug and planted. He put a little muscle on his bone, got the calluses he was looking for. The first week of October was brooding, full of uncertain silences, idling looks. There were times Guy and Claire would pass without speaking, yet still intensely aware of each other's presence. Once, of an evening, as she was tossing a basket of shucked corn-silk on the compost pile, he walked near, carrying an armload of kindling, and paused. Smoke from a distant fire was crossing the oval moon, giving it a reddish hue, while a wind came up with a gentle whoosh, eddying the scattered dry leaves between them on the ground.

"*The skies they were ashen and sober,*" he said quietly, "*the leaves they were crisped and sere….*"

"*The leaves they were <u>withering</u> and sere,*" she whispered.

"*It was night in the lonesome October/Of my most immemorial year.*"

They stood in place for a long minute; watching, not speaking, savoring and delighting in the way they were uncannily able to finish each other's poetic quotes, as if that were somehow emblematic of the irrefutable unity of their consciousness. And then, like birds of a flock, at the same unsignaled moment, both turned, in stride, and walked off to their separate nests.

At other times they'd engage in protracted conversations about garden planning, and everything else as well: religion and politics, the madness of diets, the merits of the latest new television comedies, *Monty Python* versus *Saturday Night Live*, the genius of Copeland, the limits of Jung, the imagery of the Symbolists, the undistilled power of elegiac poetry. She would touch his arm a little too long, he'd brush a lock out of her face. They laughed a good deal, sometimes to breathlessness.

But then there were the moments after the laughter faded like a flashfire that's consumed all its oxygen, suffocated by the circumstance of its own overheated existence. And in those moments they felt limp in each other's presence, blank as the sky, timeless as the seconds after that paroxysm of love the French call *petit mort*. They yearned for a little death like that.

Guy spent some of his days off in the local church. He'd had the foresight to hang onto his University of California faculty ID so he plausibly convinced the parson he needed church records going back into the last century for academic research purposes related to the Galway works of Yeats. After that the cleric left him alone in the damp rectory to plow through decades of births, deaths, marriages, christenings, divorces, conversions, baptisms and jailings. There were, alas, gaps in the record, missing pages, bad penmanship, confusing genealogies.

He spent some time in the local cemetery, reading the slate headstone carvings, communing with the dead, asking whatever spirits might be hovering around to give him guidance. One marker read: *Nor sex nor age can death defy/Think, Mortal, what it is to die.*

He thought. Death was an emptying of the vessel. Only the shell was left, the living soul moved on. The dead body: nothing. It was no more than a gradual dissolution into organic matter, until that broke down to long-chain carbon molecules, eaten by worms who proceeded to shit out rich soil. And who would remember the dead man? A few friends, or children, might... until they died. In short order, nobody; ultimately nobody to remember anything at all. In a few billion years the sun would go nova, vaporizing the earth, turning all the remnants of what had once been Guy into elementary particles, propelled into deep space, to mingle with electrons from across the galaxy, maybe to congeal one day into another planet, another life form, another husk.

None of that affected the soul, of course. The soul remembered its earthly existence as it hovered in limbo between lives, mulling over all the lessons learned in its last incarnation, in the once-animate body of the lifeless corpse. But even the soul developed amnesia once it moved on, out of the timeless void of waiting, once it inhabited its next physical manifestation. The embodied soul tended to forget – unless it happened to animate some questing physical being who pulled that unrecalled memory out of the ether, wrestled it to the ground, stared it in the face. Guy wanted his face-time with that last life.

The parson asked, one day, how the research was going. Guy mentioned some of his difficulties – unmarked stones, gravesites of children without record, deaths recorded without physical evidence of graves. The parson asked if there was a particular tomb he sought. Guy said the name Deloup was mentioned in one of Yeats' monographs, so Guy was attempting to trace the Deloup family back to its earliest roots – attempting but failing.

"Ahh, I can solve that one for you," beamed the cleric. "Until this century they were all buried in private plots. On their own estates for the most part."

Guy's eyebrows went up. "Really."

"Quite. I suppose you know all about that bad business with Lord Gantley back in the day."

Guy took a stab. "The unfortunate rancor with Earl Deloup, you mean. The murder."

"Of course murder was never proved, there was no body, you know, no actual physical evidence."

"When was that, exactly?"

"You've asked the right parson, Yank. Bit of a local historian's what I am. Eighteen hundred eighty-six was the year."

"They were neighbors, I understand, they feuded."

"Worse than that, it was. Lord Gantley underwrote a bawdy house, right in town. Earl was a pious man; he hated what Gantley was doing, all the more because Gantley was a lord. They were neighbors and they quarreled often, often in the public square. Gantley's mastiff got loose one night, took a piece out of Earl Deloup he never forgot, they say. One day soon after that Gantley just up and vanished. October of the year."

"Hunter's moon, then."

"Might well have been."

"And Earl? What became of him?"

"Died of natural causes, I'm led to believe." He furrowed his forehead in a private, interior discussion, then nodded as he drew his own conclusions. "Buried in the family plot, I should think."

Guy walked the estate again, but saw nothing like a family plot. When he questioned Claire, she shook her head, said she'd never heard of anything like a graveyard on the grounds. But she liked the idea, in theory, of lying beside her true lover for all eternity. "I'd be literally exploding with happiness if I could do that – wouldn't you?" she smirked. "I could care less." He smiled, conspiratorially rubbing shoulders with her, savoring the delicious moment of touch, the shared private joke. She rubbed the smooth back of her hand up the coarse bristle of his cheek. Some days it was hard to walk away.

Some nights he watched her from the garden, across the yard, under cover of cloud, through the brightly lit windows of the mansion. She'd waft by in a gossamer nightgown, or pause in the framed opening, inch up to the window, looking out – looking out like she knew he was there watching her from the chilly October night, his breath steaming; she could almost feel it, the hairs of her arm standing straight up, her own respirations quick and thin, her breasts pressed against the cool glass. And he would see her there, his palms tingling with the imagined tautness of her skin.

He felt like a peeping Tom, so furtive, so compelled. It was disturbing to think of himself such; but exciting, too. It made him feel naughty, and erotic, and aroused. He sometimes remembered a piece of verse scrawled on a bathroom wall at college, credited to Pound by some dormitory wag: "*My darling grace/I love your face/I love you in your nightie/When the moonlight flits/across your tits/O Jesus Christ Almighty.*"

Some nights he sidled very close. Once, huddling outside, just below the kitchen window, he reached his arm up to the place where her hips were pushing against the inside of the glass. He paused, nearly motionless in that position, watched her arms rise up to the curtain rod, about to draw the drapes closed, the movement lifting her short nightgown to expose her thighs, which rested against the window just above the sill. And dear God, she held that position. And Guy, inches away, at the outer wall, moved his fingers over the smooth, hard window, barely half a centimeter from where her mons pressed the pane, warming the cool glass almost imperceptibly in just that spot, just that spot against his fingers; and she held that position, for him.

One night Guy found himself staring at the number she'd written in the margin of his journal: 77. It was her private line, she'd said. He had an urge to call now. He didn't know why, it felt exciting and scary and secret. But what would he say? Profess his deathless love without having to face her, without having to resist how much he wanted to engulf her, kiss her, dissolve into her? And anyway, wasn't Eric home now? What if Eric picked up? Eric the Foul. Still, Guy felt impelled. He put his hand on his phone, the white Princess. Could he sense Claire through the wires? Feel her heat? They were linked, he knew. But how?

If bad behavior in one life generated karmic debt which had to be repaid in the next, was Claire the payer or the payee on Guy's wheel of karma? And if groups of souls reincarnated together, over and over again, working out their entanglements over many existences... just what was Claire's role in Guy's preceding lifetime, and what was Eric's? All Guy knew for sure was he had a revulsion of Eric, a magnetism with Claire and everything about her – the tilt of her smile, the satin hair, the melodious timbre of her voice, the exquisite geometry of her shape, her walk, her intelligence, her spirituality, her smell. Her smell.

He grabbed the filigreed perfume vial, the one that had fallen out of her pocket. He rolled it around in his hand, felt the cool glass, roughened by the gold metal design enwrapping it. He brought it up to his cheek, held it there, then pressed it to his ear, as if perhaps he could hear distant voices calling to him from distant times. Maybe it was like listening for another ocean in some involuted sea-shell, maybe you could sense another life in the attar of some blown glass ampules. Hesitantly he uncorked the vial, tremulously brought it to his nose and sniffed deeply.

The scent was so strong he had to hold it away from his face for a moment, almost had to sit down before he fell in a heavy swoon. But he kept steady, propped himself upright against the chair, brought the vial back up to his nose. With great care he inspired, drew in the musky odor. It was so profoundly like the aura of his seizures, it brought him right to the edge of that altered state, that off-center consciousness. It was like the time he'd taken peyote in college, the moment he teetered right at the cusp of the hallucinations, straddling two worlds. Now he held the ornate perfume vial high before him – stared through its lavender glass at the ivory round moon outside the window.

The hunter's moon, it was called. Its shine was diffracted by the glass, broken up by the filigree, twisted into wavy lines that began turning slowly into set shapes, triangles at first, and then elongating into squares, then three-sided squares that tied into each other in a turret configuration, like ramparts of brick scraping stone in a gravelly bark....

Somewhere, a dog barks.

A gaslight flickers above an alleyway. A weathervane, shaped like a snarling wolf with rust-red teeth, turns slowly, creaking, silhouetted over a full moon balanced near the top of the sky. And a knocking, a repetitive knocking, like a shutter banging in the wind.

An older man appears at the alley's maw. He's nineteenth century by his look. A disturbing scar runs from his left ear across his cheek down to his chin, like a twisted broken spine.

A pretty woman arrayed in purple bruises and perfumed clothes walks past him on the cobbles. She has a limp. The scar-faced man flares his nostrils, as if aroused by the perfume, and follows her.

She quickens her pace, moistens her lips which have become dry with fear, with foreboding. He says something, but the words are garbled, a strange and ancient language. "Youyig... Youyiguh... Youyiguhmihud... Youyiguhmihudan. Youyiguhmihudan. Youyiguhmihudan. Youyiguhmihuda... huda... huda... da... da... aa... a... a... a... a hunter's moon, that is," he says.

She doesn't turn around, she just keeps walking as she answers. "What are you hunting then, Luv?"

But she gags as soon as the words are out and she looks back at him. She tries to speak again but now no sound comes out, as if she's too terrified to get any air through her windpipe. He pulls a scalpel from his vest. It shimmers of ivory moonlight. He stabs her in the back. Over and over. She falls, turning.

He slips the blade into her abdomen, twists. Her lips twist, as if mimicking his gesture. He pinches her lip hard, to still it, and twists the blade in her belly again, until the beveled steel gets bound up in some glutted knot of tissue and he slices through that with a stroke, like a matador's flourish, and reaches his hand into the gash and comes out holding some fetid stump of intestine, reeking of fear and her last meal, fish gone bad, disguised with tamarind and anise. Blood gushes from the wound, pools around the knife, overflows her belly, cascades down her sides. Eyes glazed, she dips her finger in her own blood, writes two words on the ground. **RED CHAOS.**

Then she writes a longer number. A growing number. **52426.**

Somewhere, a dog barks. The moon is full. The repetitive, irregular knocking continues in the distance. The pretty woman dies.

A shovel is digging a grave. The knocking continues. The shovel rolls the pretty woman's body into the grave.

Her body plunges into a depth of dark water, a swath of pale light illuminating other floating, dead bodies.

The man fills the grave back in with his shovel. He pats down the mound of earth on top of it. The shadow of the wolf weathervane falls across the mound of earth in the bright moonlight.

Guy was having a seizure on the floor of his gardener's cottage, rattling into the table, bumping his head repeatedly on the floor, knocking over the lamp, the books, the bookends, the white Princess phone. Drooling spittle, biting his lip until he stopped; he lay there quietly for a minute, two, three, four. Finally he took a few deep breaths, remembered where he was, what he'd been doing – the perfume, it was like the perfume had brought his mind so close to the edge of epilepsy it actually triggered the seizure, launched another vision. And he remembered every moment of this one, every sound, every nuance, every soul-gashing act. He could even understand their words, now, the words started out cryptic as always, but became intelligible this time, it wasn't like a foreign language anymore. *"That's a hunter's moon, that is."* *"What are you hunting, then, Luv?"* It was clear English. In fact it was all becoming clear. He pushed himself shakily up on one elbow, saw the full moon outside, grabbed the table, pulled himself to his feet and stumbled out, limping badly.

The mist had cleared, the night air was sharp, and chill enough to condense his exhalations, like dragon's breath steaming. Guy looked over the grassy area surrounding his little cottage, glanced up at the wolf weathervane, turning one way, then another on the low peaked roof; turned his eyes to the sky again, found the moon, located the dark shapes cast by all the things of the earth that blocked out its light. He found the shadow of the weathervane, where it was spread upon the ground.

Dragging his foot, he limped over and stopped short with a sense of both shock and inevitability: the copper wolf's shadow lay elongated over an old, grassy hummock – a mound of earth roughly the size of a body. It was the size and shape, in fact, of the grave in his dream, the grave the pretty woman had been pushed into, rolled into by the man's shovel, the dirt patted down again on top of her, burying her freshly dead.

He dropped to his knees, ran his hand over the thick, century-old grass, covering the subtle six-foot, grave-shaped curve.

Then he limped to the side of the cottage, to the tool shed, where he pulled open the rickety door, grabbed a shovel, raced back to the wolf's shadow on the grassy mound.

And with an obsessed gleam in his eye, he began to dig.

He dug all night, October 8, the night of the full moon, the hunter's moon, and kept digging into the morning of the 9th. Sweating, dirty, standing in a hole four feet deep, six feet long, three feet wide, he just wouldn't stop digging, so weary, ready to dig until he dropped. And then he dropped.

On his hands and knees in the grave now, he put the shovel up on the grass and went to scrabbling with his hands at the loosest dirt. His fingers were sore, blisters under his calluses, unused to this much intense manual labor. Every handful of scraped-up soil hurt, seared him down to the bone, but he ignored the pain, kept on digging, looking for sign, all the while feeling there was a lunacy rising in him, as if the deeper he dug the closer he got to some dark empire, and that proximity was overpowering him.

When the loose earth was all gone, he grabbed a small pointed spade, and then a gardener's claw tool, to break up the hard-pack. One of his eyes was swollen half shut from flying debris, and sweat blurred everything – but he saw something in his peripheral vision, out of the corner of his good eye, something at the other end of the pit he was excavating. Saw something that made him stop. Quite nearly made his heart stop.

It was a bloody, dead mastiff lying on its side, its jaws still open, as if ready to attack even in death.

Guy lurched backward, rubbed his stinging eyes, opened them again – and the thing was gone.

It was just his imagination. That or a ghost, maybe; or a twisted vision from another time; or truly, a madness risen from hell.

Guy scrambled up out of the hole, rolling backwards, away from the visual echo of the giant, dead dog – and rolled into a pair of legs.

"What the hell do you think you're doing?" demanded Eric.

"It… it looked like a grave mound," Guy stammered. "So I started digging."

Eric grabbed his collar, yanked him to his feet. "Part of your gardening duties?"

"No, I, the shadow of the wolf crossed it last night, I saw it in my dream and then I started digging, it looked like a grave and the dead hound was lying there, all bloody."

"What asylum did you escape from, Laddie?"

Guy tried to pull himself together, to recover some sense of dignity. "I know it sounds bizarre, but, but it looked like a grave and what if it turns out the man your great-great-grandfather killed is buried here? Or maybe the man's dog, the one that bit Earl…."

Eric pushed Guy against the cottage wall, hand at his throat. He spoke with quiet venom. "You're insane and you're fired, and if you're here in ten minutes, you're dead."

"Eric, leave him alone!" Claire was walking up now, fuming, trying not to succumb to the premonition already worming into her heart, the sense of her world about to change.

Eric turned to her with a scowl. "This is the fool you're having the affair with?"

She slapped him. He punched her and she fell. Enraged, Guy rushed him.

The two men brawled against the tool shed. Rakes and hoes came slamming down on top of them, smashing a pot on the ground, cutting Guy's leg with a shard. Eric grabbed a scythe, swung it at Guy, who ducked and tackled. They went rolling down a slope, pummeling each other, as Claire stumbled to her feet, screaming.

"Stop! I'm calling the police!"

Eric kneed Guy in the groin, kicked him into the grave. But Guy grabbed Eric's ankle and they both went in. Eric landed on top, went right to ripping at Guy's eye, as Guy turned his head away and pushed up on Eric's chin. Neither one felt any pain, steaming hard on adrenaline. Claire began whacking Eric across the back with the shovel handle.

Eric jerked the shovel out of her hands, thrust it at her, hitting her square in the chest, knocking her backwards. Guy punched him in the jaw, punched with his whole body. Eric went down, but came right up with the claw tool, swinging it at Guy's face. Guy grabbed his wrist – twisted the claw tool, rotating it slowly, against the intense resistance of Eric's hand, inch by inch, closer and closer until its rusted steel fingers reached out to touch Eric's face. And then Guy found his last ounce of strength and pushed another inch further still, into skin and muscle, gouging a deep, ugly gash down the length of Eric's cheek.

Eric roared back with the strength of untempered rage. It was as if a boil had been lanced, releasing all the repressed, restrained, toxic angers that had been simmering in the cauldron of his life for as many years as he'd been filling it. He grabbed the small pointed spade lying in the dirt, raised it high to plunge into Guy's heart, wanted nothing so purely as to see Guy screaming in pain and then dead in the dirt – when Claire brought the shovel down like a club on the back of Eric's head, knocking him out cold.

Exhausted, disoriented – terrified at what had nearly just happened to him, horrified at what he himself had done – Guy pulled himself out of the grave, past Eric's unconscious body. Claire hugged him.

"Oh, God, is he dead?" she breathed.

Guy looked at Eric, whose chest rose and fell in a deep, regular rhythm. "No," said Guy. But he couldn't stop staring at the horrific, bleeding gash down Eric's face.

It was a gash that gaped open raggedly from his left ear, across his cheek, and down to his chin.

"No... no..." Guy murmured, shaking his head with a sense of growing comprehension, a terrible dread of understanding, a knowing that something is inevitable, and unstoppable, and dire. "It can't be like that."

"What is it?" said Claire.

"The cut on his face...." Guy looked at it with horror. "I just gave him the scar I've been seeing in my dream."

Claire was confused. "The scar you showed me in your journal?"

Guy nodded numbly. "The man in the dream is older than Eric, too. Thirty years older. And he has that scar, look at Eric's cheek, that's where the scar is." He grabbed Claire's arm, shook it to make her understand. "Don't you get it? I haven't been dreaming about a past life at all. I've been dreaming a _future_ life." He stared at Eric with an overpowering dismay. "My next life, after I die in this one – my next life, thirty years from now – when Eric, here, is thirty years older, and his cheek is scarred, and he's a murderer...."

Guy stumbled back, staggering away from this unmoving, bleeding man; retreating in wild dismay from the manifest evidence of Guy's own potential for uncontrolled violence.

Stumbling away from the scarred face of the killer in his future.

7

CHAPTER SEVEN

October 16, 2013
9:42 A.M.-11:56 P.M.
Before Someone Gets Hurt

Eric was sixty-six years old now. He called himself Mark Dent, the director of a stage play in Chicago, a play about a murder in Victorian England. He was a man with a trim beard, a long memory, and a plan.

He finished splashing water on his face in the small bathroom sink of his backstage office. Stood up to look himself in the mirror, his hair hanging straight, like a Saxon prince. He patted his beard dry. He was in the habit of using eyebrow pencil to tint the snow white lightning streak that ran through the otherwise black hair covering his left cheek – but his latest brand of coloring wasn't fixing very well and the dye tended to bleed out at the first whiff of soap and water.

He moved his finger along the ribbon of white-hair that traced a path from his left ear across his cheek and down to his chin; palpated the thick ragged scar that ran beneath the beard. Felt the black pain locked in that dead, insensate tissue, like a memory sealed and tagged. Brought his little dyeing brush up, layered the dark color over the white striation, short strokes, seamlessly matching the tone to the dark of his facial hair.

That's when he noticed Vicky standing behind him in the doorway, watching.

She seemed embarrassed to be caught frozen there. He smiled, though, to put her at ease. "So. I touch up. Now you know my secret little vanity."

"I think it looks very dramatic. The pale streak, I mean. If it were me, I wouldn't cover it up, it's like totally potent."

He walked toward her, smile fading slightly. "It grows white because of a scar underneath that I've had a long time. Not an experience I want to share on a daily basis."

"I'm sorry, Mark, I shouldn't even have been standing here, I just wanted to...."

"But we all have hidden scars of some kind, don't we? The only important thing is not to hide them from ourselves."

Unbidden came the image of her mother's surgical scar, which she hadn't seen until the woman was dead. Red and puffy covering eleven inches across her belly, it had never quite healed, yet the stoic lady had never mentioned it. And then there was the cut on Vicky's lip from the one time her father had hit her, that left a tiny scar for many months. And that brought to mind the razor blade that had cut her two months ago; she still had a scar from that, reprising the injury from her father, and she unconsciously reached up to her mouth to touch it.

He noticed. "In the matter of scars, I'm reminded of the story of Jacob, Genesis 32:24 and thereabouts, when God comes down and wrestles Jacob all night long, but Jacob prevails in the end, so God touches him on the hollow of his thigh, and scars the sinews there so Jacob limps ever after and God tells him his name is now Israel, which means one who struggles with God. He who is touched by God." He ran his finger down his white-haired streak from ear to cheek to chin. "I've been thusly touched. I've struggled with my Spirit and I've prevailed and been marked for it." With exquisite gentleness, he brought the tip of his index finger up to the small bit of scar tissue on Vicky's lip. The mark of the razor. "You've been touched, too."

She stretched to find something appropriate to say, without wanting to follow him down the trail of his personal melodrama. "What a coincidence," she allowed. And when he tipped his head, she continued: "That we both have scars on our faces, I mean."

"Jung said the premise of probability demands the very existence of the improbable." He brought his fingers up into his beard, felt along the line of the old wound; closed his eyes, remembering.

Vicky wanted to put his mind to rest insofar as her witnessing was concerned. "You don't have to worry. I won't tell anyone what I saw here."

"I know you won't, dear." He didn't smile at all. "It's our secret."

Later, on the set, Mark strolled onstage in time to see Ratner, at the end of his scene, backing into the shadows.

"I told you twice!" Mark shouted. "You end that moment with arms upraised, in angry supplication of your God! Underplay it like you just did again, I'll bury you alive."

"No need to be so theatrical, Mark." Ratner was in costume, in character. Dressed as a Victorian gent. Had Guy been here to see him – journeying from 1976 – he might have felt a *frisson*: Ratner was sporting the clothes of the killer in Guy's seizure dream.

But of course Guy had been dead for over thirty years now.

"There actually is a need to be theatrical since theater is what we do here," Mark explained to his star. He'd jettisoned his British accent years ago, by design. It emerged at moments like this, when he was trying to suppress anger with sarcasm. "If you can't take direction, Will, we might as well say good luck and call it quits."

"Don't say good luck," Otto called out from the wings. "It's bad luck."

"You and your stupid superstitions," said Teddy, dressed as the stable boy.

"Know my favorite superstition?" said Otto with a hint of leer. "The one about the size of a man's foot being reflective of the size of other parts of his body." And he boldly flirted with the notion of Teddy's foot size.

Mark clapped loudly. "Places, everyone. Remember, I beg you, the title of this play is *The Last Tempest*, so let's try to put just a bit of tempestuousness in our performances, shall we?"

The actors took their places on the set of a 19th-century street. A set designed with a large element of surrealism. Almost looked like a drug-twisted vision of reality. Or a seizure-induced nightmare. Vic didn't know why he'd developed those particular design elements. They'd just... come to him.

"All right," said Mark, setting the tone, informing their characters, suggesting motivations: "You're both talking around what you mean, but you both know what's really going on below the surface, so everybody's dissembling and being coy and noncommittal, and... action."

On stage, Ratner and Otto walked and talked down the surrealistic street. "I can't put my finger on it, Doctor," said Otto as the Med Student, Doyle. "You're just not yourself these days."

"And who do I seem to be, Doyle? More a denial of my self, would you say, or a mockery? More a metaphor, or an emblem? Or perhaps larger than life even, an exaggeration, even a caricature? Come, man – who are you to assert such a slander?"

"I am your student, sir, and your friend."

"Cut, stop, cease," shouted Mark. "Otto, your last line needs to be filled with layers; you say you're his friend but we have to wonder about your true intentions, there has to be subterfuge in your eyes, and betrayal, and subtext, dammit! Here, watch the way I do it."

As Mark ran up to the stage to confer with Otto, Vic sat in his office going over paperwork with a Pandora East Texas Blues radio station playing in the background. A Steve Earle song came up, not exactly a blues, though – *Galway Girl* – interrupting his train of thought. *And I ask you, friend, what's a fella to do, 'Cause her hair was black and her eyes were blue.* It gave Vic pause, he didn't know why. But it made him think of Vicky, made him want to see her badly. Made him worry about her.

He put on her gift to him, his new burgundy satin-lined black suede jacket, exited his office and walked backstage, up to Ratner. "Will, you seen Vicky around?"

"I think she said she was going shopping with your mother this morning."

Vic tried to hide the alarm he felt now that his antennae were up about his mother's once-red car. A fact he'd not yet mentioned to Vicky. "You know where they went?" he asked casually.

"The mall," said Ratner with a confidential smirk. "And if I know women – and I think I do – they'll shop until somebody gets hurt."

Vic pulled out his cell phone as he walked to his office, where he could talk with some privacy. To call Vicky. Before someone got hurt.

Vicky was standing on the roof of a parking structure at the open trunk of her car, bobbling boxes in a light drizzle as she prattled on about this great new Cuban restaurant in Lincoln Park, *Habaneros*; Gloria had to try the place, they made the most incredible *mojo de ajo*, it was a meal in itself, and flaming rum-soaked *plantanos* for dessert.

Earlier, at the beginning of their girl's-morning-out shopping trip, Gloria had directed Vicky to this rooftop parking slot near the elevator and Vicky'd backed into it, also at Gloria's suggestion. So now Vicky was standing at the edge of the ledge, overlooking a long drop – as Gloria, right behind her, reached out a strong hand toward her back. Easiest thing in the world to just tip her over the rim, slippery with rain, watch her take a long header to the pavement. But Vicky turned, and their eyes met.

"Watch it!" Gloria shouted. And pulled the surprised girl away from the precipice.

Vicky looked at Gloria with a touch of merriment. "That's okay, Gloria, this isn't *Vertigo* and I'm not Jimmy Stewart. Not afraid of heights."

Gloria smiled back. "Really. What are you afraid of, sweetie?" It was an innocent enough question.

"The usual." Vicky laughed, putting the Macy's packages into her trunk. She still thought of the place as Marshall Field's. "Failure. Meaninglessness. An empty life."

"Ahh. Not afraid of the heights. Afraid of the depths."

"My work and my man are definitely taking care of those fears, though." The thought of Vic swept over her, a sweet and filling éclair of a notion. She glanced at the tiny diamond on her ring finger like it was a special secret. "It's such a dream to be working on the same project with him," she said. "Like my life is actually a unified, integrated whole – which, come on, how often does that happen on this planet?"

Gloria tried to keep her tone neutral. "Won't that get a little claustro-phobic at some point, though? Working together, living together, sleeping together?"

"If it does, we'll deal with it. Right now, I couldn't be fuckin' happier."

It was the first time Vicky'd ever sworn in front of Gloria, which is to say, had used her real voice. They knew this was the crossing of a frontier. A moment of Vicky letting Gloria into her true world. Inching closer, and Vicky liked the way it felt.

For one thing, it was a token of her love for Vic, that she was willing and able to open up to the other important person in his life. For another thing, Gloria was a pretty cool old broad and Vicky could see where it might be kind of fun to actually hang out with her sometimes.

Gloria, for her part, could see the girl adored her son. It was simply turning out to be unexpectedly tough for Gloria to let the boy go. Vicky was obviously going to be a handful for him – able, pretty, flamboyant, intelli-gent, demanding, narcissistic, tough, brash. But Gloria had always loved brash most of all. It's what she'd lacked so long in herself. So she decided to honor it now in the prospective daughter-in-law with a brash proposal of her own. "I have an idea, hear me out. The two of you ought to get away for a couple days. I've got a room booked at the Paradise Villa, up in Union Pier, it's right on the lake; I usually like to get away this time of year – why don't you use it, my treat? You can leave tonight, stay a couple days, just get away."

Vicky was touched by the offer. "That's so sweet, Gloria – but it's too crazy right now. We're rehearsing practically 'round the clock, opening night is in two days; we were going to open tomorrow night, but Otto gave Mark such crap about bad luck opening on hunter's moon, Mark changed it."

"Hunter's moon, I haven't heard that expression in a long time. Mark is the producer?"

"The director. He's an odd one, I have to say. Kind of a self-absorbed, temperamental older guy with a scar down his cheek that gives him this white streak through his beard, and – oh, damn, I said I wouldn't say any-thing about it."

"A scar, really." Gloria tried to sound nonchalant, but the words caught in her throat. Some women found men with narrow foreheads disturbing, some reacted viscerally to tattoos or divergent eyes. Men with facial scars is what undid Gloria. "Like a dueling scar?"

"I don't know. I don't think so but how would I know? Anyway, you have to promise me you won't tell anybody about it, he keeps the whole thing hidden with eyebrow pencil over his beard."

"Why does he hide it, did he say?"

"No, he just started quoting Jung and the Bible and I got out of there."

"He sounds like an educated man."

"He is, and a Brit, I think. They get a pretty formal education over there. Not much accent, though."

"A Brit. What did you say his name was?"

"Mark Dent. Sound familiar?"

"Dent. I don't think so." She smiled tightly. "But I'll have to come down to the set, now. He sounds interesting."

Vicky was about to say she didn't think Mark and Gloria would hit it off, when her cell phone rang. Caller ID said Vic. Vicky answered. "Hey," she said.

But her face turned cloudy, listening to Vic, as Gloria loaded shopping bags into the trunk.

They met later at the Chinese restaurant. Vicky wasn't working here today but it seemed like good solid ground, away from prying ears on the set. They sat at a back booth while Oma set tables for the lunch bunch. *Galway Girl* was playing on the PA system.

"That's weird, I just heard that song," said Vic.

"Yeah, songs are like that, Baby, they play more than once."

"Something about that one, though." He shrugged. "I don't know. Anyway I just wanted to say I feel bad about what I did to poor Tully."

"Forget the 'poor Tully' shit, that's the least of this late breaking news. You're telling me Tully is innocent of everything and you think your mother is stalking me?"

"I'm not saying for sure."

"I was just with her, we were shopping all day. She was, I don't know…."
She flopped her hands in the air. "How is this possible?"

Vic wasn't sure where to start. He wasn't a real introspective guy – that
had been Vicky's first impression of him way back when and things hadn't
changed much in that regard. To help himself work it out now, he grabbed a
napkin, began folding an origami bird. Vicky held out her hands, palms up,
like "Well?" So he took a stab at his family-of-origin story. "Okay, my father
abandoned us more or less when I was born. Mom said he didn't have the
balls to raise a family but I think she always felt like it was her fault, she
wasn't pretty enough or she was too flighty or who knows what the hell."

"Why do you think he left?"

"Happened right after I was born, so I gotta believe I had something to
do with it. Doesn't matter, really. The point is, as long as I can remember
Gloria's been kind of overprotective about me. Not ever wanting me to get
hurt, you know, physically or emotionally, and also using me as her biggest
support. It was probably, I don't know, messed up; I look at it in retrospect,
it wasn't healthy for us to be that close."

"Did she like… molest you?"

"No way, it wasn't like that, it was just, I don't know, it could feel like a
big weight sometimes, like she needed me too much. I mean, there were
great things about it too, I felt loved, like we were a team, like nothing could
separate us for very long."

"Including me, I couldn't separate you? Is that where this is going? You
working up to saying she's trying to scare me off?"

"Or worse. I mean… maybe something like this happened before."

She was a quick study. She connected the dots. "Kendra."

They let that image percolate a few seconds. He'd laid out the foundation
and the backstory. Now for the evidence. "The whole time I was growing
up, Gloria used to have a purple station wagon," he said. "She drove me
everywhere in it, all my lessons, my games, my teams. My dates. Even after I
grew up and our lives separated, she still drove that old purple car. Then I
met Kendra." He paused, seeing Kendra's face clearly in his mind for the
first time since Olivetti had asked about her.

Vicky saw the look on his face, and felt a little stab in her heart. "You
loved her."

Vic nodded. "First love. For both of us. We spent every second together. Weeks would go by and I wouldn't see my mother at all. Then whenever I did bring Kendra by Mom's house, things didn't go so great. Kendra thought Mom was weird and Gloria wasn't crazy about Kendra."

"But she likes me, right?"

"Yeah, but here's the thing. Gloria left town for a couple months, some kind of papermaking workshop out in Pennsylvania. Drove off in her purple station wagon. While she was gone is when Kendra died. When Mom came home a week later, she was driving a different car, an old green Chevy she said she picked up cheap when her wagon gave out."

Vicky was confused. "But you said – Detective Olivetti said – Kendra was hit by a red car."

Vic squinted, like this was all migraine-painful. "Something just clicked in me when he said it and I flashed on you getting your car repainted and that gave me this cockeyed feeling of I don't know – intuition, I guess. Which I absolutely never have. So I went over to Gloria's garage and checked her car." He took her hand. "Vicky, there was red paint under the green."

Vicky felt nauseated. "You have to tell Olivetti."

He shook his head. "I need to be more sure in my own mind, first. I mean, this is my mother we're talking about."

Vicky thought, No, this is me we're talking about. But Vic was her fiancé now. She was sure he'd do the right thing. "So what are you gonna do?"

"The razor you got cut with, the Triple O Cutt-Ex – it's an artist's tool. Like for cutting matt board, for framing. I'll see if she has that exact brand in her garage, where she keeps that kind of stuff."

"What will you say to her when she asks what you're doing?"

"Nothing yet, I hope. I'll go when she's not home."

"She's not home now," Vicky suggested.

"How do you know?"

"She went to the set. She told me she wanted to meet the director. Don't ask me why. It sure seemed like she had something on her mind."

Gloria walked around the empty stage. Nobody here but a few hands painting scenery, hanging lights, while the actors were all out at lunch. Except one older actor, dressed like Victorian nobility, wearing a brocade dress-coat, performing and gesticulating to a blank wall. Gloria approached him.

"Excuse me," she said.

He turned. Looked her up and down, the way piggish guys sometimes do. Unashamedly approved of what he saw, and smiled like a scamp. "If you're here to inquire about the role of the beautiful starlet, I'm afraid it's already been filled."

Gloria'd had a lifetime of holding her own against men's lies. Her bullshit radar could tell in an instant which ones were basically good guys underneath and which ones were putrescent at the core. This one was a working mix of both, but she didn't plan on having much to do with him to sort it out so she beamed a smile and a wink in his direction. "That much blarney, you must be at least part Irish."

He bowed. "William Ratner, at your service."

"Gloria Stone. Actually, I'm Vic's mother – the tech director? I just came to see his set."

"And a fabulous set it is. The boy's a genius and a credit to your upbringing, I've no doubt."

"You're too kind."

"He's a fine lad and couldn't have picked a prettier lass than Vicky to marry."

"She's a lovely girl," smiled Gloria. Noticed his brogue was getting thicker by the second.

"She's a fine actress and a fine looker, round in the corner and buff in the bow...." Now he was degenerating into talking in sea chanties. "With a waist like a black widow spider – not that I mean to alarm you, I'm suggesting physical proportions, not temperament."

"I wonder if you could point me to the director's office," she jumped in before he started talking pure Long John Silver. "I'd like to say hello to the captain of the ship."

"The director," Ratner echoed, as if intrigued by such a novel idea. "Do you know him?"

"No, I just wanted to introduce myself."

"In that case, allow me to show you the way."

He walked her off-stage, past the costume rooms, past make-up rooms where inventory was being organized, past empty dressing rooms, and finally to the director's office. He knocked, opened the door in a single sweep, called inside as he stepped in. "Mark? Are you in?"

He ushered Gloria inside. They looked around the cramped space. "What a shame," said Ratner, "nobody home." No big surprise to him, though; he knew full well Mark had gone out to lunch with everyone else. He slipped behind Gloria, eased the door shut with a hint of innuendo. "I suppose that means we're alone," he said, lowering his voice an octave.

Gloria turned to face him, and found his hands all over her before she could speak. So she kneed him in the groin.

Not a physically strong man, he crumpled. She stared down at him. "You shouldn't do things like that."

No one had dropped him so unceremoniously in twenty years. Even if his attentions were unwanted, he generally felt protected by his elevated status, his well-established tenure. Now all he felt was pain and humiliation. Not remotely given the respect he was due. And from whom? From this unremarkable old hag who should have been grateful anybody would give her a tumble, let alone the great Will Ratner.

He stared up at her. "Neither should you."

An hour later, lunchtime over, rehearsals about to resume, Vic came back from another foray to his mother's, this time uninterrupted. Somebody said Vicky was waiting for him in her dressing room so he knocked on the closed door and went in without waiting.

Found Vicky standing there, one foot up on a chair, her dress hiked up to her hip, inserting a tampon. She glanced at him in the mirror, shaking her head like she couldn't believe it, like the last straw had just landed on her back. "This is perfect, isn't it, practically opening night and I'm getting my period; that's all I need now is more blood, right?" She read his face as he shut the door. "She had the razor blades, didn't she?"

"In her garage," said Vic. "I took 'em."

She brought her foot off the chair, back down to the floor, fluffed out her dress. "Fuck. This scares me, Baby."

"I won't let anything happen to you."

"Okay, let's go tell the police."

"I already called Olivetti."

"What'd he say, is he gonna pick her up?"

"He wasn't there, so I left a message. They said he's out all day on another case."

"So tell someone else at the station." She was annoyed. This wasn't complicated; why was Vic being so obtuse?

Vic nodded, considering all the angles. "We're dealing with Olivetti, let's stay with him. Besides, I kind of want to talk to Gloria first. Ask her what she was thinking."

"She's not thinking anything, Vic, she's crazy. If she put that razor in my food, she could do anything." What fresh hell was this? Was Vic actually cutting his mother some slack on stalking and assault? Let's face it, the woman sounded like a killer, maybe a serial killer, and he wanted to know what she was thinking?

"Maybe I can find her a shrink, get her some help."

"Help me!" she shouted, her voice harsh. Scared and angry, feeling cut loose, the words burst out as if there were someone far down inside, calling out.

"I'm trying to help everybody," he said, his own voice rising. Felt his stomach knotting up, took a couple deep breaths, from his diaphragm. This wasn't so cut and dried, he wanted to say to Vicky, and if his mother was really sick....

"Fuck this help everybody shit, I'm the one being attacked with razor blades and I could use a little consideration here. I mean if you're not up to actually protecting me...."

"I am protecting you!"

"Yeah, by cuddling with your mommy while I'm out here swinging in the breeze." She could feel her cheek stinging, just like it had when her father'd slapped her for the crime of announcing the bad news that she'd been molested. That's what Vic's reluctance felt like. A slap. She didn't want to be protected like that anymore.

Vic stared at her, a bleak anger filling his craw like a bubble in a tar pit. Cuddling with his mommy? That's what Vicky thought? He ground his teeth; he wanted to smack her but knew he couldn't do that, that would take him to a very bad place. So he told himself to relax and tried to retreat into the dark closet in his mind where he could regain equilibrium; but he couldn't find it right now. So he just spoke as quietly as he could, measured his words. "I'll give Olivetti the blades."

That wasn't a good enough promise anymore, though; there was still too much wiggle room, and she was feeling lost at sea. "When?"

This was a new, pushy side of her he didn't care for at all. When the chips were down, that's when you discovered who someone really was. Unrelenting, that's who she was. Unsympathetic. Unnerved. And why wouldn't she be? Somewhere deep down Vic knew Vicky wasn't wrong to be pushing this hard, which made him angry at himself as well, which made capitulating even harder. But he did it, since that's who he was when the chips were down. "Okay, I'll call Olivetti again tonight. I'll go see him first thing in the morning."

She wasn't letting him get away with anything now, though. "How do I know you will?"

"Because I said I will!" he shouted.

"Well that's been a real fuckin' comfort so far!" she shouted back even louder, stepping up even closer.

"Get off the rag, Honey, I'm sure things will look up." Right in her face, and one quick impulse away from hitting her.

Playing the menstrual card against her meant game over, as far as she was concerned. She pushed past him out of the room, knocking him to the wall, hot tears in her eyes.

He grabbed a jelly jar full of makeup brushes and threw it full force against the door jamb, smashing it into a million pieces. Didn't win the argument, but it let off enough steam to settle the kettle.

Late in the afternoon Olivetti got back to the station, looking weary, notepad in hand, as Detectives Wiley and Shaw were on their way out for the day.

"Oli, come on, I'm buyin'," said Wylie.

"You guys go ahead, I have to finish." He gestured to his notepad. "DMV says Gloria Stone has a Chevy registered in her name. I traced it back to the dealer where she got it, their paperwork says it was a red Chevy. I'm thinkin' maybe the woman's got a jones about her son's lady friends."

"Speaking of, her son called before, wanted to talk to you," said Shaw.

"What about?"

"Didn't say. Said call him, or he'd call you back tomorrow."

"Wanted to know about this, probably." Olivetti flicked his fingers at the **LOVE DIES** paper, in a plastic evidence bag on his desk. "Which is another sinker on his mama's line. Lab says the ink is non-acidic, which is common in artists' pens, which is what his mother is, an artist. I'm thinkin' maybe it's time I should go have a talk with her about that dead girl Kendra, the son's first fiancée, got run over by a red car."

"Come on, have a drink first."

"You guys go ahead without me. I ought to go talk to the mother."

"Talk to her in the morning. Talk to me tonight." He put his arm around his old friend's shoulder. Like a plea. "I hardly see you anymore, you dumb fuck."

Olivetti hated breaking stride, hated not moving forward on a case that felt like it was gaining momentum. On the other hand, it didn't seem like an emergency so much as fitting pieces into a jigsaw puzzle. And maybe a drink was exactly the thing he needed to get a new bead on the picture. See it from a new angle. "Maybe you're right," he nodded to Wylie. "I guess I can let Vic's mom get one more good night's sleep."

Gloria got out of the shower that night, dried herself, put on her comfy, tattered nightgown. Needing a little comfort. The incompetent sexual assault by that idiot actor had undone her; or maybe this was all about seeing Vicky today, talking about marrying Vic, Gloria feeling how final the closure was going to be on this phase of her life. Her boy was moving on. Made her all alone in the world. Like she was standing on the platform and the train had pulled out of the station, whistling heartache.

She got under the covers, tried to read for a while, a thin book of poems by Christina Rossetti, but was too distracted to concentrate so she put it down and turned out the bedside lamp. The nearly full October moon shone brightly through her window, starkly outlining a partially defoliated elm tree whose shadows fell across her floor, moving in the wind like the aimless scrabblings of a dying animal. There was a foreboding to it, a thickening of the air in the night quiet when there was nothing else to do but think.

She thought about that bizarre scary attack a few weeks ago, the man who'd pushed her down in the park, held her face in the dirt and lit her dress on fire. Such a random piece of urban violence she hadn't even reported it to the police. Hadn't told a soul, actually. Didn't want to ramp up her sense of panic, wanted to think about what it really meant - and if it possibly had to do with Vicky's director, a man with a facial scar. Gloria had the queasy feeling of being watched, these days, it was like a stale breath on the back of her neck.

A crash echoed from downstairs.

She sat up, eyes wide. Instantly seized by a pounding heartbeat, shallow breath, acute hearing, all those visceral internal alarms raised by the sound of a window breaking downstairs, the shatter of a protective shell on the soft underbelly of a life that seemed so safe. Someone's down there. And they mean no good. You strain your ears in the silence that follows, knowing the intruder is taking extra pains to stay extra quiet now, hoping you were asleep before, willing you to stay asleep.

But the crashing on Gloria's first floor repeated. And then continued, violently, on and on. As if whoever was smashing everything didn't know Gloria was home. Or even worse, wanted her to hear.

She reached for her cell phone, then realized it was charging in the kitchen. She picked up the landline at the bedside, to call 911. No dial tone. Someone had cut the wires. Dread paralyzed her for a few long moments but she refused to be a victim. Ever again. Forced herself to get out of bed. Looked around for some kind of weapon, anything to defend herself. Grabbed a fireplace poker. Tiptoed out her door, to the landing. Peered down the stairs into the darkness. The sounds of breaking glass just went on and on, almost celebratory.

And then the noises stopped. Gloria focused her every sense, but couldn't hear a thing, no footfall, no muffled breathing, no scratchy cackle. Could a wild animal have broken in, then escaped? Maybe. She didn't believe that in her heart, though. Too many coincidences. More resigned than fearless, she began inching down the stairs.

At the foot of the steps she paused. Looked into the living room. It appeared unoccupied and untouched. Maybe she should just leave, run to the neighbors, cry for help. She sidled over to the front door, turned the knob... but it was stuck. She turned it the other way, pulled harder, rattled it back and forth. Didn't budge. Somebody'd jammed it shut. She was locked in.

Her panic grew. She pulled aside the front curtain, tried to lift the window. Immobile. She shielded her eyes, shattered the glass with her poker, smashed out most of the fragments, tried to climb out. But there was a thick plastic sheet sealing the opening on the outside of the building. Some kind of industrial tarp. She whacked at it with her poker, but it didn't break, didn't tear, didn't give. Someone had gone to a lot of trouble to keep her from leaving.

She gripped the poker, stalked into the dining room, swinging it back and forth wildly, angrily. But there was nobody here, either. Just the familiar shapes of furniture, picture frames, piles of books, lamps. On the table beside her lay one of her matt cutting blades, a Triple O Cutt-Ex. She picked it up, dropped it into the side pocket of her nightgown. Just in case she ended up at real close range.

Outside an autumn breeze was whiffling the dry leaves around the driveway, rattling the windows insistently. At least, she thought it was the wind rattling the windows. The sound was coming from the rear of the house, from the kitchen. Looking back there, something seemed different, though she couldn't tell what at that distance. Something out of place, out of sync. She raised her weapon. Walked down the hall.

At the entryway to the kitchen the first thing she noticed was that the back window had a circular hole cut in it, the curtains moving in the dry, stuttering air currents. She didn't know why she noticed that, it just struck her; it was an anomaly that stuck out. She took a couple steps into the room – but almost as soon as she entered, her bare foot came down on a piece of nasty broken glass. She jerked back, pulled her leg up, felt the sole of her foot. Warm, wet blood, slippery and dreadful. Her heart beat palpably. She stepped to the side of the shard on the linoleum, moved deeper into the room, grasping her brass club more tightly than ever – and saw for the first time, the contents of the refrigerator dumped all over the floor.

Fractured bottles, beer foaming in a puddle of glass slivers. Leftover stew, leaking milk containers, a blood-rare shank of lamb on a cracked ceramic plate, marrow dripping from the bone's core. Curdled cottage cheese uncartoned, like some decomposing tissue in the half-light. Whipped strawberry Jello, shimmering in a crystalline bowl, a sickly vivid pink and slick. Everything looked hyper-real, unreal, and surreal at the same time; it all meant something that it was manifestly not. It passed through a detached part of Gloria's mind that by some definitions this was a work of art.

Yet more than that, really. For not just the contents of the refrigerator but the shelving itself was strewn over the floor. Torn out by someone possessed, someone in the throes of an insane and passionate anger.

The fridge door was open a crack, sending a streak of pale light across the glass-and-food-covered floor tiles. Gloria reached out to shut it. That's when the refrigerator door burst open.

Out leapt a bizarre figure, wearing Ratner's stage costume and a blank, white nylon, eyeless mask, with just a small, round mouth-hole to breathe through. Like some Victorian demon come to dance. Gloria jumped back in shock, legs suddenly shuffling with fright and fatigue. The figure kicked her in the crotch, knocked her down hard. The poker flew out of her hand.

He raised a scalpel. Stabbed her. She lifted her arms to defend herself. He stabbed her arms. She scuttled backward across the floor, into the wall – and her palm accidentally landed on an unbroken wine bottle lying on its side. She recognized it by its feel, grabbed it, it was heavy with a dark red port, the thick green glass making it heavier still. She swung it ferociously at his head. Connected like she was going for center field. Nothing on this earth could he do but stagger backwards.

She scrambled over to her fallen poker, picked it up. Swung it wildly back and forth in front of her, hoping to hit anything within range. He was ready this time, though. Dizzy but ready. He hung back until her pendulum swing reached its furthest extension, its moment of stillness before pulsing the other way; and he yanked it out of her hand, clubbed her in the head on the backswing. She was out before she was down.

He wobbled across the floor to the overturned garbage can. Turned it flipside, emptied all the trash onto the floor, the wet coffee grounds, membrane-slimy egg shells, sugar-sticky melon balls, beef gristle, squeezed out lemon rinds, congealed puddles of bacon fat. Pulled the empty black plastic trash bag out of the bin. Slipped the bag over Gloria's head and shoulders.

Pulled it tight around her face, bunching it up at the neck so it looked like a shiny black, featureless mask. Then lay down beside her. Stuck his fingertip against the black plastic that covered her mouth – pushed hard, and deep, until his finger broke through, making a fissure in the plastic, scraping past her teeth. He brought his face up to hers, slid his tongue through the small hole in his white mask, extended it further, through the hole he'd just made in the black garbage-bag plastic covering her gaping mouth. Eased the tip of his tongue past her lips, then the full meat of it into her mouth, sliding it around that warm, dark memory hole.

And felt complete, for just one breathless moment, for the first time in a very long time.

8

CHAPTER EIGHT

October 9-December 4, 1976
Time, With A Gift Of Tears;
Grief, With A Glass That Ran

Claire kissed Eric's swathed skull, then sat back in her chair at his bedside in the Galway hospital where he'd been admitted, St. Mary's. He was still unconscious from Claire's shovel blow to his head. Bandages covered half his face as well, over the now sutured gash to his cheek from the garden tool. Almost as soon as the fight was over, Claire told Guy to leave, to run away, to stay gone, and he'd stumbled off like a madman gibbering, a man at sea, lost in time. She'd called the police, told them about some imaginary intruder, a man in a mask who was looking for jewelry he'd said his cell-mate had told him was buried somewhere in her back yard, she thought he sounded insane; she sounded half-mad herself, and felt quite more than half.

Eric had a subdural hematoma, the doctors told her, a blood clot on the surface of the brain where he'd been knocked. The surgeons evacuated the clot, relieving the pressure, but Eric still hadn't regained consciousness. Now he had a serious concussion, they said. He might wake up in hours, he might wake up next year, he might not wake up at all.

Claire no longer knew what to make of her life, it had drifted so far from the dreams of a young actress, drifted into gilt prisons and guilt trips, empty longings and dark hope and bright despondency, like a life lived as a photographic negative; and the next time she looked up from Eric's hospital bedside there was Guy leaning in the doorway, staring at her with a tender ache.

She got up, joined him in the hall. They stood there awkwardly, Claire feeling exposed, naked to the soul; Guy imagining his life had become one long seizure.

"You probably oughtn't to be here," she said.

"How's Eric?"

"They had to remove a blood clot from his brain."

"I'm so sorry," Guy said, while Claire was saying, "I apologize for his...."

They both stopped. Then Guy tapped his temple with a drained smile. "I don't know, it's either irony or karma, somehow both of your men are head cases, now." She didn't appear to find it terribly amusing. He continued, more apologetic. "I mean, I know it must've sounded crazy, those things I was saying about Eric – future lives, murders...."

"You'd just had a horrid row," she said, giving him the benefit of the doubt. "I felt a bit unhinged myself."

Guy's face turned stark sober. "But what you have to understand is, what I said wasn't crazy. I've never been so clear about anything." That got her attention, but didn't do much to quell her dismay. He held her gaze. "That's what I came to tell you. To explain it better, so you'll really understand."

She shook her head. "Understand what, Guy?" Her voice was nearly inaudible, and she didn't want to hear what he had to tell her.

"It's like this," he said carefully. "I thought I'd been having reincarnation dreams, they seemed so Victorian, so previous. But it turns out they were pre-incarnation dreams. About my next life."

"Guy, please, you need to leave before...."

He took her by the shoulders. He wanted so badly for her to get it. She was all he had anymore. "From the very beginning I've thought I was the scar-faced killer in the dream. I felt so intimately connected to him, like he was the killer inside me or I was inside him or I don't know what, it just felt like I was the one doing the stabbing – but now I understand I was wrong, I was misinterpreting the meaning of the dreams. <u>Eric</u> will be the killer, he's going to be the older man with the scar."

"Oh, God, Guy, you're mad." She was near tears.

"I beg you, just hear me out." He paused as she closed her eyes. "If Eric is going to be the killer – and it's clear to me he is – then I can't be the killer. Because Eric is already alive, he has a soul – so I obviously can't incarnate into him." He started to pace, looking for flaws to his logic, finding only confirmations. "But if I'm not the killer, I must be the victim in the dream, the pretty woman with the limp; that must be why I've got a limp now, that's what connects me to her. I should have understood that from the beginning, I shouldn't have dismissed that clue so quickly. But the thing is, the victim must not even be born yet – because I'll have to die before she <u>is</u> born so my soul can migrate into her body."

He looked at Claire expectantly. She felt like she was falling, or just falling apart. This must be what it was like when two atheists fell in love, and then later, some soul-shredding day, one of them found God. It opened a chasm between the lovers that just could not be crossed. Once, Claire had thought Guy might be there for her – but now she saw he couldn't, never would. The realization glutted her heart with an implacable grief.

"The doctor said Eric could wake up any time," she said softly. "It would probably be better if you weren't around when he did."

Her response sliced into him like a ragged shard of glass. "Any time," he said, his chest run through with salty grief. "I used to think I had no time at all, and now I'm drowning in it."

He gave her the good-bye look. "I'm sorry for everything."

She nodded once, too tired to lift her head again. He just limped away.

He took a taxi back to the gardener's cottage, packed up all his notes and journals and books in a sturdy archive box, got a fleabag room in a transient hotel in Galway called the *Jackson Park Arms*. And there he stayed for many a dreary week, meticulously studying the meanings and implications and ramifications of his revelation about sequential existence.

It shouldn't have been that big a surprise to begin with. After all, according to some interpreters of Hindu text – and Yeats, for that matter – all incarnations are happening right now. The soul exists beyond what we perceive of as space and time – a soul's next life could appear as easily in the past as the future. For Guy to be dreaming of the previous incarnation, or the next – it was all one.

The remarkable thing, as it had been from the start, was that he could see another one of his lives so clearly, so intensely, at all. That was relatively rare. In most Hindu teaching the only way to do so was to keep presence of mind at the moment of death, to have a spiritual depth, a closeness to the heart of God that enabled the fleeting soul to hold all its recollections dear. But maybe Guy's memories – future memories, at that – had somehow been preserved, or accessed, by his tumor – that was his way to experience other incarnations.

This, of course, begged a whole host of scientific questions related to the nature of tumors, neural connections, sensory functions and cognitive perceptions – but the most critical import of the whole business to Guy was the realization that because he was, in fact, seeing his next incarnation… these upcoming events weren't necessarily indelible anymore. They weren't written in the stone of history.

And that meant that now that he understood the murder was going to happen in a future existence, he had a chance to prevent it. It was certainly theoretically possible to prevent it. It was rare, in Hindu teaching, for anyone's karma to be absolutely fixed. Almost all karma could be changed, or redirected. And to make that happen now, to undo the murder he'd witnessed thirty years in the future, he must first figure out exactly when it was going to take place. That way, forewarned with the specifics of the pathway that led to the killing, he could change his behavior, find alternative forks in the road, set a different course, modify his karma, alter his fate. And the fate of the future victim.

Could he really do it? He had a chance, he had a shot at it, he had maybe a small window of opportunity; but more than that he had a sacred obligation. He had to try, that's all he knew.

The first order of business was striving, yet again, to understand the details of the dream. Why, for example, had it looked so Victorian if it was happening in the future? Was it a metaphoric vision, requiring interpretation? Or would there be people in the future who actually dressed the way he'd seen them? Would Victoriana come back in vogue? Was there to be a revival, like a retro fashion craze, or a theatrical…? Maybe that was it. A play. A play about a murder in Victorian England, a play about Jack the Ripper, or… Jekyll and Hyde? Or was he just imagining that connection because *Jekyll and Hyde* was one of his fields of study? Like *The Tempest*, or *Macbeth*. He picked up his well-thumbed copy of the Scottish Play, opened it to a dog-eared page, and read: "'*Tomorrow, and tomorrow, and tomorrow, Creeps in this petty pace from day to day To the last syllable of recorded time….*'" But all our yesterdays have lighted fools the way to dusty death and all these threads were running together for Guy now, he couldn't untangle them, couldn't find the bright line to follow.

He put those meanderings on hold and moved ahead to the business of narrowing down the dates of the pre-visioned homicide. If it wasn't strictly an artifact of a theater production he'd envisioned, it looked like the killing was going to happen under a hunter's moon. So he bought a Farmer's Almanac, and from that made his own calculations of every date the moon was going to be full in October, between thirty and thirty-five years in the future. That's how much older Eric looked in the dream, and that's how old the pretty woman victim looked, and he assumed she'd be born in the next couple years, because he assumed he'd be dead before then, dead of his tumor at the very least. That would put her age around thirty-something at the time of her murder.

He wrote these dates on sheets of paper and taped them to the wall. And then he cross-referenced those dates with the other numbers in his dream: 52426. He didn't know what the relation was, but it had to be significant. Was 52426 a date? Like 5/24/26, as in May 24, 1926? Or could it refer to May 24, 2026, was it that far in the future?

Or were the numbers inverted, or rearranged, possibly encrypted? He bought several mathematics books on numbers theory, mathematical games, numerical code breaking. He bought a hand calculator. He ran sequences, looking for patterns.

Numbers started to fill his walls. He looked for meaningful relationships between the numerals 52426 and lunar events in October, and the potential correlations between that and autumnal equinoxes, which preceded the hunter's moon by anywhere from one to four weeks. Was there a recurrent progression? If so, was it arithmetic or logorhythmic? Was it predictive? Was it chaotic?

There were, after all, the words **RED CHAOS,** scrawled in blood by the dying woman. So he bought books on chaos theory and threw that into the mix. Just coming into fashion at the university, chaos theory was originated by a meteorologist named Lorenz back in 1960, who was looking for underlying patterns in seemingly random weather data and ended up describing what had come to be known as the Butterfly Effect. It was the computerized proof that even the infinitesimal flapping of a butterfly wing in Japan can generate effects that may result in turbulent wind storms a month later and half a world away.

Was this the nature of endless incarnations, that immeasurably small actions in one life could have devastating results in the next?

Chaos theory predicted fractals, a mathematics of self-similar repetitions, like the branching of a tree into smaller and smaller limbs, or the bifurcations of bronchi into bronchioles into bronchioli into alveoli, or the increasingly finer netting of veins that webbed into a muslin of venules throughout the body. Is that all that reincarnation was, a series of self-similar repetitions, coded into our DNA? And if so, could those repetitions be predicted, analyzed, altered?

Guy's walls were soon encrusted with pinned-up references and equations, covered with minute calculations scribbled in his fine handwriting directly on the paint-faded plaster surfaces. And strewn around the floor were all his journals recounting his dreams, all his sketchbooks detailing the minutest visual details, rendered in delicate pencil chiaroscuro, all his noted thoughts and feelings on the philosophy of reincarnation.

But he was thinking too fast to write now, his mind was racing into tomorrow and back, it was trying to run in two worlds at once. So he bought a hand-held cassette tape recorder to record it all, to congeal his thoughts into words and nail them down before they flitted into the ether. He lost track of time, it was all the same to him. He was becoming dark as a singularity, blindered as a monk. The other things people fill their lives with – food, sleep, entertainments, human contact from the most mundane to the most intimate – those things slipped away, like foam on a receding tide.

The first time he sat on his fleabag floor, surrounded by the documenta-
tion of his obsession and talking into his new tape recorder, this is what he
said: "So begins my last journey. The yogis teach us we can change our destiny by several means, the first being pilgrimage – and to Galway have I
come for this pilgrimage. We can change our fate with ritual and my journals are my ritual, my offerings to the forces that guide my soul. And we can
change our fate through discipline, such as forsaking the small pleasures and
loves we may be given in this life, and yes, I've forsaken love; and we can
change through fasting, which I must be doing since I can't remember the
last time I ate." Though he added, with a whiff of Western irony, "Of course
I'm not sure you can call it fasting if you're just not hungry. Maybe I'm
simply suffering from existential nausea. In any case – what goes around
dies around. So let's begin. Again."

He held up one of his drawings of the pretty woman being stabbed in the
back. "The details must be critical," he spoke into the recorder. "And the
first detail is, the victim limped. Did I mention that? It's key, of course, it's
what connects me to her, our lame legs. And she looked to be thirty or so.
I've calculated the dates hunter's moon will fall on, thirty years from now,
with an under and over of four years and six on either side. That span should
encompass the events I've foreseen, assuming I die in the next couple years,
which seems likely, given my condition."

He pushed PAUSE, to gather his thoughts. He caught his reflection in
the window. Hollow-eyed, thin, his left leg slightly atrophied notwith-
standing all his recent exercise; death seemed more like a reprieve than ever.
Except it was also a death sentence for the woman who was to be his next
manifestation. How could he warn her, from a lifetime away? He shuffled
through the archive box beside him, looking for clues he might've written
down without realizing their import. Something even as miniscule as the
flutter of a powdery butterfly wing.

And still, nothing struck him. He took the recorder off PAUSE.

"I need more seizures, to get more clues. To find out who the murdered
woman is – who I will be, when I incarnate into her." This made him smile
at a memory which he shared with his dictaphone. "The first time I met
Claire, she told me I was seeking my inner woman. So now I have to get a
message to that woman, the woman I'm going to be – a warning to myself,

to my soul inhabiting that woman – so I can stop her murder. My own murder. If I can just put all the pieces together..." He closed his eyes tightly. What was he missing? "She limps, did I say that?"

Time went by. Eric's concussion improved and he woke up in the hospital, went through a course of inpatient rehab and came home, shaky but on the mend. Claire tended him. The violent outburst that had brought them here had been catharsis, in a way, an explosion of cleansing intensity. Things were quiet between them now and they didn't speak of the fight. She told him that she'd told the police he'd been attacked by some anonymous burglar. Eric just looked at her and nodded. It seemed he actually didn't remember anything leading up to the injury – retrograde amnesia was not uncommon in cases like this, the doctors said. He may get those memories back, he may not.

And there was a flatness to his affect now, as if the blow to his head had crushed some prickly aspect of his personality. Something inside her relaxed as well, like a soufflé settling. She brought him meals, took him for short walks, doted on him, actually; a combination of guilt, grief, and fury spent.

His hair was short, barely grown in from surgery. The scar on his cheek was fresh, red and raised. His doctors assured him plastic surgery would do wonders with it, some months down the line. But for the foreseeable future, in light of his recent coma, they said they'd just as soon rather not submit him to any kind of anaesthesia quite yet.

He slept a great deal. Claire was told she needed to be very patient with him. His total recovery might take some time, the doctors advised her so often she grew tired of hearing it. Complete recovery might not happen at all, they insisted. His psychological state might remain altered indefinitely.

Eric's flat affect did change over time, in fact, and he slowly became more paranoid. He loved being hand-fed, for example, especially by Claire – but expressed an irrational fear that his meals were poisoned. He bought a dog, a Rottweiler puppy that he kept in his lap or by his side at all times. He began entertaining himself with secret, elaborate revenge fantasies, describing precisely what he was going to do to the doctors who failed to cure him, for example; or to the accountant who was undoubtedly stealing his money; or to the nurses; or to Alice, the maid, who didn't come quickly enough when he rang. And of course Eric's most delicious vendetta was reserved for that anonymous felon who'd whacked him after digging up the yard in search of buried jewels, should that damned soul ever be so foolish as to show up around here again. He retained that particular memory of the event, it seemed – the one Claire had invented for everyone.

On a particularly dazzling, crisp day in early December, Claire – who was now showing, well into her third trimester – was feeding Eric mouthfuls of beef broth at the drawing room window as the Rottweiler dozed contentedly in his lap. Eric was able to feed himself quite well now but he preferred to have Claire wait on him. It was Alice's day off.

"It's a bit chilly but I think if you put on a sweater we can walk in the garden today," she suggested.

"I don't like the garden anymore."

"The park, then. The doctor says you should be getting out and about more by now."

"The doctor's trying to kill me. And I'm too tired for a walk. I suppose that's what happens when love dies."

"You're being melodramatic again, Eric."

"You're right, Darling, the doctor's not really trying to kill me. But you can't deny the other thing. That love dies. After all, everything dies eventually. Why not love?"

She couldn't bring herself to answer.

He pressed. "All right, if you won't admit love dies, at least tell me something, then, will you?"

"If I can."

"I won't be a bit angry, no matter what the answer is. Promise me you'll be honest?"

"Of course, Eric." She didn't like this. She could hear the tone in his voice; it had a familiar strangulating quality.

"You two were having an affair, weren't you? You and that Lawrencian gardener who worked for us once."

"No, Eric, we weren't."

"I just want it all out in the open, exposed to the light. Then we can start fresh, no secrets."

With a flash of anger, he reflexively squeezed the dog in his lap. It woke up with a yelp, jumped down and ran away.

Claire tried to stay composed. "This is as open as I can be, Eric. I never had a romance with Guy."

"I'm not saying romance, *per se*. I'm just suggesting you fucked him. There's nothing *a priori* romantic about fucking."

"Eric, please, why do you go on this way? It's simply hurtful and I'm trying to support you."

"The thing is, my darling – and you are my darling and ever will be so, no matter how you may stray – I had him checked out. I hired a detective, who told me something very interesting."

"I don't really care to know about it."

"The detective said Guy was living in Great Britain last year, doing some kind of literary academic research in Edinburgh and in London, something to do with Robert Louis Stevenson and Yeats, and then, most interesting, he spent time in Galway. Our very Galway. He left only eight months ago, to return to the States – but now here's the really curious part – he came back here to Galway just a few months after that."

"And that's curious why?"

"Did I mention he left eight months ago? That's right 'round when you got preggers, isn't it?"

She felt her face flush with anger. "Would you please stop accusing me of this imaginary crime?! Guy is not the father of...."

"I know the baby's not mine, Claire," he said, the way a disappointed parent speaks to a dissembling teen. "But I can't forgive you until you've admitted what you've done."

She stared at him with a chilly wind in her heart, hating him for the false accusation. And she'd be damned if she'd admit to <u>wishing</u> she'd had an affair with Guy – though that's apparently the sin she was being punished for.

9

CHAPTER NINE

October 17, 2013
12:57 A.M.-4:44 P.M.
Night Of The Hunter's Moon

It was barely an hour after the violent, insane kitchen kidnap. Gloria'd awakened in darkness, jostling on her back, the smell of decay assaulting her senses, a kind of caked fish rot, tangy with mold and thickened with moist air that never circulated, just kept becoming more itself.

Gloria was moving, though, accompanied by a black noisy rattling; then out of the dark, into a dimly lighted room. Until finally her rumbling motion ceased, and the silence was immense.

She was lying on her back, on some kind of bed, a bed on wheels; it must have been a hospital gurney, that's what she'd been moving on, and now it was stopped. She tried to get up but couldn't. Arms and legs bound to the bed rails with straps that cut into her wrists and ankles like dull blades. She heard footsteps scurrying back and forth, a man's presence, rustling papers and objects. She turned her head toward the sounds. "I haven't done anything to you," she whispered. "Why are you doing this to me?"

A hand punched her unconscious.

She was in fact tied to a gurney in the damp basement near the mostly sunken thousand-gallon storage tank, dead rats still floating in the putrid water. Rats and centipedes and human parts you couldn't quite name, or would rather not. A few feet away from Gloria, just out of sight, the man who'd attacked and kidnapped her turned on a searing bright surgical lamp while the vicious mastiff growled in its pen behind the slatted door.

Gloria's arms, hands, and legs were lacerated, badly knife-cut from the fight in the kitchen, fat and deep tissue exposed. But the man sat beside her gurney and began the steady, studied manual labor of suturing her wounds. No anaesthetic, of course, and no sterile field. A rough job, done with thick black polyester dime store thread off the shelf. The man still wore his Victorian costume. Still wore his white nylon featureless mask. Phantom of the Basement.

He took the ornate, lavender glass vial with gold filigree off the table. Opened it, sprinkled its perfume all over Gloria's head. Leaned down, deeply inhaled its scent, lingering in her thick mane of white hair, the hair that used to be so raven black, buried his face in the sensual aroma, so evocative, so compelling, so carnal. Fondled her breast. Moved his mouth to her unconscious ear, and whispered.

"Grrrrrrr, darling Claire, my Little Red Riding Whore, it's time to come home to your big bad wolf."

He brought his teeth down on her arm, tearing through the flesh, and – as she regained full consciousness with a terrible jolt – tasted her pain.

Later the same morning, near eight o'clock, Olivetti knocked on Gloria's front door. No answer. He'd returned Vic's call before breakfast and listened to his troubled admission. Turns out Vic had snooped in his mom's garage, found a painted-over red Chevy and a box of Triple O Cutt-Ex blades, was afraid she was involved in everything that had been happening to Vicky and felt like hell that he hadn't done something about it sooner. Olivetti'd thanked Vic for the 411, told him he'd done the right thing by telling everything he knew, and gone straight to Gloria's house, figuring he'd walk her easy through her sob-tale confession; she might get off with Not Guilty By Reason Of, that might even be the best way to go. But now nobody was coming to the front door.

He tried looking in the window, but it was covered over with a reinforced translucent plastic tarp. Looked like the window was broken behind it, and somebody was temporarily sealing off the hole. Warped casing, maybe, some carpenter halfway through fixing it? No. Something about it made the hairs on the back of Olivetti's neck go up like tiny antennae. Something not right about this.

He went around back. Saw the circular hole cut in the kitchen window, the back door partly open. Same kind of hole as the one at Vicky's apartment. That was the worst sign imaginable, more of the same pattern and Olivetti a day late. He drew his gun, pushed the door wide and quiet. Went inside.

The place was a wreck. Food all over, broken shelving – and what looked like blood on the floor. He called for backup, searched the house in the meantime. All the downstairs rooms, then upstairs. Nobody here, dead or alive, and no other rooms trashed. He went carefully over the kitchen.

It'd be interesting to find out whose blood was spattered all around. He hoped it wasn't Vicky's, hoped the girl hadn't come here looking for Vic, only to find a demented mother-in-law-to-be with a butcher knife and a mission. But he didn't think that was what had happened. The circular cut-out window said otherwise.

Of course, it could have been Vicky glass-cutting her way in – but then why would she have cut open the back window of her own apartment, the night the puppy had disappeared? Might have been Gloria's doing tonight, glass-cutting her way into her own house to make it look like forced entry. But why would she do that? Anyway, she was an artist, not a big-time felon, and this wasn't any comic book heist, it was a real-world B and E. Okay, here was another idea: what if it was Vic? What if he was the bad guy?

Vic could certainly have run over his first girlfriend, Kendra, with his mother's red car. But leave that aside for the moment, just concentrate on the current series of crimes. Easiest thing in the world for him to vandalize Vicky's car, spraypaint **WHORE** on it. He knew right where it was parked and when. He was onstage when the razor went into her sandwich, he could clearly have slipped that in himself. He was pretty handy with a tool, he might easily have cut out the back window of her apartment while Vicky was sleeping, gotten rid of the little dog. It totally fit, as part of a series of stalking events, if he was trying to get a rise out of her. Make it look anonymous at first, then when Olivetti started getting too close, blame it on his own mother? And now, for who knows what reason, this? Breaking into his mother's house? And what? Killing her? Could he really be that psycho?

Like a split personality, maybe, not even know he was doing it? Olivetti had had one case like that in his thirty years on the job. Guy who killed his sister's boyfriends with one personality named Veronica, thought he was actually a woman, thought he was jealous of the two-timing boyfriends he was killing. Then his main personality, Tony, never knew about it. At least that's what the shrinks said. Couple other personalities mixed in there for the hell of it. If Vic was as far gone as Tony, then he could've done all this shit no sweat, never had a clue he was doing it, and Vicky was next on his hit list for sure.

Through the translucent plastic covering the broken front window, he saw a blue-and-white van and the crime lab pull up to the curb. Okay, good, let's get some prints here, some DNA on the blood, some hair and fiber. Time for him to pay a visit to Vic again.

At the crack of noon, the stage crew was putting final touches on the scenery, setting up for the last dress rehearsals. Lights were hung, gels placed. Vic and Vicky, both hurting and raw after the acrimonious argument they'd had the day before, were tense, civil and avoiding each other. The other actors, not as spry in the a.m. hours, were just drifting in when Mark stormed onstage, addressing cast and crew and all the ships at sea.

"Ratner's gone missing, probably on a bender, the sot, if past history is any indication."

"He has to show up," said Vicky. "Opening night's tomorrow, and he knows it better than anyone." This was the last straw; her leading man a no-show, it was all she could do not to pile onto Ratner's case. But if she let herself go there, she was afraid she'd just start screaming. This was really more than anyone should have to put up with.

"We have a full dress rehearsal in five goddam hours!" Mark went on. "Who the hell does he think he is?"

"The great William Ratner," said Vic drily. "The Goliath of Greasepaint." And he visualized Ratner as a giant, messy overflowing jar of greasepaint.

"He's fired, that's what he is," Mark came back.

There was a dark pause.

"You can't fire him," protested Otto. "Who can you get to play the Doctor on one day's notice?"

"I'll play the role myself. I know the lines and the character better than that old drunk ever did anyway." He lowered his eyes at Vicky. "And then I'll get to kill you in the alley under the" – he continued in character – "'hunter's moon, is what that is.'"

He grabbed a knife from a windowsill on the set – and plunged it into Vicky's chest.

Her eyes went wide, her breath caught, her heart took a stutter-step. Vic went from zero to sixty at the speed of thought, leapt forward, grabbed Mark's wrist, slammed him against the wall.

Mark slowly brought up his other hand. Touched his fingertip to the point of the knife he was holding – and pushed the blade, on its spring mechanism, into the hilt. "Prop knife, Vic," he said softly. "This is all make-believe, remember?"

Vic let him go, looked over at Vicky, who was both rattled and annoyed that she was rattled. "I'm okay," she said. "It was just a bad joke." She kept her voice flat; she wasn't ready to reconcile with Vic just yet – even though he had jumped to her defense. She just couldn't deal with sorting it all out right now.

"Had you going," chuckled Mark. Then to everyone: "All right, scene work until four, then we'll break for an hour, and then full dress run-through until we get it right, and if that means all night, I've got nowhere else to go."

The old scar on his cheek felt like it was burning with thrill beneath his beard. Like a bright, twisted, undercover exclamation point.

His phone rang and he touch-screened *Answer*. "Olivetti."

It was the lab, they had some good latent prints from a fireplace poker on the kitchen floor, and a prelim on the blood, two different types; did he want to come down and check it out?

Yes, he did, indeed.

That afternoon, close to five. Gloria opened her eyes in the dank cellar. Still on her back, tied to the gurney. Living the nightmare she'd been running from so long she'd almost forgotten she was running.

Everything hurt. Brain, skull, neck, arms, hands, back, it was all excruciating; she couldn't focus on any one pain, she never knew it was possible to have so many all at once. She lifted her head up as far as it would go. Lacerations on her arms had been sewn up, but the skin around the black thread was red, puffy, crusted with dark blood, oozing serous fluid. And was that a bite on her arm, a little chunk gone, oh, God, and bordered by teeth marks? Tooth marks. Tooth mark. Mark tooth. Mark Denture, Mark Dent. Dent, Vicky's director, a man with a scar on his cheek and a name like a fang, and why hadn't Gloria waited outside the playhouse until he'd shown up yesterday? Scared to find out in the flesh what she already knew in her heart.

She saw a man walking toward her. She flinched, tried to pull away, couldn't move.

It was the figure in the white mask, the berserker in Victorian clothes who'd attacked her. When he reached the gurney he pulled off his mask, pulled his lips back stiffly in a kind of *rigor sardonicus*. She saw it was in fact Eric, the scar on his cheek thirty some years older than the last time she'd seen it.

There were a couple cuts on his chin as well, fresh shaving cuts, they looked like. He rubbed his smooth cheek with satisfaction. "I've shaved for you, my darling Claire," he said. The old scar followed the crooked line it always had, but was grotesquely thicker now, like a frayed cable. "Pretty, isn't it? It's called a cheloid, an abnormal growth of scar tissue; comes from a genetic flaw, I'm told, so every time the doctors tried to repair it, it came back bigger. Like a child's tantrum." He smiled philosophically.

Of course she'd known who this masked madman was from the moment he'd leapt out of her fridge – as strangely terrifying an entrance as any demon might conceive. But really, in the end, who else could it have been? After Vicky talking about her director's scarred face, his age, his slight British accent. Even his name, Mark Dent. Dent, like a Romance Language code for tooth, Tooth of the Wolf, this predatory sharp Tooth, this glinting twilight shadow from her past. She hadn't been wrong, just drowning in denial. A tear burned the corner of her eye.

But oddly, at the same time, seeing his face now was almost a relief. She'd been holding her breath for so long, it felt good simply to be done with it.

"Hello, Eric."

"I'm called Mark now. Mark Dent. Dent, as in Tooth." It wasn't half so clever as he seemed to think it was, but then that had always been true about his so-called witticisms. When she didn't gush about the symbolism, he went on. "I'm the director of the play your son is technical directing, and his blushing bride-to-be starring in."

"You don't have to do this," she said wearily.

"Oh, but I do, Claire. I owe it to you. And to myself."

It was probably too much to hope, but maybe she could paint him a new picture of her life, make him see everything was different now, sweep away the past and answer his old delusions. She just needed to find out how he saw things. If this was still about the jealousies he'd been nursing all those years ago. "Just tell me what you want, Eric. Tell me what this is about."

"About bringing down the curtain on your stunning career as a world class slut."

"Please, Eric, I'm not, I've never been."

"But before your final bow we should stage a run-through. With a stand-in."

He walked away, came back wheeling another gurney, this one covered by a sheet that he pulled off with a flourish, voila! And tied to the gurney, Gloria could see, was Ratner, the fool actor who'd accosted her on the set yesterday. There was a gag stuffed in his mouth, one of his eyes bruised shut. Ratner and Gloria exchanged a look of abysmal terror.

Mark picked up the filigreed perfume vial, showed it to Gloria. "Remember this?" He smiled. He passed it slowly under her nose, sprinkled some of it on Ratner's neck, chest and groin.

Mark – or Eric, or some third party that had set up shop in the hellhole of his brain – but whoever it was, he closed his eyelids, like a young girl waiting for her first kiss, and brought his face to Ratner's neck, to sniff the perfume straight in to the power source, to the place where all his nightmares and memories and fantasies merged.

Ratner's eyes rocketed this way and that looking for escape, his heart doing one-sixty; Jesus, what was going on? But Mark just followed the scent of the cologne, dragging his face down Ratner's body, past his chest; it smelled like sweet blood and sweetbreads. Red filled Mark's mind now, the color of the nectared perfume. Red's what a wolf likes, sniffing down Ratner's chest to his crotch, and then over to his arm and down to his hand, the hand bare naked flesh beyond the sleeve. The wolf inside Mark was alive to the play of Ratner's chubby little fingers twitching like worms on a hot-plate – and suddenly Mark bit down hard, jerked his head wild back and forth a dozen times until he came away with Ratner's pinky finger in his mouth.

Ratner screamed, spitting out the gag with the sheer force of his monstrous exploding fear.

Mark wheeled Ratner blabbering on his gurney over to the slatted door where the beast was kept.

He opened the door.

With a hindbrain snarl, the doggish thing in its cage – more wolf than dog, yet more vile than wolf – sprang forward out of its room-sized enclosure. It was stopped short by a leash around its neck, secured to the back wall. Chained like that, so close to its prey, it gnashed apoplectic.

Ratner strained to get free from his bonds, they cut into his wrists where he pulled with every muscled ligament, every bone and sinew, as the stump of his little finger poured blood onto the gurney, where it puddled slickly, and then dribbled to the floor. He couldn't see the animal, but he could hear it snarling and he was hardwired to dead-run from that sound.

Mark spit Ratner's finger at the dog, whetting its appetite. Then he turned a crank on Ratner's gurney, tipping it upright at a 45 degree angle. Now Ratner saw the beast salivating for him and his heartbeat kicked into overdrive, fueled by the adrenalin of primal fear, pain forgotten.

Laughing inhumanly, Mark pushed Ratner's gurney into the dog's chamber. "Claire!" Mark called brightly, turning toward her. "Are you watching this closely?"

The gurney rocked, rocked, nearly tipped over but leaned against the wall as the wolfish hound tore into the bound actor. Ratner, denied fight or flight or bargain or reason, was reduced to making frantic gurgling noises in response to the tearing apart of his flesh.

Mark walked back to Gloria and turned her head so she had to watch Ratner writhe and squeal as the mastiff ate him alive. She tried to close her eyes but Mark pulled her lids open, held her head up. She turned her eyes away, her searing blue eyes, but he put his face close in front of her so she had nowhere else to look. It was either the maniac or his work.

In any case, no matter what she did she couldn't erase those images of carnage from her mind, couldn't begin to shut out the grunting din of unbearable, insufferable death. If she could've ended those sounds by dying herself, she would have.

Mark leaned down, whispered to her. "I had to get rid of him anyway, so I could take his part in the play. So I could kill the girl onstage. So I had to get rid of him – but this way I can show you your future."

She didn't want to know the future, though. Not the present, either. Certainly not the past, all those times thirty years ago when her life with Eric began to go so dreadfully wrong, and she wondered now in the dark chasm of her soul if there were anything she might have done differently.

10

CHAPTER TEN

December 6, 1976

7:21 P.M.-7:34 P.M.

Strength Without Hands To Smite;
Love That Endures For A Breath

Claire sat in her kitchen, alone at the table, stirring her Chamomile tea. How had her life reached this strange, low point, she wondered? A problematic baby on the way – she rubbed her hand over the tense roundness of her belly – and a husband who silently hated her, recently back from the Galway hospital where they'd managed his latest relapse. Then there was her American friend, Guy, headlong spinning deeply into fantasy; she hadn't seen him in many weeks now, he might have fallen off the face of the earth for all she knew. Casting her gaze about, she found the moon hanging low in the sky, like God's baleful caseous eye, watching her sad life and finding it wanting.

December's full moon, the long night moon it was called, because it came so close to the longest night of the year, the winter solstice; and because it hung in the sky that night so much longer than usual. But for Claire the entire year seemed like one long night, getting darker and darker. The long night year, like a great black hole in her life.

A spectral figure materialized in the gloaming outside the window and stood there watching her like a dark memory, a ghost from another life come to lay unabridged claim on her immortal soul. She gasped, dropped her spoon – then realized it was Guy.

She opened the back door, let him in. He was carrying his archive box full of notes and sketches, he carried it everywhere he went, now. His limp was worse. He looked gaunt and ill. He seemed practically insubstantial.

"I didn't mean to frighten you," he said. He looked at her solemnly, as if from a long way away.

She hugged him silently. "How have you been?"

"As you see." He offered a worn smile. "And you?"

"My blood pressure's a tad high, my legs are bloated as the Pillsbury Doughboy. The baby doesn't like being cooped up, is my best guess."

Guy paused. "And what about Eric?" He couldn't even say the man's name without clenching his teeth.

"He's upstairs sleeping. He was back in hospital for a while. They had to operate again, there was what they called re-bleeding in his head." It pained her to think about. "He was getting so paranoid, he'd begun training these savage dogs to protect him from…." She stopped, choked by a swelling of emotions: guilt, regret, anger, fear, blame; but finally, just a weariness.

"I hope he gets better," said Guy. He could say that and mean it, no matter what else.

She found herself trying to explain her life to Guy. "I know you think I should have left him ages ago, but you have to understand, Eric wasn't this way when I met him, you know. When I first met him, he was dashing and sophisticated and he threw himself into grand adventures with everyone from Bohemians to Lords of the Realm; it seemed as if he had a thousand friends, he was so loving…." But she stopped again. What was the point? It was a distant memory, it had nothing to do with today's reality. Love never endured, in her experience. Her parents had died, and her brother, and now her once-loving husband twisted beyond recognition. The life seemed to have left everything she knew. She was out of air. "You shouldn't have come," she said without much fuel.

Guy was wrestling his own monsters. "I just came to tell you – I've calculated the dates, over thirty years from now, when the hunter's moons will appear."

Not this again, please don't start, she thought. "Guy, I beg you, stop this fixation."

"But I can prevent the murder," he rushed on, his eye glinting. "If I know exactly when it will happen, if I know every little detail, if I can warn the victim who I know I'm going to become, maybe I can change the course of things, maybe it's not writ in stone, maybe the future can be bent."

"Enough!"

He stopped. She looked near tears – and then she burst out laughing. Crying and laughing at the same time.

"I thought you were going to save me," she whispered, seeing this love, too, evaporating in a breath of wind. "I thought you were my getaway plan."

There was a profound regret in his tone. "I could never have been that. I've got a fatal brain tumor, I've had it since June, and now I've stopped taking my medicines."

She took a moment to assimilate this news, then just shook her head, confused. "But why did you never tell me that? And how serious is it? You don't truly mean fatal, do you? And why would you stop taking your medication?"

"I'm terminal," he said, answering all her questions. "So why prolong the inevitable? And why burden you with more bad news? You already have more than your forty-acres-and-a-mule's worth."

"But if you have medicine to take…" she began uncertainly, not knowing which of a dozen questions to ask first.

He shrugged. "If I don't take my meds, I get to have more seizures, more intensely, more unfiltered."

"You want more seizures?" She didn't understand.

He nodded. "They let me see the future. If the future becomes clear enough, maybe I can see how to escape it."

Her face was a bleak mask. "There is no escape."

"Different escapes for different traps, that's all. I have to try to stop my own future murder. You have to try to get out of a suffocating, destructive marriage. Doesn't mean we can't help each other along the way."

"I can't even see what the way is."

"The way is to keep starting your life over and over until you get it right."

"But I don't believe in reincarnation." She sounded so thoroughly beaten.

"That's okay, you don't have to. You just have to believe in Shakespeare. Remember what Antonio said in *The Tempest*? He said, '*We were all sea-swallowed, though some cast again, And by that destiny, to perform an act Whereof what's past is prologue, what to come, In yours and my discharge.*'"

"Ah, so Shakespeare was a Hindu yogi, after all."

"I think he just meant you can start your life over as often as you want. Don't even have to die to do it. But it's 'in your discharge,' you're in charge of doing it. We all are."

She gazed at him, pining for all the submerged feelings between them, all the things that might have been. He held her stare, took her hands, spoke softly. "I love you," he said.

Her eyes overflowed with a strength of emotion she could no longer hold, a rage that made her want to strike him for insisting on his love; but she couldn't hit him because there it was in her, too, enduring.

So she just wrapped her arms around him, her voice husky. "I love you, too."

But a sudden painful spasm in her belly made her flinch. She stepped back, held herself with both hands, broke out in a sweat.

Guy looked scared. "What is it, are you all right?"

The spasm faded. Claire relaxed a bit. "I've been having contractions, so I went to the doctor today. My baby has a medical condition. Something congenital."

"What is it?"

"It's called spina bifida."

"Is it serious?"

"They don't think so. It'll probably heal itself, as time goes by. It may need surgery, though, even more than one. Might even result in a permanent limp."

The word struck Guy like a punch in the heart. "A limp."

"I'm not due for another month, though, so...."

"A limp. Your baby's going to have limp. Like the murder victim in my dream."

"Guy, please...."

"A limp. Like me."

"What are you talking –"

"That's the last piece!" he said, voice rising. "I'm going to be reborn in your child. When you give birth, or maybe before you give birth, I'm going to die and my soul will migrate into your baby and she'll have a limp and in thirty years she'll be killed by Eric unless we –"

"Stop it, please stop it, I want you to stop!"

"– she'll be killed by Eric unless we can figure out how to –"

"If you have any feelings for me at all, for the love of God stop saying these things!"

He stopped. He tried to settle, to rein himself in. But he had to make her understand. "Don't you see? The limp makes it clear," he explained slowly, as to a child. "I'm going to be the girl with the limp. Your baby."

"My baby's going to be a boy, Guy, all right?" Her own voice was escalating in volume. "Not a girl. A boy."

That stopped him. He looked confused, trying to rearrange the pieces in his mind, make them fit again. He pulled a sketch out of his archive box, stared at it, perplexed. It was the pretty woman, limping past the alley, just before she got stabbed. "But if you're going to have a boy," he said to Claire, "why does the murdered girl in my dream have a limp?"

11

CHAPTER ELEVEN

October 17, 2013
7:05-7:18 P.M.
Out Of The Past

Vicky limped onstage for the gaslit street scene, dressed in the torn, tatty garb of a Victorian harlot, for the full after-dinner dress rehearsal.

Mark, now all done up in Ratner's leading man evening wear costume – including the long, elegant, brocade frock of a well-to-do Victorian physician – barked at her in his director's voice from the surrealistic alleyway. "Pull back on the limp, dear; you're not supposed to be a complete cripple, you know."

Vicky adjusted her limp.

Mark was freshly clean-shaven for the part; he'd done it secretly, during the dinner break, and everyone on the set kept stealing surreptitious glances at his face. Fascinated horror at a scar the likes of which none had seen before, the kind of thing people can't look at and can't look away from. The make-up man offered to pancake it but Mark gave him such a withering stare as to make the poor guy slink away like a dog cowering from a great surly bear.

Mark gathered everyone. "Okay, let's get this out on the table. I have a large, ugly scar on my cheek, it's who I am, *l'escar c'est moi*. But beyond that purely existential note, I believe it will help inform the character of the Doctor. Everybody look, stare at it long and hard; now's the time, so we can get past this and move on to the business at hand, which is that opening night is tomorrow, so let's do it, people. From the top."

And in the next moment, everyone was taking their places.

Victorian extras crossed upstage to down, left to right, right to left. A scruffy lad – played by Teddy – lit a gaslamp as the effects tech turned that single light to flickering, dialing it up on his board in the lighting booth. Vicky exited the door of a roominghouse of ill repute, cast a brazen glance at a slumming duke who shook his head at her. She shrugged and walked the other direction, past the maw of the glooming alley. Mark emerged behind her, Mark the actor now, in character, intense.

"Lovely evening," he said, his accent full-on noble British, where it was born and bred.

"Lovely for some things," said Vicky's character, the trollop.

Walking behind her, Mark pointed to a glowing globe, hanging from the rafters. "That's a hunter's moon, that is," he said.

"What are you hunting, then, Luv?" she cooed.

They finished the scene; there was a blackout, a set change, the stage got flooded with red gels. The play was a sort of non-linear meditation on Stevenson's *Jekyll and Hyde*. Titled *The Last Tempest*, for that frenzied state accompanying a tortured soul's moment of choice between good and evil. After the murder sequence came a series of flashbacks and flashforwards that revolved around the Doctor's experiments on the nature of the human spirit. The first act ended in his laboratory, beakers bubbling with dry ice; static electric discharge globes, bought at a novelty store downtown, crackling melodramatically, as the Doctor – played perfectly by Mark – contemplated drinking down the steaming, transformative brew while Doyle the Med Student, played by Otto, and the Doctor's Maid, played by Joan, pounded on his door.

"Please, sir, come out of there!" pleaded Joan.

"Let us help you, Doctor," Otto beseeched.

"There is no help," Mark intoned, staring bleakly into his cloudy drink, his crystal future. Cloud and crystal, he was double-visioned: no help for Mark the Doctor; no help for Mark the wolf.

"Let the past fall away, Doctor! You can start clean as a crucible, no one will know."

"There is no past. All life's but a single thread, a continuous present – the worm Ourobouros devouring his own tail, like the infinite solitary face of the Mobius strip that binds our wretched memories."

Vic and Vicky watched the performance from the wings, near the pay phone on the wall of scribbled phone numbers. She was in costume, he was in his black suede jacket with the burgundy satin lining.

"You played that last scene well," he said. Trying to give her an opening, so she could admit going over the top in yesterday's fight.

She shrugged. "I'm still mad at you."

He shrugged back. "Whatever." She always over-reacted to emotional issues on the day of her heaviest flow; he knew it, she knew it. He knew it was politically incorrect to bring up the influence of her period in an argument but he figured she had it coming after that comment about him cuddling with his mom. So he was damned if he was going to apologize first.

They stood like that for a full minute. Finally, when she spoke, she was still looking at the players onstage, not at him. "How did you get his beaker to glow like that?"

"Put a waterproof battery and light-bulb inside the glass." Pride of craftsmanship, just a touch of smug. He knew Vicky valued stage tricks like that. Okay, maybe bringing up her menstrual cycle had been irrelevant to what they'd been fighting about; and okay, she did have a good point about talking to Olivetti. But... but what? He watched her out of the corner of his eye, pleased that she was nodding appreciatively at his design of the Doctor's glowing beaker.

"That's what Hitchcock did in *Suspicion*." She nodded.

"Looks kind of like the beaker has a soul of its own, is what I was going for," he allowed.

She was on the verge of a reply, maybe heading toward softening the rancor that still lingered between them, when Teddy walked up to Vic. "Package just showed up for you, Vic. In your office."

"From who?"

"Return address says Gloria Stone. That's your mom, right?"

Vic furrowed his brow. His mother hadn't mentioned sending anything. A gift for opening night?

"Maybe it's an engagement present," said Vicky. "Or here's a really wacky idea – maybe it's a bomb."

"That's extremely humorous." They were still thinking Gloria was the stalker, of course; events were moving way faster than they knew, they'd have to play catch-up in a hurry pretty soon. But for now it just reopened the cause of their fight, their differing responses to Gloria's presumed aggressions.

"I'll look at it later," said Vic.

"No, I think we should look right now," said Vicky.

"You're right in the middle of dress," said Vic. But she just shook her head, said this could be important information, and besides she wasn't on for at least twenty minutes.

He shrugged why not – he was kind of curious himself – and they headed back to his office. Vic was, in fact, afraid the package had something to do with all the recent troubles, something ugly. Something to do with the red underpaint on her car, or the artist's razors he'd taken from her garage.

As if reading his mind, walking down the corridor – or maybe she just couldn't not ask any longer – Vicky asked him, "So did you tell Olivetti yet? About your mother's red car and razor blades?"

"Told him this morning."

Thank God. "And?"

"And he hasn't gotten back to me yet. He's probably working on it."

They entered his office. Small and cluttered. A large carton wrapped in brown paper sat on his desk. Addressed to Vic.

"It's Gloria's handwriting," he confirmed.

"Go on, open it." But she had a momentary flash of the movie *Se7en,* visualized opening the box and finding Kendra's rotting head inside. She shivered once, shrugged herself still.

He tore off the paper. Inside was an archive box.

It looked familiar to Vic. Something about its shape, or color, or… he didn't know what. Of course he couldn't possibly have suspected this was the box a cancer patient named Guy Daniels once dragged around with him everywhere, back in the fall of 1976, filling it up with the obsessive ephemera of his life. Stuffed it with his dreams and visions until it somehow found its way to Vic's desk here, now, nearly forty years later.

Vicky pulled off the cardboard lid, they looked inside. Filled to the brim with papers, journals, textbooks, sketchbooks, monographs, an old answering machine, a dated, white telephone. But on top of the pile was a new envelope, addressed to Vic, in Gloria's handwriting and with her name in the return address corner. He opened it, started reading aloud.

"*Dear Victor – I'm hoping, if anything happens to me, what's in this box will help you sort it out....*"

"If anything happens to her, what does that mean?" Vicky asked nervously. Was she planning some kind of big "*Top-o'-the-world-Ma*" finale, blow herself up standing on an unrefined fuel storage tank, screaming about the bitch who stole her baby? Maybe if they turned on the radio they'd hear all about it, WGN, this just in. Maybe opening the box now would give them a clue about Gloria's precarious state of mind. Vic kept on reading his mother's letter.

"*The things in this archive box belonged to an old, dear friend of mine, who once told me if we know every little detail, maybe we can avert disaster, maybe we can change the downward plunge of our fate. This is a box of details and they say that's where the devil is. I'm sending it now because Vicky told me about your director, Mark Dent, the man with the scar on his cheek – and I'm sick with fear about where this is leading. It's giving me a very bad feeling. So if I don't see you again, maybe the details in here will help you navigate the way. I don't know what else to do. I'll always love you. Your loving mother....*" Vic lowered the letter uneasily. "'If I don't see you again'? What's that about?"

"It's kind of disturbing, is what that is," said Vicky. Didn't sound like a madwoman's rantings. Sounded like a mother trying to protect her kid. And not from Vicky.

They began pulling papers out of the archive box, glancing through journals full of writings and sketches. Vicky opened one well-thumbed, page-stained notebook, and started reading the meticulous handwriting that Guy had inscribed so long ago.

"'*Souls aren't the only things to reincarnate,*'" she read in Guy's journal. "'*Situations recur as well, and so do relationships, and not just relationships, but the emotional briar patches of relationships, the tar and the sinkholes, the loves and hates and passions and recriminations, over and over and over and over again. We sense these recurring intertwinings whenever we're drawn to people or places without reason – but the reason we're drawn is that we remember them from another time – the problem is that we simply don't* <u>remember</u> *that we remember them. We also sense these ancient, repeating relationships whenever we experience déjà vu – that tinted window which allows us to see, just for a fraction of a moment, when the same thing happened in another life.*'"

"I don't believe in *déjà vu*," said Vic absent-mindedly.

Vicky thumbed through other pages. Vic began reading from what seemed to be Guy's diary. "'*These dream elements are hard markers of every life I've cycled through, every revolution on the Great Wheel of reincarnation. The murder is always there. So is the full moon. A barking dog. RED CHAOS. The wolf, in some form....*'"

And from Vicky, reading another page: "'*The interpretation of the dream is key. Dreams have a secret language, it's like a code. The numbers **52426** are a crucial numeric code, if I could only decipher it, but I don't have the key, the Rosetta Stone of my own internal clockwork. I have to break that cryptogram to see the reality of all the lives I've lived over the centuries. The reality of the three people. The murder. The wolf. The perfume. The barking dog. The hunter's moon.*'"

"Hunter's moon," said Vic. "That's tonight."

He reached into the archive box, pulled out another item. A rusting metal weathervane in the shape of a wolf. "I wonder if this is the wolf he keeps writing about." But as he examined the jagged thing more closely, he cut himself on its barbed tail.

He jumped, dropping the eight-inch weathervane into the side pocket of his black jacket. A thin line of blood welled up on his index finger. He brought it to his mouth.

"You okay?" asked Vicky.

"Yeah, it's nothing."

"It's blood. First I'm bleeding, now it's you, we can't fuckin' get away from the stuff. This is creeping me out, Vic; let's just put all this crap back, we'll deal with it after we open."

He could hear in her voice she was warming up to him again, but he still couldn't quite get over that she hadn't apologized, especially after he'd told her he had let Olivetti know about his mother. Not letting go of being pissed off, it was one of his failings, he knew that; and he was working on it. But for the moment he just wasn't ready to give her much back yet in the way of kiss-and-make-up.

He pulled his finger out of his mouth, put pressure on the puncture. Didn't hurt all that much but it felt deep, like it had touched something to the bone. Animated something at the edges of his mind, he couldn't place what. That's when – casting his glance down to try to retrieve the thought – his attention was drawn to the answering machine in the archive box. And he couldn't have said why, but he had an urge to listen to it.

He took it out of the box, put it on his desk, plugged it in. It was an old model, a black plastic Panasonic with a tiny cassette tape snapped in place, from the dark days before digital. Vicky looked conflicted, reticent but curious, unsure she wanted to hear what the tape had to say. After all, this was kind of strange; it was at the very least a huge distraction and she was still trying to stay somewhat in character, she was on in less than ten minutes. Vic turned the VOLUME wheel to 10 and pushed the PLAY MESSAGES button. First came the OGM, the Out-Going Message, spoken in the voice of a young Irish woman.

"This is Claire, I'm not in right now, leave a message at the tone." The tape was so old, the voice wasn't that clear.

"She sounds familiar," said Vic. There was a beep on the machine, and the incoming message began playing. A man's voice, scratchy from the degenerated tape quality, but no tape could have hidden the deep melancholy in that voice. Neither Vic nor Vicky could have known it, but it was Guy.

"Claire," said Guy on the tape, "I realize now there was a third person in my dream. Not the killer, not the victim – but the witness who was watching it all. And here's the thing – I think I'm the witness. I'm going to be the witness. So now I don't know who's going to be murdered but I'm afraid somehow, in some way, it's you – because the victim in my dream has your perfume vial in her pocket…."

And then the line went dead.

"That's very fuckin' disturbing," said Vicky.

Mark strode past the office, slapping the doorframe as he went by. "Five minutes, onstage, let's do it again." They could hear him knocking on every door along the hall.

Vic and Vicky looked at each other silently a moment, hesitated, almost said something. Then simply put the journals back in the box.

That's when Vicky saw something else in there, something that glinted like a bauble, caught her eye. She pulled it out. It was a small, ornate perfume vial. Gold filigree over lavender glass.

She uncorked it, curious. Brought it to her nose and sniffed.

12

CHAPTER TWELVE

December 6, 1976
11:20 P.M.-11:23 P.M.
Night, The Shadow Of Light,
And Life, The Shadow Of Death.
With Life Before And After
And Death Beneath And Above

Guy uncorked the filigreed vial, brought it to his nose and sniffed the weighty vapors. The perfume filled his senses, aroused him, made him vertiginous. He pulled it away from his face. It wasn't time yet. He needed a clear head now, he needed to think, to work out all the clattering voices inside him. He re-corked the vial, dropped it back into his archive box.

He was sitting on the damp grass outside the gardener's cottage, in the now-abandoned efforts he'd begun months ago to salvage the ruins of the vast garden, in the shadows under a rising moon, watching Claire move around past the windows of her house, watching her from across the expanse of wide, torn-up lawn. In his mind he was going over the conversation he'd had with her in the kitchen a few hours earlier. And he was thinking about killing her.

It was the clearest path to salvation he could come up with. His own personal, physical salvation, certainly. The most direct way to prevent his own death and to prevent the murder of his reincarnated soul in the next life. If he killed Claire, after all, he wouldn't have to die now to provide a soul for her new baby. And if she didn't have the baby, there would, of course, be no victim in the next go-around, nobody for Eric to kill. Thwarting two deaths by dealing one. Of course he couldn't be sure that's the way it worked but there was a resounding internal logic to it.

Unfortunately the death he was contemplating was the murder of the woman he loved. He could hardly believe he was even considering it; he wasn't the kind of person who'd ever do such a thing. What was it he'd told his old friend Alan, so many months ago, that bicentennial night at the Venice beach house when his seizures had first kicked in? "Taking a human life is just evil," he'd insisted to the good doctor, the moral relativist. And yet… here he was, watching Claire's graceful form glide back and forth across the kitchen window and wondering how he might reasonably do just that.

Poison? There was strychnine, arsenic… but he didn't know poisons, didn't know how to get possession of them, or how to administer them, or which ones were painless, or how to disguise them. A knock on the head from behind, that would be the way to go; it was quick, just a loss of consciousness and she'd be departed. But what if his aim was off, and he just split her skull, and she gushed pain-screaming blood over the floor and staggered around and saw him? The horror of that sight stopped him; he couldn't stand thinking that might be the last thing she saw in this life.

But how could she do this to him?! She said she loved him! How could she have a baby now that guaranteed his death? It was intolerable, it was profoundly impossible, he wouldn't accept it, he couldn't; he'd suffocate her first, he'd put a pillow over her head while she slept, she'd never know, she'd even say that's what she wanted if it meant that her true love, her soul mate, would live.

He slumped, he wept. This was useless. He felt ashamed, horrified at what he was considering. He could no more kill her than kill himself. Less, since letting her live was in fact tantamount to his own suicide. So be it. She'd suffered enough at the hands of selfish men; he wouldn't add to her torment, though it cost him his life. Cost him twice, if he couldn't come up with a way to warn his next incarnation of the peril that awaited.

Or maybe kill Eric, maybe that was the way to go. With Eric dead, Guy wouldn't have to warn his next incarnation – the actual murderer would be gone. Why hadn't Guy thought of this before? It was perfect, it was more than perfect, it was deeply satisfying, positively exalting, there was a lustiness about it that nearly made him salivate at the thought; he could feel it in his fingers that had become so strong from physical labor, feel his fingers wrapped around Eric's neck, the exquisite pleasure of strangulating the life out of the vile, hated... but wait. The ecstasy of killing? Guy blanched at this hint of who he was becoming. Who he was about to become. Had he changed so much, then? Gone from Jekyll to Hyde in the blink of a tumor?

This wasn't the Guy he'd always been or known. That old Guy never quite understood, at a gut level, how a person, a good person, could get any joy or juice out of hurting someone else. So what was this new Guy about? What dark lust was driving the glorification of his own one-man death cult? And what kind of karma did he suppose that was going to generate? Could he ever, in a million lifetimes, pay off that karmic debt?

No, there had to be another way. Back to the beginning. Or to the end. A way to warn himself, in his future life, of the killer who stalked, and stabbed in the moonlight, and dug shallow graves.

In the kitchen, on the other side of the yard, Claire moved sinuously past the window, her arms wrapped around herself, touching the soft shoulders Guy couldn't touch, weaving sensually, gracefully dancing alone to some poignant melody Guy couldn't hear, encircled by a fragrance Guy couldn't smell; she was a breathtaking vision, an unworldly vision, swaying on his watch, and a line from Swinburne came unbidden to him, "*His life is a watch or a vision/Between a sleep and a sleep.*"

A watch or a vision of some past or future life, before and after, bracketed by the blind, dreamless sleep of death beneath and above. Seizure visions, seizure watches, seizures to see across the chasm of those long muffled sleeps, he needed more seizures, to gather more clues. If he wasn't going to kill anybody, he needed signs, tokens, to warn the victim. If life is a watch, he had to keep watch, this murder was on his watch and to stop it he needed inklings such as he could only find in seizure. Convulsive intimations. He'd already tossed his Dilantin, so he was much more receptive to the effects of the tumor discharging its electrical energy through his brain. Now the time had come again to invoke headier spirits. Unleash the causative agent.

He pulled Claire's filigreed perfume vial once more out of his archive box, uncorked it again, brought it to his nose and inhaled the essence. The compound's aromatic esters always gave him a rush of adrenalin, like the first taste of a drug to a junkie. This was more than just a chemical rush to him, though; it was more like a sacred ritual. It served a higher purpose.

He tipped the vial's mouth against his index fingertip, rubbed the perfume across his lip. Rubbed it over his forehead. Down the bridge of his nose. Like an Apache applying war paint. Ready to ride into battle with his nightmares. *Hoka hey.* This was a good day to dream death.

The scent of his seizures cloaked him like a meditation. He watched Claire recede from the kitchen into the depths of the house as he sank into the depths of his pre-consciousness. Inducing his seizures was becoming easier the more he did it; those pathways were getting hardwired, set off by his olfactory trigger. And now as he sat on the ground he felt it coming, like a downhill train, open-throttle. The lights of the main house began to twist, to crenellate, to turn into parallel lines of turrets – and as his fingers began to twitch, his eyelids fluttered with a harsh baying, growling bark....

Somewhere, a dog barks.

Gaslights, alleyways. Distorted, as in a dream. The weathervane of a wolf turns slowly under a full moon. A hunter's moon. A drop of blood glistens on the wolf's tooth, glinting in the moonlight like hell's morning dew. There is a repetitive, irregular knocking.

A scar-faced Victorian gentleman walks behind a limping, pretty woman dressed in tatters, her hair perfumed, her face bruised, her eyes looking for escape. He points up at the yellowing moon.

"That's a hunter's moon, that is," he says.

October 17, 2013, 7:20-7:21 P.M.
"What are you hunting, then, Luv?" asked Vicky.

Vicky and Mark, in threadbare tart's dress and gentleman's frock, cockney and courtly, in costume and in character, were rehearsing the scene on the Victorian street set.

But Vic hadn't left his office. Still going through the journals in the archive box his mother had sent him. He couldn't tear himself away, felt compelled to keep reading, gazing at the drawings, until he turned a page in a sketchbook – and stared mutely at the image drawn there. Stared in shocked disbelief. And ran out of the room.

Ran down the corridor of empty dressing rooms, past hair and make-up, to the wings. Just in time to hear Vicky, onstage, saying her line, "What are you hunting, then, Luv?"

December 6, 1976, 11:24 P.M.

"Hunting you, then, Luv."

The old scar-faced man raises his scalpel high over his head. He stabs the pretty woman in the back. She turns to look at him with a death's-head grin and crumples to the ground, on her back. He sinks his scalpel into her belly. It catches on some knotted tissue but he slices through it.

The pretty woman dips her fingers deep into her abdominal wound, pulls them up dripping slick, thick blood. Another chilly smile.

Once more he raises his blade high above his head, to stab deep.

October 17, 2013, 7:22-7:26 P.M.

Onstage Mark raised the prop knife high over his head, eyes gleaming, poised to stab Vicky in the back. But he paused at the sound of running footsteps. And as he turned back to look, Vic raced across stage, tackled him hard, spilling them both to the ground, arms and legs flying as if they were marionettes discarded by a furious puppeteer. The prop knife flew out of Mark's hand, hit a backdrop, skittered across the floor.

Mark jumped up flailing. Enraged. "What the bloody hell do you think you're doing?!"

Vic scrambled over to the fallen knife. Picked it up, gripped it, jammed its point into the wall. It stuck there, buried half an inch in the wood. The blade didn't slide into the hilt.

"Not exactly a prop knife this time, is it?" demanded Vic.

Everyone looked shocked. Mark stood up, grabbed the knife out of the wall. Looked at it closely, flipped a tiny catch at the base of the hilt. And now the blade slid easily backwards on its spring mechanism. "Somebody forgot to release the lock," he said.

"Why in God's name didn't you check it before you used it?!" shouted Vic, nearly out of control and not much interested in stopping himself at this moment. There was a time for anger management and there was a time for anger.

"I thought that was the tech director's job," Mark answered in a stony, lowered voice, the implicit accusation loud enough for everyone in the room to hear.

They faced off darkly, the knife in Mark's hand electrifying the air with the imminence of bloodshed. Vicky, shaken, stared at Vic. Was it his job to check the catch? Had he dropped the ball again, left her in the lurch? No, she couldn't fathom this as his fault; he was the one who'd rushed in to save her at the last possible moment – but in that moment of her uncertainty, Vic saw the look in her eye and she saw him recognize it.

Angry now, she stomped up to Mark, forcefully pried the knife away from him. He held on with a perverse smile; then uncurled his fingers from the hilt.

Testing the device herself, Vicky pushed the knifepoint back with her own middle finger, but as the blade started to slide smoothly in on its spring mechanism, it caught – and the point pricked Vicky's skin, a moment of unexpected pain. Pain was a gift, an acting teacher had once told her. An intense punctuation, a moment to focus on, to call back to when a role demanded it. A pure sensory cry of life; but then the slippery flipside of it was always the echo, the shadow, the promise of death.

And almost in slow motion, now, a drop of blood beaded on her fingertip, where the knife had punctured.

December 6, 1976, 11:25 P.M.

The pretty woman lies, bleeding, on the ground. She writes **RED CHAOS** *in her own blood. She writes the numbers* **52426** *in her own blood.*

Her body is motionless. Lifeless.

And then it plunges into a depth of dark water, her tattered clothes flowing like seaweed, a swath of pale light illuminating other floating, dead bodies, dismembered body parts… .

The scar-faced old man stands over her. He leans forward, smiling, curious to watch her die. But suddenly her arm shoots out of the water, swings up and she slaps him… .

October 17, 2013, 7:26 P.M.

Vicky slapped Mark as hard as she could. "You could've killed me, you goddam bastard!"

"Might've improved your acting," he said.

"Fuck off."

She stormed out. Mark followed.

December 6, 1976, 11:27 P.M.

The pretty woman stands up, bloodied, as if risen from the dead. She storms off. The old scar-faced man follows her.

She walks off the Victorian street, to an area behind a long velvet curtain. The street appears to have been a stage set, a collection of facades belying their true meaning. She is now backstage. She stalks past a full-length mirror, the scarfaced man right behind her.

But there is another person's image in the mirror. A third person, watching them. The witness.

October 17, 2013, 7:28 P.M.-7:29 P.M.

Vicky charged backstage, Mark at her heels. He grabbed her arm, jerked her around.

"All right, I'm sorry, it was an accident," he said. "But it's done now, and nobody was hurt, so get over it."

Vic caught up with them. Paused to watch their interaction. To witness. Tried to slow himself down just an inch, knew he was balancing very close to going over the top, took some deep breaths. Glanced at his own reflection in the mirror, saw equanimity was hopeless. So he just stepped forward, roughly pulled Mark off Vicky. "Let go of her."

As Mark's hand was yanked free, it caught on Vicky's pocket – knocking to the floor the small filigreed perfume vial she'd taken from Gloria's archive box.

The two men were still on the thin rim of violence, face to face. Cast and crew stood frozen, like they were watching a train wreck about to happen. All so slow-motion, the way these things sometimes are, time elongated and magnified by events.

Mark backed down though it clearly galled him. Turned to address the room. "All right, we're all jumpy. Opening jitters. Everybody take the night off. Get drunk, get laid. Get back here noon tomorrow." Then he turned back to Vic and glowered. "Happy now?"

Vicky bent down, picked up the filigreed perfume vial off the floor where it had fallen, put it back in her pocket again. Tossed one last glance of disdain at Mark. Exited.

December 6, 1976, 11:27 P.M.-December 7, 1976, 4:42 A.M.

The scarfaced old man grabs the pretty woman's arm, backstage, near the mirror. He knocks a perfume vial from her pocket. The image of the other man, the witness, stands in the mirror, watching. A man wearing a black suede jacket with a burgundy satin lining. The witness looks at himself in the mirror. Screams echo out of the mirror as the glass turns red, begins to crack and then shatter. The witness turns around and faces the wall.

*The words **RED CHAOS** are written in blood on the wall. The screams get louder. There is a payphone on the wall. Phone numbers are scribbled all around it. Many numbers. The numbers **52426** are there. But not in isolation now. The number is growing. There are two more numerals that can be seen beginning the sequence. Two **5**'s. Now the whole number sequence reads **555 2426**.*

*Everything fades away but those numbers. **555 2426**. And the words **RED CHAOS**. And the screams. The screams go on for hours....*

Guy stopped convulsing. He lay on the grass outside the cottage for a long moment, willing his eyes to open, wiping the bloody saliva from his chin. He crawled over to his archive box, pulled out paper and pen. Wrote down the numbers he'd just seen in his seizure. **555 2426**. It looked very like a phone number. Like an American phone number.

He looked up at the main house. The lights were out. The moon was low. Hours must've passed since his seizures began. Slowly he stood, and slowly entered the gardener's cottage.

He flipped open his notebook to the page Claire had written her private house phone line on – 77. He picked up the white Princess phone off the table and dialed. He got Claire's answering machine.

"This is Claire, I'm not in right now, leave a message at the tone."

There was a beep, and Guy spoke into the phone. "Claire, I realize now there was a third person in my dream. Not the killer, even though I've always felt so connected to the killer, and not the victim, who limped, like I limp – but the witness who was watching it all. And here's the thing – I'm the witness, I'm going to be the witness. So now I don't know who's going to be murdered but I'm afraid somehow, in some way, it's you – because the victim had your perfume vial in her pocket."

He looked up to see the lights go on in the kitchen of the main house. Eric appeared at the window. Guy hung up the phone. He looked at the scrap of paper in his hand, where he'd written the number from his seizure dream. **555-2426**. He stared at the number in some confusion. It was certainly a phone number but he didn't think it was in the format of any Irish number he'd ever seen. Still, he dialed it, uncertain. It rang once, twice, three times, four. The line disconnected.

Guy hung up, increasingly frantic. He looked across the yard to see Eric open the back door of the main house, run to his car and drive off. Guy moved to the doorway of his cottage, to get a better look. Eric had simply left the rear entrance of the main house wide open. Guy had a terribly sinking feeling.

"He's killed Claire," he whispered with hollow certainty. And started running lame toward the house.

October 17, 2013, 7:31 P.M.-7:36 P.M.

Vic pulled an emotionally fragile Vicky into his office, hugged her until her breathing quieted.

"I can't take any more, Vic," she rasped into his shoulder. "My trashed car, the razor in my sandwich, my nightmares, Tully out of prison, your mother, my period, our fight; Vic we've never had a fight like that, I hated it, and then I swear to God this psycho director almost killed me, if you hadn't…." She stopped before pursuing the thought to its conclusion.

He just kept holding her, rocking her, his hand on her head. "Sshh," he said.

She didn't say anything, just tried to absorb everything that had happened. But among all the bizarre recent events, all the premonitions and intuitions and uneasy revelations, something stuck out that really, really didn't make sense. "Vic – why did you come racing in like the Lone Ranger just now? How did you know the catch on the knife blade was locked?"

He wasn't sure he wanted to tell her. But she asked, he supposed she deserved an answer. Gently he released her, pulled the top journal out of the archive box. Opened it to the first page. Started reading to Vicky.

"'*September 23, 1976. Dream journal. Images of the murder….*'"

"This is not helping my freak-out," said Vicky.

"This is what saved your life. A drawing from this book that was done thirty-seven years ago."

He thumbed through a dozen pages of sketches, darkly detailed, hyper-realistic. Until he came to a close-up of the old scarfaced Victorian gentleman of Guy's seizure dream.

Vicky startled. "That's Mark." Nobody else had a scar like that, its thick angles turning ear to chin, first this way, then that.

Vic flipped the page. The old scarface, dressed in a long, nineteenth century Englishman's coat, was stabbing a pretty woman in the back, a woman in a tattered dress very like the one Vicky was wearing at the moment. Vicky stared at the image. She turned pale. "And that's the scene we were just rehearsing. These are like storyboards for our play. How could these have been drawn thirty years ago by someone I never heard of before?"

Vic turned the page one more time. Now the pretty woman who was getting stabbed had her face turned toward us. It was a portrait of Vicky.

Vicky began to shake, unnerved to her core. "Vic, what is this? What's going on?"

"I don't know, it doesn't make any sense. All I know is I saw this drawing of Mark stabbing you, and I just knew it was true, I knew it was really going to happen and I had to stop it."

"We have to get out of here, Baby." She began pacing. "I mean I don't know, what the fuck, this is all like *Twilight Zone* time, all I know is we have to get out and not come back."

"If you did that, who'd play the victim?" said Mark. They turned to see him standing in the doorway.

Vicky looked taut. "I don't give a fuck, Mark. You were so far out of line, the line's gone."

"You're an actress, you were paid to do a job. Now I expect you to do it."

"The job didn't include getting murdered," said Vic. He took Vicky's arm. "Come on, we're going."

"You're not going anywhere," said Mark.

Vic started to shove past him. Part of him really wanted to leave without a fight; part of him wanted to pound Mark senseless. But Mark had his own agenda, and put his hand on Vic's chest – slammed him against the wall. All three of them froze for a long moment. Then Vic punched Mark in the cheek.

And the fight was on.

December 7, 1976, 4:47 A.M.

Guy ran in the back door of the main house, turned on the kitchen light. The place was empty; but more than that. The very air had a terrible emptiness about it, an expectant stillness, like a premonition.

He hobbled to the edge of the hallway, the looming shadows like clusters of night. He called out, afraid of the reply he might get – or not get.

"Claire?!"

A low shape emerged from the darkness, a nightmare shape, issuing a primitive, disturbing growl. Guy took one step back, he couldn't help himself; he wanted to stand fast, but his feet moved by some atavistic reflex.

The shape came closer. It was Eric's Rottweiler, baring its teeth.

Guy stumbled backwards, reaching around to grab a weapon, any kind of weapon, a kitchen knife, a pot, a cookbook – but a hand came out and grabbed the dog's collar, holding it from advancing on him – and then Alice, the maid, stepped forward, restraining the animal.

"Mr. Daniels," she said, surprised.

"Is Claire here?" he asked. "I saw Eric leaving...."

"She's at hospital, sir. St. Mary's."

"What happened?"

"Contractions. Too early for labor, but she insisted on taking herself, and now Mr. Deloup's gone after her."

"Your car, can I have your car?"

She nodded. "It's in front of the garage. The key's in the glove box."

But he was already running out the door, and the dog was straining at the leash to charge after him.

October 17, 2013, 7:37 P.M.

Vicky, Mark and Vic grappled on the floor of Vic's office.

It was one of those mean, scary you-don't-give-a-shit-if-you-get-hurt-or-not fights. Teeth, fists, feet, knees. Grabbing anything hard you could find, swinging wild at heads and backs, necks and faces. Vic's shirt was torn off with a chunk of skin, Vicky broke her foot and didn't even notice, Mark's ribs got cracked in a glancing blow from a falling filing cabinet. Like they were playing out an ancient blood feud. Like they wanted to kill each other.

December 7, 1976, 5:24 A.M.-5:25 A.M.

Guy drove Alice's car dangerously past the speed limit, sometimes spilling over onto the wrong side of the road, but no policeman stopped him and no innocent bystander got in the way. He came as close to the hospital as he could, then just left the car idling in the street and loped the last two blocks, bumping into hapless pedestrians. A newsstand told him it was December 7, and for some reason he thought of Pearl Harbor Day, the day that would live in infamy. This was just such a day. The sky was turning a ceramic gray in the pre-dawn as he reached the wide front entrance of the hospital.

He paused at the vehicle turnaround. Cars, taxis, shuttles, patients, nurses and visitors milled around the concourse – and then he saw Claire, leaning against a parked car on the far side of the road, holding her belly in pain. She was at the curb, across the street from the hospital, looking for a break in the busy traffic so she could cross. Guy shouted her name and stepped into the street to cross to her, looking left for cars.

But the car that hit him was coming from his right, the way they do in Ireland.

It hit Guy with a sickening thud – and all arms and legs, like a crane, he went airborne, he took flight.

October 17, 2013, 7:38 P.M.

Vic went airborne, hit the wall with a sickening thud. Mark kicked him in the groin, but Vic grabbed Mark's ankle, brought him toppling down. Mark landed on top, askew, and went right to ripping at Vic's eye. Vic turned his head away and pushed up with all his strength on Mark's chin, trying to bend the man's head backward to breaking. Vicky began whacking Mark across the back with a prop shovel handle, hitting him like she meant to do damage.

Like Claire had done at the open grave near the gardener's cottage, so many years ago.

Mark jerked the shovel out of her hands, threw it at her, hit her in the forehead, knocking her back. Vic punched him solid in the jaw. Mark went down but came right up with a letter opener, raised it high to plunge into Vic's heart – when Vicky brought the shovel around like a club, knocked the weapon flying across the room, breaking Mark's hand at the same time.

Mark jumped to his feet, slammed her backwards, grabbing the shovel out of her hands as she fell. Vic stumbled up a moment later, lurched into the wall – but even then, Mark was coming around with the shovel full force – landing it square into Vic's sternum.

Vic hung there a second, teetering. Then his eyes went up into his head and his legs crumpled and he hit the floor deadweight.

December 7, 1976, 5:25 P.M.-5:29 P.M.

Guy hit the pavement deadweight, came to a twisted stop as the sports car sped off. Claire saw his motionless body.

"Guy, no…." She ran unevenly to his unconscious form, knelt beside him. "Oh, God, no… somebody help him, please…."

Guy's eyes fluttered open. He looked in all directions, undone. "I have to remember this," he whispered. "All of this. Remember every detail, for the next time…."

"Guy, be quiet, please, don't waste your strength...."

"There are methods, there are exercises for staying awake at this moment. Presence of mind... closeness to the heart of God. Pilgrimage, this was my pilgrimage to Galway. And to you. And rituals, I had the ritual of your perfume vial, it was a sacred ritual, it was a sacrament actually. And meditation, do you think seizures are a form of meditation? I think mine are, I think I've been doing seizure meditations for months. But do you think that's long enough? Do you think it's kept me near the heart of God? Do you think...?" Then, looking desperately into Claire's eyes: "I have to remember this."

She took his hand in hers, his frail hand, and held it to her cheek and dropped a tear on it. "I'll remember for both of us," she promised.

He smiled at her kindness, but then floating by in his stream of consciousness came a fragment of verse from his youth: "*'Because I could not stop for Death/He kindly stopped for me....'*"

"You are not going to die," she scolded him angrily. "Do you hear me?"

He pulled his garden-roughened hand back slowly from her tender grasp and looked at his long, spindly fingers, in some essential way still fragile beneath the callus. He furrowed his eyebrows. "I wanted to work with my hands. Will I get to do that next time, do you think?"

"I'm sure of it," she choked, her voice barely under control.

"Don't cry," he whispered. "It's nothing to be sad about, I promise. You just gather your memories around you... and then you die. And then you hold onto them when the new you wakes up later." His eyes glazed. "Hold onto them... hold on."

"I'm holding you," she whispered.

A glimmer of panic crossed his features, a fleeting presentiment. "But if I should forget this beautiful life... you have to help my next incarnation. My notes – give them to the next one, to the body I inhabit, to your daughter. To stop the murder...." He held Claire's gaze, a far and loving goodbye – and his eyes dropped shut.

She shook her head, refusing to accept what she saw. "Don't go," she murmured. She felt for his pulse. It was wispy, thready – but it was there. Or was that her own pale pulse she was feeling? She leaned her ear down to his mouth – held motionless there, trying to push away the cacophony of traffic noise that was drowning out all other sounds – held her ear even closer to his sweet lips… until she felt, at last, the slightest movement of warm air, a hint of ebbing breath.

She sat up tall, like a sentry sounding the alarm, and started to call for help again; but then another spasm came, worse than any of the others, and she grabbed her belly, crying, "Ohhh… my baby…."

October 17, 2013, 7:39 P.M.-7:41 P.M.

"Baby, please get up, come on…." Vicky was crouching beside Vic's motionless body, shaking it.

"He's dead, you stupid bitch," said Mark, checking Vic's carotid pulse. There was no pulse. There was no chest movement at all, no muscle tone, no breathing. No life stirring.

Torn with black grief, Vicky started pummeling Mark, wild fists and nails and grunts of wanting nothing so much as to kill; she was all over him, sobbing as she beat at his face until he finally got some traction and muscled himself upright and kicked her in the head. She was out as she hit the ground but somehow the keening continued to echo from her mouth, a pitiful, endless, unconscious wail.

December 7, 1976, 6:35 A.M.-6:45 A.M.

Claire wailed at the clenching of her last contraction as the obstetrician eased out the baby.

"One more push, it's crowning," he said. "Take a deep breath, here we go, the last big push…."

Claire pushed. Her baby was born. Eric was watching nearby, looking anxious, looking grim.

"Cut the cord, please," said the obstetrician to his nurse. And there was a flurry of activity but it felt like a pause, a soft clatter of instruments, a muttering of nurses trading opinion. "Come on, hurry up…." And then, more quietly: "Let's get some oxygen going."

But Claire heard with the acute ears of a new mother. There was something new in his voice now, a hidden urgency. "What is it?" she breathed. "Is my baby all right?"

But her baby was not all right, not at all. It was premature, for starters. Small, poor color, eyes closed, body limp, respirations thin and wheezy, not responding. Apgar of 3.

Eric saw it. Nobody needed a medical degree to see there was something not right with this baby. But Eric's response wasn't concern. It was hatred, anger. "Something's wrong," he said quietly.

Claire heard that, too, heard his words, and something behind his words. Dread rose in her throat like a backed up drain. "What's wrong, somebody, anybody? Eric, what is it?"

But Eric was already slipping out the door.

Guy lay on his back in the hospital bed, his eyes closed. He was conscious, but floating, somehow. He knew he'd been hit by a car but nowhere did his body hurt. Had the doctors given him drugs for pain? Probably so. This wasn't like drugs, though, he'd had narcotics after his brain surgery in the summer – and this feeling he had now wasn't like that at all. This was more like being hypnotized. A state of timelessness is what this felt like. He was aware but immobile, his mind calm yet racing. It was as if his spirit were separate from his body, watching this world from a parallel existence. Could this be what death was like? Was he actually dead? If so, it was serene, he felt a blissful indifference. No, not indifference, it was more akin to curiosity. And he was aware of a gentle fullness of being, of oneness with everything. He wondered if he tried to open his eyes, if it was his soul's eyes he'd be opening, if he'd see the famous white light at the end of the tunnel. See spirits of dead loved ones beckoning him to a greater beyond. If he only opened his eyes. He opened his eyes.

Eric was standing over him, watching him with an unflinching, glassy loathing.

"You're the father of Claire's baby, aren't you?" said Eric in an eerie, stilted cadence.

All at once the myriad senses of Guy's physical surroundings came rushing in on him. The tug of the IV in his arms; the soft green clear plastic oxygen mask covering his mouth and nose; the sticky tape on his chest connecting him by wires to a cardiac monitor that beeped regularly, once per second, behind his head; the smell of alcohol and Betadine and floor disinfectant; the gleam of the surgical instruments on a tray at the bedside, in case Guy required emergency intervention; the pain of his broken bones, bruised muscle, laboring lungs.

And infusing all of it with new meaning was the malign intent of the face leaning over him.

Venom sparked for just a moment in Guy's heart: here was the man he hated. With a last effort of will, Guy thought about springing up, grabbing the scalpel at the bedside and plunging it into Eric's throat. Right here and now: he could kill the beast.

But then who was the beast? The one who killed, that's who. The beast was the one who forgot the lessons of life's wondrous ardors, death's untroubled meditation. *And wrought with weeping and laughter/And fashion'd with loathing and love/With life before and after/And death beneath and above.* Guy felt the zeal of his earthly attachments sublimating like dry ice, as if they'd been solid rock in his gut since the day he was born, now simply dissolving into the ether, leaving Guy empty but whole.

He shook his head weakly at Eric, meaning to comfort the man. "No... I'm not your child's father," he whispered, "but we're all children of time."

Eric shook his own head with considerably more vehemence. "That pathetic stillbirth isn't my child, I can tell you that."

He pulled the pillow out from under Guy's bruised head. He unstrapped Guy's oxygen mask, laid it on the bed beside him and raised the kapok-filled pillow with calm purpose. Guy couldn't move, he could only watch the pillow lower onto his face, blotting out all air, all clatter, all light, except the lights in his mind that began to sparkle at the edges of his peripheral vision, suffused with an abiding peace amidst a cacophony of internal senses, especially that familiar musky perfume, the barky raw scratching....

Somewhere, a dog barks.

There is the irregular knocking sound. And out of the blackness a full moon emerges. But incense is burning thickly now, cloying like perfume, and the dense smoke drifts across the face of the moon, turning it a dark red, swirling like red chaos, and a cacophony of words spilling out of the smoke, strange words from an ancient language. Youyiguhmihudan youyiguhmihudan youyiguhmihudan. And the blood, the screams, the bodies floating in dark water smelling of fish rot and tamarind, her tattered clothes flowing like seaweed, a strange swath of light illuminating the chaos, punctuated by the irregular knocking, it all mingles to crescendo.

And then the light of the moon elongates, brightens into an intense concentration of yellow fire, pulls out into a weaving of fine threads of light that twist and crenellate into turrets... .

October 17, 2013, 8:05 P.M.-8:07 P.M.

A crenellated turret stood in silhouette relief against the huge yellow moon. It wasn't any dream, though, it was a real turret. An architectural detail on top of a crumbling, condemned building rising eight stories above the desolate, trash-littered empty lot.

At the base of the building, at its rear entrance, a car pulled up and rolled to a stop. Mark popped the trunk, got out. He was still in costume, his long cloak flowing in the wind like something out of Sleepy Hollow. His body hurt in ways both deep and superficial but that was small price to pay for the joy he felt at bringing his wrath to bear upon his betrayers. Tonight would come a great reckoning.

He walked to the back of his car. Vicky was curled there, in the open trunk, still unconscious, her Victorian harlot dress in tatters from the fight and splayed all around her like shredded angel wings. Mark jammed his bruised, swelling broken hand between her legs, then with his other grabbed a fistful of hair on her head and hoisted her body from the boot, slinging it easily over his shoulder. He was a strong man.

He slammed the trunk lid shut, fireman-carried Vicky over the pot-holed landscape to the rear entrance of the condemned, turreted building, where the faintest aroma of tamarind and dead rodents lingered in the doorways. He leaned her against the dirty wood, rummaged around in his pocket until he came up with his keys. Unpadlocked the door of the condemned building, swung it wide, and hefted the insensate girl through the dark opening.

December 7, 1976, 6:46 A.M.-6:59 A.M.

*The pretty woman's body is rolled into the dark opening of the grave. There is an irregular knocking. A bouquet of spices and maggots eating flesh. There is **RED CHAOS**. Youyiguhmihudan.*

And now her body is plunging into dark water, her tattered clothes flowing like seaweed, a strange swath of light illuminating other rotting, floating bodies. Dead. All dead....

Guy twitched his last convulsion under the asphyxiating pillow Eric pressed into his face. There was one final convulsive spasm, Guy's hands gripping for whatever life was left him; but it was tissue thin. The convulsion was followed by a long, motionless breath-holding moment; and then a brainstem, animal struggle for air, more a reflex than an intention; and in the end it was this simple: Guy's chest ceased to rise and fall.

The cardiac monitor went flatline.

Eric removed the pillow, put it back under Guy's head. Put the oxygen mask back over the unbreathing mouth and nose. The urgent flatline alarm was triggered on the monitor, the continuous *eeeeeeee* of modern hospital death. *Eeeeeeeee....*

"Eeeeeee!" wailed Claire's baby, finally opening its mouth, coming to life under the desperate resuscitation of the doctors and nurses. Crying out its first breath, it was a new soul, brought to life; or an old soul, at the moment of migration, an old soul newly incarnate....

An intern checked Guy's pulse. A nurse disconnected the cardiac monitor alarm, making the room go suddenly silent as... well, as the grave. The intern put a stethoscope to Guy's chest, left anterior, right anterior; pulled open Guy's eyelids, pupils fixed and dilated. The intern stood straight again, shook his head. No pulse. No respirations. No heartbeat. No brain function.

Clearly there was no point in pursuing resuscitation. The nurse indicated a note in the patient's chart – the man had terminal brain cancer, it had said so on the card in his wallet, along with a medical advisory that he was a DNR. Do Not Resuscitate.

The intern pronounced him, noting the hour and minute for the record.

Guy was dead. Long live Guy's soul.

13

CHAPTER THIRTEEN

October 17, 2005
7:52P.M.-9:38 P.M.
Dead Men Don't Dance

Vic was dead.

On the floor of his office. No pulse, no heartbeat, no respiration. No signs of life the way we measure it with our volumes and pressures and finely calibrated instruments.

But after a span of time – not that long in one framework, a lifetime in another – his muscles contracted once; powerfully, convulsively, every fiber in tonic spasm for two seconds. And then every muscle, maybe every cell, in his body went completely lax, all the vital force within them spent.

Except then, somehow, some visual sense was reawakened, a kind of reanimation, as if his eyelids had fluttered open.

He saw blurry, distorted faces moving over him, surrounded by a bright white glow. This was death, then, he thought. Spirits moving through a tunnel of light, waiting to guide him to whatever came next, if anything did. He felt like he was suspended in a fluid, ethereal portal, a place for coming into something grand and wondrous, a reborning into some glorious new life. He'd never believed in heaven before; he'd grown up agnostic, he thought this white-light-to-heaven stuff was a fairy tale for those who couldn't deal with death, or with the meaninglessness of life it implied – gutless people who dreaded the nothingness of lying unliving in the ground for all eternity. And Guy didn't want to live his life in a world of fairy tales. Yet here he was, experiencing a curious, anticipatory feeling. Anticipating the manifest presence of an afterlife. No pain, no fear, no time, no sound... but wait. Now there was sound.

A melody, actually. What was it? So familiar. Then it came to him – it was that Steve Earle song, *Galway Girl*. Now that was strange. Why was that melody floating through his deathly unconscious consciousness? But then the melody faded and other noises rose and swirled around him.

Unintelligible noises, actually, like people talking in tongues. Or in some arcane, ancient, dead language. Or something unearthly, even, something like alien communications. Had he been snatched by creatures from another world? Extraterrestrials, benign or malevolent? Were they going to experiment on him with anal probes, put him in a zoo, throw him in a crock pot to stew and eat, teach him the irreducible truth of the cosmos? Was heaven really just a universe of space beings in a galaxy far, far away?

"Recharging," one of them said. This was Paramedic One.

"Hang on, I got a pulse," said Paramedic Two.

He nodded at Paramedic One, who removed the defibrillator paddles from Vic's chest and taped down the IV in Vic's arm.

So he wasn't dead. Or rather, he had been dead briefly; dead and then defibrillated. The white light of defibrillation, the rebirth into this brave new world of... where, exactly, was he?

Vic was lying on the floor. Crouching above him were the two paramedics, and standing behind them, watching anxiously, were Otto in an open, silk kimono, and a shirtless Teddy.

"Looks like sinus rhythm," said Paramedic Two.

"Is he gonna make it?" asked Teddy.

"Depends how long his heart was stopped," said Paramedic One.

"I started CPR right away, and Teddy called as soon as –" Otto began, but Paramedic One interrupted when he saw Vic's eyes stutter open.

"How you feeling, pal?" asked the medic.

"Not... sure...." Vic rasped shakily.

"Can you tell me what happened?"

Otto, upset, wanted to help. "I told you, there was a terrible fight, we heard crashing."

Paramedic One ignored him, though. Engaged Vic directly. "Aside from the bruise on your chest," he said, "you have any medical problems we should know about? Heart problems? Epilepsy? High blood pressure? Diabetes? Are you taking any medications?"

Vic shook his head vaguely, still somewhat disoriented. "Vicky... where's Vicky?"

"Any pain in your neck?" the paramedic went on, palpating Vic's vertebral column and wrapping it in a cervical collar. Vic only stared at him blankly. He still didn't quite get what was going on, who these men in white were, or where he was. He thought he'd been reborn, but it looked like the same old shit as far as he could tell.

Paramedic Two laid a strong cotton blanket on the floor, rolled Vic on his side. Paramedic One slid the blanket under him. With Vic on his side, a mass of scar tissue showed across his lower back.

Teddy got grossed out. "His back's all gnarly, man, isn't anybody else squicked by that? I mean, maybe you shouldn't move him."

Vic spoke weakly. "It's okay... old surgical scar... spina bifida when I was a kid... they fixed it."

The paramedics rolled him back onto the blanket. Then each took an end, muscled him onto the nearby gurney.

Otto pulled Teddy aside. His whisper was a combination of vindication and regret. "I'm telling you, this entire show was cursed from the moment it got wrapped around the hunter's...."

"Otto, shut up," said Teddy.

But then they hugged emotionally, the way new lovers do; and the paramedics wheeled Vic out on the gurney.

Vic grabbed Otto's arm as he passed, though. "Call the cops," he whispered desperately.

"We already did, that was the second thing we did," said Otto. "They're on their way."

"Detective Olivetti," demanded Vic. "I need to talk to him... has to find Vicky."

But his voice was failing and the paramedics moved him out the door, as Teddy and Otto embraced.

An hour later Vic was lying in a bed at Sacred Heart Hospital, same place he'd taken Vicky when she'd bit down on the razor in her sandwich. Plugged into an IV, O2 sat clip on his finger, cardiac monitor, oxygen tubing, call button hooked to the sheet near his right hand. His eyes were closed, his mind perched on that funny cusp of consciousness, not sure if he was on his way up or down, like a dream you knew you were dreaming, not sure if you wanted to wake up.

And it was odd, he never knew much poetry, didn't really like it, always said he didn't get it; but now here was a little piece of verse floating to the surface of his mind from the depths of his childhood. *Mary Anne Barnes was the queen of the acrobats/She could do wild tricks that'd give a cat the shats.* He smiled to himself. That's what he'd just done, okay, the biggest damn cat-shitting trick of his life. Died and un-died, thank you very much.

There was a knock at the open door and he opened his eyes still smiling. Detective Olivetti entered.

"All I gotta say is, you're lucky those gays were screwin' upstairs. They heard you gettin' killed and called 911 and started doin CPR – about which, by the way, your face is pretty cut up; if it was me I'd want to know which one of them was doin' mouth-to-mouth, and get an HIV screen on him. But that's just me. Any case, you got more pressing problems than that to worry about at the moment." And he tapped Vic's bruised chest, right over his heart.

Vic shrugged dismissively. "It's just a cracked breastbone, the doctor says. From getting hit in the chest with that shovel."

"Yeah, a cracked breastbone which he also says happened to kick off the irregular heartbeat that stopped your ticker."

"Just for a minute, though. There's no permanent damage, I'll be as good as new in a couple days."

"Guy I took care of in 'Nam, MPs brought him in from a bar fight, some-body whacked him in the chest with a bottle of Chivas, just a little cardiac contusion, no big deal, everything's rosy, then two days later blam, he had a coronary. This shit, I'm telling you, it's nothin' to sneeze at."

This was a kind of macho banter, Olivetti essentially telling Vic that his kind of potentially lethal injury is what happens when civilians try to take the law into their own hands, Vic telling Olivetti he was damn well healthy enough to pursue the matter better than Olivetti ever could, cardiac contusion or no cardiac contusion. But they'd established their positions now. Time to move on.

"The point is," said Vic, "how's Vicky?"

Olivetti was concerned by the question, and it made him wince involuntarily. But he didn't want to upset Vic more than he already was. "We're not really sure."

"Not sure," Vic rasped. He still couldn't generate much volume. "Did Mark do something to her? Did he hurt her?"

"The boyfriends upstairs at the theater saw him carry her to his car, dump her in the trunk and drive off. We got a BOLO out on him right now."

Vic closed his eyes, his heart aching and not from contusion. He was in pain remembering the big argument with Vicky, the things he'd said to her, so mean, and his tone so cold, so harsh, and then he'd never told her he loved her afterwards, not that night, or the next day, or anytime since, he'd never even said how sorry he was. And now his small meanness, his cold disregard, was the last thing she was going to remember about how he felt, and... fuck fuck fuck. Vic began getting out of bed. "I have to find her."

"Whoa, shall we dance?" Olivetti smiled, easing the impatient patient back down into bed. "Settle down, pal, you're not goin' anywhere. I'll find her, don't worry, that's what I do."

Olivetti paused. He wanted to spare Vic any more details. But Vic could see he was holding something back.

"What?" said Vic.

Olivetti bobbed his head. "I'm afraid your mother's in trouble, too."

Vic's breath quicked up. "What do you mean? You can't think she's involved in this anymore, I mean I know what I told you about the razor blades and the red paint on her car...."

"Because of what you told me, about the razors and so on, I went over to have a word with her this morning. No answer when I knocked. So I headed around back, saw there was a window cut open. Same as at Vicky's place,

when the puppy got stolen, big glass cutter circle. So I went inside the house
– and it looks like there was foul play."

"What? What was it?"

"Things smashed up, your mother's blood type on the floor…."

"Oh, God."

"And I gotta admit, right around then you were getting to be my prime
suspect."

"Me." Incensed.

"Look, you were always around when somethin' bad happened – the
spraypaint, the razor, the puppy – and then it seemed like maybe you were
tryin' to shift suspicion to your mom. I mean, you said you found those
razor blades in her garage, but who knows."

"Yeah, and I suppose I hit myself in the chest with a shovel; I figured a
cardiac arrest would really throw suspicion off me."

"I'll cut you some slack with the sarcasm this time, you had a nasty experience. But here's the thing. The lab says there was somebody else's blood in
your mother's kitchen, and some partial prints on the fireplace poker match
prints we just lifted from Mark Dent's office, so now I'm thinkin' this Mark
character ran over your old girlfriend or fiancée or whatever she was to you,
the Kendra chick, and now he's grabbed your mom and Vicky both –
because for some reason that we haven't figured out yet, he has some kind
of ding against you."

"Why would he do that?"

"You tell me."

Vic thought hard. It didn't make any sense. He hadn't even known Mark
before the play started. Did Mark know him from somewhere? There was
some kind of familiar feeling about the guy, Vic just… couldn't figure it. "I
don't know," was all he could say.

Olivetti stared into Vic's eyes, weighing the truth. No reason for the kid
to lie, not at this point; but maybe Vic knew something he didn't know he
knew. Best thing to do in that case was give the kid some space, and some
time, to ponder. "I'll get back to you when I find anything," Olivetti said
simply, and left.

Vic lay there in bed, looking for his own truth. Why was this happening,
why now, why to him? Bruised everywhere, his chest hurt like hell, his life

upside down. *And by that destiny to perform an act Whereof what's past is pro-logue, what to come In yours and my discharge,* he thought. And that might've been the weirdest thing he'd ever thought in his life, because it was poetry of some kind, he was sure of it and he didn't know any poetry except for *Mary Anne Barnes, Queen of the Acrobats.* So why the hell was he spouting poetry all of a sudden? Where had he learned it and what did it mean and why was it cropping up now?

And he didn't know why this would occur to him but he thought maybe there was a clue in that box his mother sent him.

With deliberate slowness he dangled his legs over the edge of the bed. Sat up. Sat there for two, three, minutes, letting his lightheadedness dissipate, gathering his various strengths.

And then he pulled the IV out of his arm.

Olivetti drove away from the hospital, talking into his cell phone to Wylie at the cop shop.

"Yeah, you got the plates on this Mark Dent's car? Okay, hang on." He pulled over, took out his little note pad, scribbled as he repeated the info. "Illinois tag 9AXD99. Got it. What about a house address on the guy?"

"I got two," said Wylie. "You want 'em both?"

"He owns two buildings?"

"What it says here."

"Yeah, go ahead, gimme both numbers."

"First one's on Lakeshore Drive, pretty ritzy for a backwater theater director."

Olivetti wrote down both numbers Wylie read to him. The second address was more interesting. "That second one, that's near Garfield Park, that's the same neighborhood where the girl works, matter of fact it's not all that far from the theater."

"Guy probably figures he can save on gas that way, he's probably one of those whattayacallits. An environmentalist."

"Yeah, okay, thanks for the info. I'll stay in touch."

"You want me to check out one of these places?"

"No, I got 'em." He hung up. He thought about trying Dent's house first. Bound to be clues there. Prints, Double 0 Cutt-Ex razor blades, a computer, maybe paperwork to support a motive. But this other address was maybe more interesting.

Second addresses, he'd often found, were like second thoughts. They were the ones that caught you up.

Vic walked halting through the empty theater. It was like a ghost playhouse now. Echoes of some terrible deed, like a lynching, like a ritual murder, lent a chill to the air, a queasy darkness to the shadows. He walked through the wings and across the stage, where his footfalls resounded all the way to the back row until they diminished like a muted recollection. He moved down the maze-like halls, past hair and makeup, past costume, past all the dressing rooms until he reached his office door.

Yellow police crime tape was stuck across the threshold as a visual warning. CRIME SCENE – DO NOT CROSS. Vic didn't think that applied to him, though. It was his office, and besides, he <u>was</u> the crime scene. At least his chest was. He touched the shovel-shaped bruise over his sternum. Winced. If that wasn't evidence of a crime, he didn't know what was.

He took out his key, opened the door. Stepped under the tape. Entered.

The place was a total wreck. Industrial shelves on the floor, props and papers strewn everywhere, big gouges in the walls, furniture broken. He moved around from surface to surface; gingerly, like a man afraid of falling. Looking for something. Something his mother had said might help him sort this all out, make it make sense. Some detail.

And there it was. The archive box full of details, tipped over, half its contents spilled on the ground.

He sat cross-legged on the floorboards beside the box, turned it upright. Got a little dizzy, just sat there a minute as a fine sweat cooled his forehead and the yellow dancing lights faded away. Started to look in the box when the sound of footsteps slowly approached from down the hall. Vic felt his heart racing. He glanced around for a weapon – a lamp, a scissors, anything – when Teddy appeared at the door, fully dressed.

"Jesus, Vic, you okay?"

Vic slumped with deep relief. The sheen of sweat that had dampened his temples began to dry; his strength was returning slowly. He took a deep breath, smiled wearily at the young actor. "I've been better, Teddy. Thanks for calling 911 when you heard the ruckus."

"Hey. Brotherhood of the theater, right? Anyway, we told Jonathan and Sid and some of the others what happened and Sid said he'd call the rest of the cast and crew, and the long and the short of it is, the play is canceled. At least it's indefinitely postponed."

Otto showed up behind Teddy, held out his hands, palms up, in a what-did-you-expect gesture. "Like I said, hunter's moon," was all the explanation he thought necessary.

"Whatever," said Teddy. "The point is…." He scrunched his eyebrows together and shrugged, though. Not really sure what the point was. So he let it go and simply, gently said to Vic: "Just go home, man."

Otto nodded in agreement, took Teddy's hand, and they left. Vic's gaze fell on the letter from his mother, lying on the floor. He picked it up and read: "*Maybe what's in the box will help you see the way….*"

He dropped the letter on the floor. Reached tentatively into the archive box. The way he might've reached into a grave.

14

CHAPTER FOURTEEN

January 7-8, 1977
And Wrought With Weeping And Laughter

Claire reached into the archive box, putting away another one of Guy's journals. She was sitting in the gardener's cottage, surrounded by the ephemera of his life. This was all that was left of him, now that he was gone: just these papers, his thoughts and drawings, and her memories of him. She held some of those memories now, like a touchstone: his long, gentle Aubrey Beardsley fingers, his dry wit, his thoughtful intelligence. And she remembered the way he touched her, warm on her skin and deep into her soul. These were the recollections of Guy that forged the shape of her life now. Her memories had a flavor of teary-eyed joy, of great loss that evoked a once great love. Once, and always.

She carried her month-old baby on her hip. Victor, she called him – so he would never be a victim, the way she felt she'd been. She'd been a victim and with luck she'd be a survivor; but her son would be a victor. She brought him to Guy's cottage frequently, hoping something of these sights and smells would register on the child, establish a subconscious link, a bond to Guy's brief, intense stay here. She didn't know why, she just wanted it so, wanted her child to know him at some level; wanted the boy to know the last man she loved.

She took the copper-corroding wolf weathervane from where it lay on the table and put it in the box.

One of her filigreed perfume vials sat on the tabletop as well. She picked it up, passed it under her nose. It was a scent she'd never wear again, it was too loaded with evocations of these days, with sense memories of Guy and associations of Eric that she wanted to repress, to banish from her memory. She put the perfume vial in the box, too.

Finally she unplugged Guy's white Princess phone from the wall, nestled it into a corner of the box, wedging it right beside her own telephone answering machine; she'd put that in here, too. It was the machine that took incoming calls on her private line; it had messages from Guy on it. It was a record of his voice, another irretrievable piece of him: his lovely, lost voice.

When she was done with this cleanup, she wanted no physical trace of Guy left, in the cottage or her house.

"I killed him," said Eric.

Claire turned to find her husband standing in the doorway. He was holding his Rottweiler on a leash. The Rottweiler growled, the way wild things have snarled since they first crawled onto land. Claire suppressed a shiver she didn't want Eric to see.

"I just wanted you to know," he elaborated. "I let him see me, to make sure he was scared, and to make certain he understood exactly what was happening to him and who was doing it to him and why. And then I put a pillow over his face and smothered him to death. It must have felt like drowning. He certainly fought like a drowning man and then he went into convulsions and died with a look of abject terror on his face." The scar on Eric's cheek was healed now, though still red and raised, just a few months old. He pointed to it. "And I'm going to keep my pretty scar," he added. "To remind me of the wounds you inflicted on me, the things you did to make me so ugly."

Claire didn't answer. She just looked at him a long few seconds, tried to remember who he was once; who could he have possibly been to inspire her love? She turned her back to him and stared into all that was left of Guy, packed into a single archive box. A tear filled her eye.

Another nearly subsonic death-rumble rose like bubbles in a tar pit from the Rottweiler's hungry throat.

The next day Eric flew to Cannes for the weekend, to meet with one of his property managers and, incidentally, to demand sexual favors from the manager's secretary. He kissed Claire goodbye and bit her lip. She yelped and jumped away and spit out the blood like poison. That was their real goodbye to each other.

As soon as he left, Claire spent the morning running around the house, sorting laundry, organizing papers, wrapping up a few phone calls. After lunch she walked back up to their bedroom, where Victor was now asleep in a baby carrier on the floor.

She grabbed her gym bag out of the closet, put it on an end table and took the dirty sweat clothes out of the bag.

Then she pulled aside the hanging tapestry depicting hunters and hounds mauling a boar. Behind it was a wall safe, which she opened with the combination she'd stolen by capturing Eric's dial-turns on a hidden video camera. When the last tumbler clicked into place she pulled wide the heavy safe door.

Inside were bundles of cash, scores of them, in thick packets of hundred-pound notes. Envelopes of bearer bonds. Trays of expensive jewelry. It was a small fortune, all tolled. She removed everything, stuck the loot in her empty gym bag. Then she closed the safe, locked it, put the tapestry back in place, put her dirty gym clothes back in the bag, on top of the stolen riches. She zipped up the gym bag, slung it over her shoulder. She picked up the baby carrier on the floor. She turned to go.

Alice, the maid, was standing there, watching. Her expression was ambiguous, her intentions opaque.

"Alice," said Claire, jolting to an unplanned stop.

"From all appearances it would seem that you think you're not coming back," said Alice, stating a fact.

Claire felt trapped, a hollow fear filled her chest. But she took a moment to bring it under control, calm with the rightness of what she was doing, steely in her purpose. She took a deep breath, walked up to Alice, unzipped her gym bag, reached inside, pulled out two packets of hundred-pound notes and extended them to the maid with a good deal of eye contact. "I don't think I'm not coming back. I know I'm not coming back," she said. "I'm starting my next life. We get to keep starting over until we get it right. You can do it, too. It's in your discharge. You're in charge of doing it. We all are."

Alice didn't move. She was carefully measuring responses, trying to navigate this unanticipated terrain, trying not to slip. Neither woman breathed, measuring what ifs and other shifting places.

"He'd hurt me bad if I let you do this, mum." She shook her head. She inched toward the phone.

Claire moved two feet to the side, to block her, to stand between Alice and Alice calling for help. Claire wondered how deeply loyalty to the Lord of the Manor was ingrained in a servant like Alice. She wondered how far she herself was willing to go, to save her own life. Her eyes darted to a sharp letter opener on the bedside table.

"He won't hurt you, Alice, he'll never know what happened. He'll know what I did, he'll never know what you saw. You never saw this."

"It don't matter, mum. He won't hold me harmless. At best I'd have to leave his service, and at worst...." She left the thought unfinished, though they both had reasonable expectations of what might ensue.

"Then you'd probably have to go away," said Claire. "I know how hard that can be." She added two more packets of hundred pound notes to the two already in her hand.

Alice turned pale and her lips got very thin, as if being offered a bribe of twice the size was twice the sin. And then she took the money.

"When Mr. Deloup gets home Sunday night," said Alice, "I'll just tell him I thought you'd gone to join him in France, then, shall I?"

A conspiratorial glimmer passed between them: a smile of "Thank you" from Claire, one of "Go with God" from Alice.

"Yes, that sounds fine," said Claire. Then she nodded at Guy's archive box on the floor of the closet. "Would you be so kind as to put that box in the car for me?"

"Of course, mum," said the maid with a curtsy.

Claire exited. Alice reached down for the archive box.

15

CHAPTER FIFTEEN

October 17, 2013
9:39 P.M.-10:17 P.M.
Red Chaos

Vic reached inside the archive box again. Pulled out a sheet of paper that just said **RED CHAOS** in shaded, block lettering.

He'd seen these words over and over in the journals and diaries. "RED" for blood, he assumed. "CHAOS" for... what? The chaos of life? Of betrayal and murder? Of confusion, meaninglessness, despair in the face of paralyzing, smackdown loss?

Frustrated beyond sense, he kicked the box with the flat of his foot, slamming it against the wall, toppling it over.

An old white desktop Princess phone rolled out. Stopped at his leg. He stared at it. Picked it up, stared more closely. Was it a sign? He didn't believe in signs. Did it mean something anyway? That he was meant to do something with this phone? He looked at the keypad. Just the usual letters, numbers, function keys. VOLUME. CHANNEL. ON. OFF. REDIAL.

But the color on the last three letters of the REDIAL button was worn away, faded to black. So the remaining, inked letters just said RED.

He looked again at the words RED CHAOS written on the journal page from the archive box. Then he looked at the phone, and thought of an interesting thing he might do with it. Something, in fact, that was usually done with phones back in the day. He plugged the phone into a wall jack.

He pushed the REDial button.

Three rings. Then a female voice answered. "Chao's Restaurant, sorry, we just closed."

Vic looked at the words RED CHAOS printed on the journal page. If RED was REDial, what was CHAOS? He picked up a pen, wrote an apostrophe between the O and the S. So the word wasn't CHAOS. It was CHAO'S.

"Hello, this is Chao's," the voice on the phone repeated. "We're closed now but if you call back tomorrow…."

And then Vic remembered.

He hung up the phone, ran stumbling and tripping out of his office, back down the hall the way he'd come, past all the dressing rooms until he got backstage to the pay phone on the wall, the wall full of scribbled phone numbers. Ran his finger over the chipping plaster until he found it: **CHAO'S CHINESE RESTAURANT 555-CHAO**. And then, in parentheses: **555-2426**.

In Galway, forty years earlier, when Guy had dialed this number, it hadn't yet existed, at that time or in that place. But here, now, for Vic in Chicago… it did. Now it was the number Guy had seen in his pre-life vision – and somehow managed to draw to Vic's attention, across the ocean and a lifetime later. Now it was a number Vic could call.

He marveled, not really understanding what it all signified. He could only shake his head, whispering to himself: "It doesn't mean RED CHAOS. It means Redial Chao's."

Olivetti pulled up to the curb, put it in park, peered dubiously out the windshield at what looked like an abandoned residential hotel. Nothing up and down the street but ruined buildings, urban desolation. He grabbed his cell phone and speed-dialed Wylie.

"Okay, I just pulled up at that second address you gave me – but are you sure this is the place he owns? It's a goddam condemned apartment building, or somethin'."

"What it says here. You sure you don't want me to come give you a hand?"

"No, I'm fine, I'll check it out first, doesn't look like it's gonna take long. I'll call if I need backup." He punched the cell off before Wylie could make anymore suggestions or insist on joining him. He wanted to do this one alone. That's the only way he was ever going to feel okay about not getting to Vic's mother in time.

He got out of his car. Never liked to have backup in Viet Nam, either, now that he thought about it. Didn't like the feeling that someone was depending on him, that he might drop the ball and then his backup would end up dead or worse.

He looked up and down the guttering block of overturned garbage cans, dead trees, human flotsam, junkies in cardboard boxes in pee-smelling doorways, weed-cracked sidewalks, boarded-up buildings. Walked to the padlocked front door of the abandoned hotel. Rattled the lock. No give. Tried to peer through a painted-over window. Nothing to see.

Adjacent streets were struggling to get renewed. Maybe Dent had bought this building as long-term investment property, to hold it, gentrify it and cash in big one day. Way it looked now, though, no gentry were coming anywhere near here for a long time. Olivetti walked to the corner of the structure. Looked down a cavernous alley. Took a flashlight out of his pocket, shined it down the lane. The shadows jumped like bad elves trying to hide from the light. He entered the depth of the passage.

Overflowing dumpsters, broken-open sacks of trash, dried vomit, sticky condoms, rusting needles, shattered whiskey bottles, porn mags torn and stained. Fat rats jumped and scurried away from his beam, and the brazen ones just stood their ground staring at him, daring him to make a move on them as he walked slowly down this narrow corridor between two buildings, it was like a tunnel into hell and the door shut behind you and your palms got damp.

Fifty yards ahead the alley opened up, though. Olivetti found himself standing at the wide rear entrance of the wildgrass-covered hotel parking lot.

The back door faced a pot-holed, debris-strewn field, surrounded by an assortment of buildings, some collapsed, some abandoned, some refurbished. The backs of a couple funky galleries, a few artist crash pads, a liquor store, a thrift shop, a coffee house. A restaurant, with an exhaust fan at its rear entrance, blowing the tang of its cookstove and refuse bins all over the backlot, tamarind and anise, burned grease and fish just gone bad.

The whole area was scattered with junked cars, working cars, broken asphalt, dumped garbage. But there, near the rear entryway of the condemned hotel, sat a newer car with Illinois plates. Olivetti took out his notepad, checked Mark Dent's plate numbers, looked at the car in front of him. 9AXD99. Perfect match. Dent's car.

Olivetti shined his flashlight into the car. Empty in front, empty in the back seat as well. Opened the front door, checked under the front seat and in the glove compartment for weapons. Clear. He flipped the trunk latch. Also empty, except for the spare tire and a couple tools. And wait a minute. There was a dark, wet streak of blood on the spare, and imbedded in it a long, blonde hair, fake bright yellow except at the brown root. Actress hair.

Olivetti backed away from the car and began methodically searching the area, playing his light over the ground. Looking for a trail.

Vic scraped up to the curb in his Chrysler, still Jimi on the box: *Something's wrong, baby, the key won't unlock the door, I got a bad, bad feeling that my baby don't live here no more.* He jumped out of the car, left the door open, ran to the window with the Chinese characters on it, the restaurant where Vicky worked. Stepped up to the front door, now closed. The sign said CHAO'S CHINESE RESTAURANT. Vic tried the door. Locked.

He pounded on it. Rattled the knob. Tapped loudly on the glass. No response. Backed up a step, looked around. Saw a chunk of brick lying in the gutter. Picked it up, prepared to launch it through the window – when the door opened. It was Oma, the woman who ran the place. She was holding papers, looking tired.

"We're closed."

"Is Vicky here?" Vic said without preamble.

"No, I told you, we're closed. It's late, I'm doing receipts."

Vic nodded. Started to turn. Then swiveled back, rushed past Oma, into the restaurant, knocking her aside.

Once in, he stopped, looked around. The place was definitely locked up for the night, no customers lingering, lights mostly doused. Alt Country music playing on the Sonos system. Oma walked up behind him, pissed off.

"What the hell's bells do you think you're doing? I told you, she's not here."

"I don't know, I'm sorry, Oma, I thought she might be here but maybe she didn't tell you, or somebody brought her here and you didn't know where they went, or I don't know, just cut me some slack, okay? I'm not sure what I'm looking for."

He wandered toward the rear of the place. Oma followed a few steps behind. He passed a back booth where three Chinese cooks were smoking cigarettes, playing mah jong.

"Vicky around?" he asked them. "Anybody see Vicky tonight?"

One shook his head; one smiled without a clue, didn't understand, didn't care. The third said, "You yi geh mi hu dan." And they all laughed, and the first one nodded and said it back faster, "Youyiguhmihudan."

"What's he saying?" Vic asked Oma.

"'Another lost fool,'" she said. "But I don't know if he was talking about you or Vicky."

"How do you know she's not here?"

Oma was getting pretty ticked off herself. "You think I don't know what's going on in my own place? Vicky's not here. This is my restaurant and it's closed. You know what time it is? Three in the a.m." She liked to stay on top of these things. The here and now.

Vic just kept walking. Checked the bathroom doors, a pantry. Looked around the kitchen, sink full of dishes, air suffused with layers of burned sesame oils, Asian spices, molding vegetable matter never cleaned out from behind the counters, dead fish spatter soaked into the grout. He breathed in all these smells, found a distant memory in them but couldn't grasp it. Like the memory of a long-ago dream of the future.

Oma didn't know what he was up to but he was looking beat down and wigged out; and she didn't care who he was looking for; if he didn't finish soon and get out of here, she was going to toss him.

Olivetti made his way to the main exit door of the condemned hotel. It was slightly ajar. He flashed his light around, saw something reflect back at him from the ground nearby. Bent down, picked it up.

It was a Triple O Cutt-Ex matt cutting razor blade. Same kind Vicky had pulled out of her wounded mouth. Olivetti wondered if this one was Gloria's and his guess was right on the money. It had, in fact, fallen out of Gloria's nightgown pocket, where she'd put it last night to use against the insane intruder in her house. To use against him but never had the chance. Fallen out of the pocket as she was carted over this ground and into the condemned building.

Olivetti put the blade on a windowsill. He felt another spasm of regret that he hadn't gone over to Gloria's house the night before, when he'd gone out drinking with Wylie instead. Letting Dent get away, letting him nearly kill Vic at the theater and now doing God knows what to Vicky. Olivetti swore to himself he'd make it up to them. He was going to nail this sonofabitch hard.

He drew his gun. Went in the door, left it wide open behind him. A nippy wind was picking up. It swung the door a few inches on its hinges.

Inside the aged building the blackness was softened by moonlight filtering through fractured windows. Olivetti passed his flashlight beam over ancient debris, splintered tables, a long warping counter, rusted barstools, a damp rotting mattress on the floor. Maybe this place had once been a diner, or the hotel lunchroom; then later a crash pad for neighborhood crackwhores, full-time drunkards, random bottom-dwellers. Now it was just a mausoleum for the roaches.

He panned his light around. Something glistened darkly on a doorframe across the room, right at shoulder level. Olivetti walked over for a closer look. Yeah, it was fresh blood. And beyond that, stairs leading down.

Back inside Chao's, Vic was heading down the rear corridor. Oma, at his heels, looked more and more annoyed.

Vic turned his head around at her, kept walking. "You have, like, storage rooms, a basement, an attic, a utility room? Any place someone might...."

"You know what?" They'd reached the back door. Oma unlocked it, opened it. "It's after hours, I'm tired, and you're gone."

She pushed him lightly backward, in the chest. In his contused chest, that is. It really hurt. He flinched, stumbled out the door. Without hesitation she slammed it shut on him and locked it.

He stood outside, rubbing his breastbone, looking around. Getting a little frantic, he didn't know how much time Vicky had left. The clue had been clear as day: RED CHAOS meant Redial Chao's. That had to be Chao's Restaurant, where Vicky worked. Chao's had to be central to all this; he knew it had to be, he just didn't know how.

His heart was beating at a good clip, maybe skipping a stroke now and then from the cardiac contusion, it made him feel like time stopped for a wild second at each missed pulsebeat, a caesura, like an unexpected gap in the fabric of his existence. He scanned the rusting car shells, the pitted asphalt, the straggly weeds, the decaying rubbish, the backs of the condemned buildings, deserted warehouses, old newspapers blowing over the ground in the wind....

In the wind, there was an irregular knocking sound.

He looked across at the rear-facing building. All boarded up. Except one door was wide open and knocking against the jamb in the rising October blow. Vic had the briefest flash, some deep atavistic memory. What was that knocking sound, that repetitive knocking? Hollow but meaningful, resonant somewhere unknowable inside him. Resounding, jarring, but he couldn't place it, it was murky as a forgotten nightmare, like the smell of tamarind and fishmold, and anyway he still didn't believe in intuition.

Yet when he stared at the open, irregularly knocking door, for just a moment he saw a faint wash of light, like a flashlight beam sweeping deep in the core. And then, like a firefly, it was gone.

But now he knew there was someone in there.

Olivetti crept along the damp wall, staying low as he moved through the darkness. Toward a distant luminescence in the room beyond. Probably where that psycho bastard Dent was right now, holed up with the women he'd kidnapped, doing dark, haunted obscenities to them. Olivetti hated men who hurt women. He was going to enjoy putting a hurt on Mark Dent.

He inched closer to the illuminated doorway that opened on the next room. He could hear voices, vaguely. Couldn't make out who they were. Male and female both, it sounded like. Heard the growl of a dog, too. He didn't like that.

He'd had run-ins with attack dogs a couple times over the years. So he knew what he had to do, though it meant stopping in his steps now, for just a moment, to prepare himself mentally. When the dog attacked, he knew, he'd try to shoot it but he'd likely miss. He wasn't a great shot under the best circumstances and this would be facing off against a brute creature in flat dark, probably running at speed. But with his gun extended out in front of him, he could let the dog sink his teeth into the meat of his arm – and then gouge the animal's eye out with the thumb of his other hand, send the beast howling in the other direction. In other words, he had to wrap his mind around knowing he was going to get damaged.

He came to the doorway. Peered through. Some kind of big holding tank not far inside. And way on the other end of the room, a couple people on gurneys. What was the bastard doing, experimenting on them? Olivetti gripped his gun tightly and stepped across the junk-filled space into the next room.

Vic walked across the junk-filled field that separated the back of the restaurant he'd just left from the deserted building across the way. The mountains of rubble looked surreal in the moonlight, like an alien landscape, like a bad-trip hallucination. He stumbled, nearly fell. Glanced down at the big pothole he'd stepped in. The whole place was pocked as a half-exploded minefield.

But he wound his way through it – past Mark's car, he could see it was Mark's – until he reached the open back door that first Mark, and later Olivetti, had gone through. Vic put his hand on the open door to stop its irregular knocking. Read the faded, old lettering on its outer face: CHAO'S MANDARIN RESTAURANT, EST. 1949. So this must be where old Mr. Chao had had his first place, long before the family had moved to the present location, the one Vic had just been thrown out of, at the other side of the lot. This was the original Chao's. Where Vic was meant to be.

Vic looked up. The top of the building was a crenellated turret silhouetted against the moon. Looked back down to the open doorway before him, and a snippet of the last Hendrix blues that had been playing in his car drifted through his mind. *Got a bad, bad feeling that my baby don't live here no more.* He took a breath, stepped through the darkened door, and into the condemned structure.

Into Chao's. Same shadows Olivetti saw, cast by moonlight through dirty cracked windows. He stepped around the rotting mattress, the broken furniture, the long warping counter, the disintegrating boards.

He tripped, fell to the floor. Whipped out his cell phone with a rush of adrenaline, turned on its flashlight, shined it at the thing he'd stumbled over. A dead cat. Its head was mostly eaten away, a family of maggots writhed in the rotting neck stump.

Bile welled up in Vic's throat from the smell. But he forced it back down, stood up, moved away from the dead mass of tissue and fur.

He scanned his LED light around the room. Bright for the first three feet, but so dim beyond that it was nearly useless. He held it out, stepped carefully. Looked in the kitchen behind the counter. Broken appliances, filthy pots, a doorless refrigerator full of mummified, unnamable foodstuffs. Just the faintest hint of the same Asian smells he'd been inhaling at Oma's place a few minutes earlier. Probably the same smells Oma's ancestors had produced cooking 5000 years ago in China. Funny how some things didn't ever change. They just kept happening over and over and over again.

He looked in another doorway. Sensed a large emptiness looming beyond it. Didn't see the bloodstain on the jamb that had drawn Olivetti's attention. But he did see the ramshackle stairway leading down into the black hole of the basement. A faraway sound echoed up to him from deep below, a sound or a memory of a sound or an echo of some soundless recollection. He took a breath, tried to blow off some tension. Started down the stairs.

The steps were wooden. Some creaked, some were completely rotted through. Vic pointed his Droidlight down in time to avoid missing an absent stair, hugged the wall until he reached the lower level. The immense blackness absorbed everything beyond the first few feet of the phone light beam. But as he stood there a minute, listening intently, letting his eyes get used to the dark, he was able to just barely make out a rough, lopsided circle of illumination coming from way across the other end of the dank, airless cellar.

He began walking that way. But a dozen steps in, something spidery harsh hit him in the face, like cold fingers.

He fell, swinging his arms wildly. Jumped up and back, dropping his phone to the floor. Crouched, ready to fight for his life, ready to kill.

The glaring beam from the Droid shot straight up from where the phone lay flat on the floor – spraying light over a tangle of corroded wires hanging from the ceiling. That's what he'd walked into. Swinging like a noose now. He quietly huffed a little laugh, shook his head at his overreaction, his jumpy nerves. Breathed in and out a few times, cleansing breaths, though the air he was taking in felt far from clean. Grabbed his phone, stood carefully, gave the hanging wires a wide berth, headed for the half light at the far end of the room.

When he got there he discovered a three by four foot hole in a thick concrete wall. Looked like it had been sledgehammered through to make entry into a contiguous section of building. He peered across this opening into the next space. A huge expanse, vast as night, even bigger than the basement he'd just crossed. Like a subterranean cavern. Filled with the strange shapes of archaic, broken machines, piles of ageless construction materials, iron rods, crumbling bricks, molding crates, animal bones. And illimitable darkness.

But Vic liked the dark, he always had. It brought him focus, shut out all the distractions, drew his mind down to a single point of essential clarity. It would serve him now. Just as his mother's closet had served him all those years ago. Inside the closet, on the floor, at the back, it was safe, and wondrous. And dark. And the dark is what protected him.

He slowed his breathing down, to settle the distraction of his nattering fear. And stepped through the hole.

The darkness welcomed him.

16

CHAPTER SIXTEEN

December 24, 1985

And Fashioned With Loathing And Love

Eric sat behind a large desk in his sitting room. His cheek scar was no longer fresh and red. It was white, mature, nine years older than when Guy had first cut him. It was long but not yet so thick as it would gradually become. He lived alone now; had done, for many years. He despised women, wouldn't let one in his house. His Rottweiler rested at his feet, unmoving but awake.

Christmas Eve, and a fine powder of snow crystallized the lawn outside the window. An icy fog draped the trees at the edge of the garden even as the tree in the corner of the den was draped with tinsel, strings of colored beads, hanging angels with mirrors for eyes. There were wrapped boxes of presents under the tree. But the silvery wrapping was just for show; the boxes were empty. And the show was for no one but himself.

Still, a guest was entering the room now, a sport-coated, middle-aged man with a military cut and laugh wrinkles at the corners of his eyes, adding a conviviality rarely seen in these halls. Not that there was anything particularly jolly about the guest; more like a cheery smugness.

He stopped in front of Eric's desk, put his hands behind his back, and waited like a Cheshire Santa.

"Well?" said Eric.

"We found her," said the man.

Eric couldn't have been more pleased if the private detective before him had been Santa. But Eric wasn't one for effusive gratitude. Instead he stood up, wound tight as a cheap Christmas toy. "About bloody time."

The dog, responding to his master's mood, stood up simultaneously and poised, baring his teeth. "Stand down," said Eric quietly, and the Rottweiler grudgingly sat, but never took his eyes off the visitor.

"She covered her tracks well, I'll give her that," said the detective, to amplify his own accomplishment. "But in the end, all paper trails, no matter how many layers deep...."

"Yes, yes, you're brilliant," Eric said dismissively. "Now where did she end up landing?"

"Chicago. In the States."

"Did the baby live?"

"Kid's named Victor, he's nine years old now."

"Tell me something I don't know."

"Your wife changed her name from Claire Deloup to Gloria Stone, had some plastic surgery. Speaks like a native now, though of course she was an actress so that wouldn't have been all that hard for her. Here's what she looks like, as of last week." He handed Eric a photograph.

It was a close-up, on a long lens, of Gloria, heretofore known as Claire. The woman Eric had once loved, now loathed. The picture showed a mature, beautiful woman. Her hair was prematurely white but her eyes still held that intense blue he'd never forget. And a new set to her jaw that bespoke a strong instinct for survival, full of tentative hope. But in the photo, as in life, she was looking over her shoulder.

"And the money she stole?" pressed Eric.

"Used most of it up on travel, identity change, facial reconstruction, buying a house in Chicago." The detective beamed a satisfied smile. "Want me to notify the authorities there?"

"No." Eric shook his head. He'd given the matter much thought; even so, he considered it for another minute. "Set up something with a local watcher. Just keep an eye on them."

"How close tabs do you want? Which boils down to how many men you want on the job."

"Whatever it takes for twenty-four hours a day. Three eight-hour shifts, I suppose."

"That could end up costing."

"Do I look like I care what it costs?"

"That's fine, then, long as you understand. How long do you want the surveillance kept up?"

Eric weighed all his options. There was no need to rush now. A dish served cold, and all that. "Twenty-four hours a day for a month or so. Then you can cut back to part-time for a few months, finally just phone taps and occasional check-ins unless there's some activity. The portfolio is, keep tabs on them until they're living a good life. And then keep tabs on their good life."

"You're talking years, then."

Eric nodded. "Until the boy grows up and finds a girl he wants to marry and everything's going just right for him and his mother." He smiled to him-self, poured some good sherry into two glasses, clinked them with his detec-tive, and drank; feeling, at last, a bit of Christmas spirit. "Until they think they're safe."

And he had them watched that way for twenty-eight years.

17

CHAPTER SEVENTEEN

October 17, 2013
10:17 P.M.-11:06 P.M.
As Time Goes Die

Vicky lay on the hard dirt floor, hands bound at her back, ankles wrapped together with plastic ties. Mark dug a shallow grave in the clay beside her, favoring his unbroken hand. He still wore the long frock of the Victorian doctor.

"Why are you doing this?" she said dully.

"Like the scorpion who stung the frog on their ill-fated trip across the river, dear. It's my nature."

"But why to me?"

"Not to you, *per se*. To Claire – excuse me – Gloria is her stage name." He nodded at Gloria, tied to her gurney near the water tank. "And I'm doing it to destroy her life. And Victor's, of course. His birth, his very existence, was the physicalization of her subtext."

"I never betrayed you," Gloria whispered hoarsely across the room. "With Guy, or with anyone."

He walked over to Gloria, put his lips to her ear – and screamed as loud as he could. "You loved him!"

She winced. From the volume of the shout, but also from the kernel of truth in the accusation. She'd never betrayed Eric in the flesh, never sexually; but she'd certainly loved Guy. She gathered her will, now, told him something she'd told him often before, but in any case she had no artifice left in her to dissemble. "Whatever you thought, Eric – my son, Victor, is your son, too."

"Liar!" he shouted through clenched teeth. He'd refused to believe it for so long, refused to believe her child had been conceived by him – yet the possibility of it still gnawed his guts.

All at once he clackered his teeth noisily at her, like a rabid animal snapping at food. It was a pit-of-the-stomach sound; it reeked of insanity, made her gag to hear it. The sound of her retching made him smile. He cranked her gurney upright to 45 degrees.

"Well, nothing works out exactly to plan," he spoke more calmly now. "Kendra, for example. I learned from my detectives that you'd bought a red Chevrolet, so I bought one, too. I ran the girl over, just to give you a big helping of grief – and then you had to go and paint your car green." He shook his head with some exasperation. "So I got more careful after that. I bought some buildings close enough to your neighborhood to keep an eye on you. And when I saw Victor going into theater tech work, I bought some buildings near him, and set up my little theater projects."

"That was how you lured me into your world the first time, too," she said with a great weariness, remembering all those years ago. "You bought our rep company, you built us a theater."

"Stick with what works, I say. Once I had your spawn and his little slut, here, in place, I got rid of Ratner – so I could kill Vicky onstage. Make it more of a public execution. Now that was an excellent plan. But Victor spoiled my fun so I had to put him down early." He grinned like a hyena at the tear in Gloria's eye. "Yes, he's quite dead. Begged for his life, the little snot, but I killed him slowly and with a great gladness." It was a lie, of course, but it pleased him to cause her more pain. He paused thoughtfully. "I suppose that's what Plan Bs are for. I suppose I'll have to abandon this place after tonight. But that's all right, my work here is done. And I do love my work."

He strolled back to Vicky, lying tied up at her impromptu graveside. "I've been spending time in your bedroom, you know. That was part of my work, too." He ran his hand slowly down her body.

Vicky shivered at the notion of this madman in her bedroom. He'd been watching her, up close, maybe touching her, for weeks, maybe more. She must've caught flashes of him in half waking moments during those uneasy slumbers, before he'd manage to hide amid the dark corners of her room. He was the source of her recurring nightmare, the shadow demon at the foot of her bed. The nightmare was real.

"If you could slip in unnoticed so easily, why'd you cut that hole in my window?"

He pursed his lips, pleased at the question. "Because that time I wanted you to feel invaded, and violated, and afraid. It was all about turning up the heat in the second act of your crisis. You know how important structure is in a dramatic, archetypal myth."

Mark took a small, lavender, filigreed vial out of his pocket, sprinkled its liquid contents all over Vicky, and called back to Gloria, "You remember this scent, don't you, Claire? I had it made just for you. It positively stinks of your transgressions." Then, softer, to Vicky: "This particular aroma makes my little wolf salivate. It's the smell of dinner for him. All that's left now is to let Claire watch."

"Watch what, you sick fuck?" Vicky snapped.

"What a wolf does to a whore," he answered, grabbing her ankles. He dragged her across the floor with his good left hand, to the slatted door of the mastiff's pen. He bent down, turned her body head-first to the door, blew through her perfumed hair, toward the open slats. The perfume drove the beast wild. It snarled, flashed its foaming jaws at the slats, just inches from Vicky's face.

Mark whispered to her. "He's going to like you."

But there was a crash somewhere else in the cellar. Mark spun around, searched the perimeter of the room. Nobody there.

He stood and ran out the door.

Vic picked himself up from the pile of rebar he'd crashed into as the pieces stopped rolling and clattering. Finally, silence. He paused, listening until the ringing in his ears diminished to a muted throb. Those were footsteps he heard in the distance. He raised his phone flashlight in that direction – and just like that, it winked out. Total blackness now. He pushed the button on his phone to bring up his homepage, to grab the flashlight function again. And maybe call the cops, maybe let Olivetti know he was here. But his homepage told him there were no bars down here and now the Low Battery was blinking. And now it was out. So no phone, no light.

What was he going to do, turn around and go back upstairs? Run for help? Nothing to do but go for it, he supposed. So he resumed his walk through this room of dead machines, walking by feel.

As his eyes accommodated to the blackness, shapes did emerge, though. Large irregular masses, small protrusions. Something flitted across the far wall, backlit by a red glow. A man-sized shape. Vic froze, crouched down. Crept around a collection of large boxes. There was a skittering noise, to his left. Again, Vic held still. Squinted into the dark. Strained his ears for a direction.

He inched around a rusted forklift, peered down an alley of plastic containers. There in the distance was an old wire-coil space heater, plugged with an extension cord into an unlit ceiling fixture. He walked quietly toward the heater's infrared radiance.

As he neared the glow, his own shadow grew on the wall to his right. When he got just a few feet away from the heater, he saw his distorted shape cast on the wall – and saw a second shadow as well, rising up behind him. He leaped forward, yanking the extension cord out of its plug as a heavy pipe sailed over his head in the dying red burn of the electric fire. The room went black.

There was a scraping, the sound of someone crawling over the floor. Crawling away from Vic. In the other direction, the entryway to the next room was even more visible than it had been, its thin light shimmering out of the void. Vic ran toward it.

He got to the open door. Entered the next room. Hunched low, he walked past some large crates and cardboard boxes, long ago overturned to spill their contents of dented aluminum ducting. He paused when he reached the two-foot tall, steel lip of what seemed to be a large water tank. Squatted behind this iron-zinc rim, peered carefully over it – and saw, far at the other end of the room, his two women. Gloria, his mother, tied to a gurney. And Vicky, his love, tied up on the floor near a slatted door.

He stood up straight, glancing down into the scummy water of the large tank he was hiding behind.

Olivetti floated there, face up, eyes open in surprise. A scalpel stuck straight out of his throat. He still gripped his police flashlight, its beam washing over his pale, dead face.

Vic fell back a step. Stumbled around the water tank, ran over to Vicky, bound on the floor. She saw him kneel beside her. Took a quick intake of air.

"Vic, thank God...."

The dog beyond the slatted door growled. Vic dragged Vicky by the ankles away from it, checking her bonds as he did.

"These are plastic tie-cuffs, I need a knife," he said.

"He's got surgical tools on the desk, by the lamp," Gloria called out. "There's a scalpel."

Vic ran to the desk. "I see some instruments, but I don't see a scalpel."

A scalpel plunged into his back. But he was turning as it came down so the blade only gashed the flesh near his kidney. As he accelerated his turn with a shout, the surgical knife was wrenched out of his back and out of Mark's swollen hand in the same motion.

The two men grabbed each other's throats, trying to squeeze them shut and rip them out, with a violence erupting straight from the reptilian base of their brains. They pitched to the floor in a death grip.

Mark, attempting to get traction, jammed his feet against the wall – pushing off into the shovel on the floor, which flipped Vicky into the shallow grave he'd dug.

The shovel rolled the pretty woman into the grave.

As the men pulled each other upright, still in choke-holds, Vicky struggled out of the grave, began wriggling across the floor toward the fallen scalpel.

Mark clawed Vic in the flank, where he'd stabbed him. Vic grimaced in pain – and in that lapse, Mark punched him in the chest, in his cracked sternum. Vic folded to the ground. Mark dropped behind him, wrapped his legs around Vic's waist, wrapped his arms around Vic's neck. Squeezed.

Gloria got herself up on her elbows, leaned forward on the gurney, stretched, tipped the balance – until the already 45 degrees upright gurney shifted forward, its foot edge coming to rest on the floor, its head-wheels turning slowly in the air. But then the center of balance shifted again, and the head-wheels came crashing down to the cement – sending the gurney coasting backwards with new momentum. Coasting towards the water tank.

Vic was losing consciousness. Scraping his fingers behind him at Mark's face, jamming his elbows into Mark's flanks, twisting and kicking and bucking for his life. But his strength was ebbing.

Vicky made it to the scalpel on the floor. Rolled over it, got it in her hands behind her. Began cutting her plastic cuffs with clumsy, short strokes, cutting the skin of her wrists in the process.

Vic kept thrashing, and in a final effort, put his hands on the floor, to try to push backwards. Couldn't budge. But his arm scraped something at the side of his black suede jacket. Something sticking out of the pocket. He felt for it with end-game effort. It was the metal wolf weathervane.

He pulled it out of his pocket and jammed it hard behind his head. Into Mark's neck.

Mark yowled, released his grip. Both men stumbled up like punch-drunk boxers. Vic gasped for air as he grabbed a length of rebar from the floor. Mark held onto the jagged metal wolf in his neck, pulled it out. Blood flowed down to his shoulder.

They stared at each other, measuring the several feet between them. Mark raised the weathervane like a knife, holding it left-handed but still deadly. Vic wielded his rebar like a tire iron in a gang fight.

Warily they circled.

But Vicky cut through her bloody wrist bond and was almost through her ankle ties. Mark saw her about to get free. Saw the odds about to change.

He feinted at Vic with the weathervane. But when Vic jumped back, poised to swing, Mark ran in the opposite direction – to Gloria's gurney – which he rolled hard against the water tank. In the next motion he up-ended the gurney, flipped it into the air. The gurney plunged, twisting out of balance, with Gloria tied to it, into the murky water, head first.

Vic looked horrified. "Gloria!"

Vicky got free, stood up shakily, holding the scalpel. "Get her!" she shouted to Vic.

Mark inched toward Vicky, brandishing his weathervane. She waved her scalpel right back at him, taunting him to come ahead, ready to give as good as she got. The thing about Vicky, she had the grit to hold fast. And once she got into character, she knew how to do wrath well.

Vic, thirty feet away, hesitated, torn by what to do. Which woman he loved was he going to help.

Vicky yelled at him again. "Go! I can drop this fuck!"

Vic ran to the large tank, took a couple deep endurance breaths, held the last one and dove in.

Plunged into the several meters deep of foul, cold dark water, a swath of yellow light illuminating Olivetti's floating dead body, parts of Ratner's corpse, decomposing rats and remnants. All of it bobbed around him, lit by the eerie glow of Olivetti's flashlight.

Vic pulled himself to a wide ledge ten feet down the cistern, where his mother's gurney had caught, dangling halfway over an even deeper plunge. Carefully began to wrestle the gurney upright.

Outside the tank Mark rushed Vicky, both of them with weapons raised. He lunged, she dodged, losing her balance, dropping her scalpel. But in the moment his weathervane found its mark in the meat of her arm, she raked her backhand across his face – dragging her tiny diamond ring across the surface of his eye.

He yelped, letting go of his blade as he brought his open hand up to his lacerated cornea. Vicky fell, twisting her ankle even worse as she pulled the corroded weathervane out of her arm and brandished it at the madman who teetered a few feet away.

But instead of pursuing her with surgical tool or shovel, Mark ran again, hobbling to the slatted door of the dog's cage. Pulled out his keys, undid the padlock.

Vic, meanwhile, was pulling at the plastic ties that bound his mother to the sunken gurney. Couldn't break them. Tried to heave the entire gurney up to the surface. Too heavy.

So he pushed up off the bottom, followed the flashlight beam to its source in Olivetti's hand. Pried the dead detective's fingers loose, pulled away the flashlight. Shined it on Olivetti's neck – pulled the scalpel out of the corpse's throat. Exploded to the surface to expel the stale air in his lungs, took another wheezing deep breath in. Then shot back down to Gloria, held the light on her bonds, began cutting them apart with the scalpel.

Up top, weak and bleeding, Vicky saw Mark opening the lock on the cage door. Heard the dog snarl. Reached into her pocket, found the perfume vial she'd taken from Gloria's archive box. The perfume that Mark had told her made the dog salivate, made the dog think of dinner. She uncorked the vial, crawled over to Mark just as he pulled off the padlock and opened the door. Splashed the Pavlovian perfume all over his back.

The slatted door burst open. The dog charged out, knocking them both over and running ten feet further on, before it could stop itself, claws skittering. Then it turned, and paused, to seek its prey.

Not a dog so much as hellhound. It actually was part wolf, its mother caught in the wild, mated with fighting dogs, Rottweilers mostly, the litters beaten and fed raw meat and trained to kill for sport. Its long snout curled back showing dirty ochre fangs, its eyes feral as a tundra, empty as a shark's. Three feet tall, two hundred pounds, fur matted with grease and blood. Not so much a hound as a beast. It sniffed the air for prey. Vicky ran.

Ran to the water tank, the wolf at her heels, pure hard muscle and death, and it leapt at her as she jumped. Caught her leg in its powerful teeth. Time froze for a long, acute moment. But she twisted free, sank into the water, her fight-shredded clothes flowing like tendrils of seaweed.

And her body suddenly plunges into a depth of dark water, her tattered clothes flowing like seaweed, a swath of pale light illuminating other floating, dead bodies….

The hound stood at the edge of the tank, licking Vicky's blood off its chops. Looking around for new meat.

Mark sniffed something. What was that smell? Turned his head, sniffed his own shoulder – where Vicky had splashed the perfume on him. And now he saw the dog sniffing, too. Taking a bead on Mark. Salivating. Mark's eyes went wide. He desperately wrapped the tail of his frock around his forearm, hoping in vain for a little protective padding.

The beast charged him.

Underwater, Vicky was holding the flashlight now, as Vic cut his mother's last bond. Gloria was motionless, eyes closed, mouth open. With the plastic tie severed, Gloria floated free. Vic and Vicky dragged her quickly past the other still bodies to the surface.

Vic hoisted himself to the lip of the tank. Vicky stayed in the water, holding Gloria up, trying to ignore the floating Olivetti's cold fingers behind her, brushing her shoulder like a call from the dead. Vic grabbed his mother under her arms, and with everything he had left, pulled her over the lip, crashing down onto the floor on top of him.

Vicky jumped out a moment later, dropping the flashlight beside her, as Vic turned Gloria onto her back. They began doing CPR, Vic breathing her, Vicky doing chest compressions.

Mark was getting mauled by the wolfen creature, his coat and his skin flayed. But he'd grabbed the jagged weathervane, he was stabbing the beast repeatedly. Both in a frenzy. He stumbled toward the door, dragging and slashing at the wounded mastiff, which kept its jaw clamped on his thigh, looked like it was trying to rip the man's entire leg free.

There was a moment of pause, as they shuffled past the resuscitation on the floor. Vic saw them, grabbed the flashlight, raised it like a club – but Mark just moved on, out the door, trading sharp wounds with the dog he'd trained, with such relish, to kill with such relish.

Gloria coughed once. Gagged, vomited. Breathed hoarsely; and then again. And then once more, more deeply this time. Opened her eyes. She was alive.

Vic hugged her. Two souls embracing, near death. Vicky put her arm around Gloria's shoulders and helped sit her up against the water tank. Vic stepped back, spoke to them both, haltingly.

"Can I leave you?" he said. "Will you be okay?"

The women nodded. "Go," said Gloria. "Make sure it's done."

Vic looked at Vicky. "Stay with her," he said.

Vicky nodded. Vic got up, limped off after Mark.

He stumbled through the blackness, tripping, falling. His chest hurt, his back bled, he was dizzy and exhausted and hyperventilating. But he made it through the obstacle course of junk, back to the rotting staircase and up, and outside the building. In time to see Mark on the ground, the dog atop him, jaws wide. Mark thrust the weathervane up into the dog's throat, and higher into its brain. The death blow. And the beast fell on top of him.

For a long moment they were still. Mark rolled the animal's carcass off into a large pot-hole in the dirt beside him. Struggled to his feet. Began limping away, spending everything he had left.

His long coat shredded, in tatters, he made it lame-gaited to his car, limping badly, bleeding from multiple bites and clawed gouges. Started to fall, but managed to hold himself up by the door handle.

"Turn around," he heard Vic say.

Mark turned. Vic was standing there, breathing heavily, squint-eyed and cold as a tombstone.

The door to the condemned building was knocking irregularly, repetitively, in the wind.

"I'm leaving now," said Mark.

"No, you're not," said Vic.

Mark turned back to the car door, started to open it. The wind whipped his hair, carrying the heady smell of the perfume in it, the odor making Vic oddly nauseated. He gripped Mark's shoulder – and Mark swung around, much faster than seemed possible – slicing Vic's jawline with the unsavory edge of the weathervane clutched in his fist. But Vic ignored the pain of the bloody knife cut on his cheek. He grabbed Mark's wrist. Slowly, with pure force of will, he held Mark's arm low, bent his wrist in, turned the blade around, inch by inch until its point was denting the skin of Mark's own belly. Face to face, staring deep into each other's eyes, searching.

Mark whispered, an unexpectedly gentle, plaintive voice. "Son…" he said. "You're my son."

Vic faltered. In that moment Mark let go of the weathervane and turned, in a single motion. Started hobbling quickly away, into the night. Long frock torn like a fallen woman's evening gown, wild perfumed hair, body cut, bruised and battered, limping into shadows made all the more stark by the contrast of the full moon's brightness.

A pretty woman arrayed in yellow bruises and tattered perfumed clothes walks past him on the cobbles. She has a limp. The scar-faced man follows her.

"No!" shouted Vic. He lurched forward, weathervane raised, just as Mark's figure was vanishing altogether. And plunged the knife-point tail of the wolf deep into the fleeing back, just to the left of Mark's spine.

He pulls a scalpel from his vest. It shimmers of ivory moonlight. He stabs her in the back.

Mark crashed forward, headlong to the ground, and lay still. His heart punctured from behind, it was the last wound his body could bear. He was bled-out and asystolic. Dead as dead.

And Vic would never know how correct his pre-incarnation, Guy, had been, right from the very beginning of his earliest interpretation of all those summer of '76 seizure dreams: Guy had felt, from the first, that he was, in fact, the murderer. The jaw-scarred killer of the limping, perfumed, ragged-gowned figure in retreat. Guy was just confused about the future tense of it all; and he never quite understood who the victim was going to be. But he was right in the essence of the thing, in the depth of his instinctive feeling: the victim had all those characteristics he'd envisioned – the limp, the ragged gown, the perfume – and he himself, in the body of Vic Stone, would be the murderer.

Vic dropped to his knees, pulled the wolf weathervane out of Mark's back, rolled him over. Mark's eyes were glazed in death, baffled by his fate, seeking an answer he'd never found in this life. Maybe never would, in any life.

The building door kept repetitively knocking. Vic looked at it, flapping in the wind. Vicky and Gloria emerged through the doorway, holding each other up, not yet quite believing in the simple fact of their survival. Vic limped toward them, met them halfway.

"Is it safe?" Vicky asked, then broke a dry smile. "Christ, I sound just like Olivier in *Marathon Man*." The girl still had brass.

Vic gestured to Mark's dead body. Then he looked at Gloria. "Was he really my father?"

Gloria regarded the corpse of the man who'd haunted her all those years. "It was so long ago," she said. "Like another life."

Vic – one of his eyes swollen shut, sweat blurring everything – looked down into the pothole where Mark had rolled the hound. The bloody, dead mastiff lay on its side, its jaws still open, as if ready to attack even in death.

"Now that," said Vicky, "was the physicalization of Mark's subtext."

Vic squinted at the torn animal, knitted his brow. Something about it was familiar, but he'd never comprehend the echoes of echoes it was generating: here was the lifeless dog Guy had foreseen a generation earlier, while unearthing what he thought was a grave beside the gardener's cottage; and now Vic was remembering Guy's pre-vision of this dead, wolvish beast.

One of his eyes was swollen half shut from flying debris, and sweat blurred everything – but suddenly Guy saw something out of the corner of his good eye – it was a bloody, dead mastiff lying on its side, its jaws still open, as if ready to attack even in death. Guy lurched backwards – and the thing was gone.

But now here it was, that same bloody, dead mastiff. Just one more of Guy's psycho premonitions.

"Why do I feel like I've seen that somewhere before?" said Vic.

"*Déjà vu*," said Vicky.

"I don't believe in *déjà vu*."

"It's not a question of believing it," said Gloria. "If you want to say you just don't get it, that's something else."

"Okay, I don't get it."

They smiled wearily at each other. They were trying to normalize all this insanity with everyday patter, just for a moment. But Gloria's smile faded under the weight of the carnage they'd endured. She touched the slash on Vic's cheek, where Mark had cut him. "You're bleeding. It's gonna be a bad scar."

He kept his macho up. "I'll live."

What's past, it turns out, is only prologue.

"Come on," said Vicky. "I see a light on at Chao's."

"I hear music in there, too," said Gloria. "*Galway Girl*. That's me."

"'*And I ask you, friend, what's a fella to do,'cause her hair was black and her eyes were blue*,'" said Vic. "I've been hearing that song all day."

"Did your hair used to be black, Gloria?" asked Vicky.

"Black as night. And the blue eyes you see. I was quite a charmer, to be sure, lass."

And the three of them limped, arm in arm, toward the back of the Chinese restaurant. Toward the rest of their lives.

Of Vic's and Vicky's next life, there was undoubtedly some promise. Some issues yet to be worked out, others maybe settled for good and all. There seemed to be, in any case, a certain poetic finality about the Eric entanglement; though maybe not where Claire/Gloria was concerned. Maybe there was still a little goes around/comes around work to be done there.

As they neared Chao's, the full moon dipped below the crenellated turret of the condemned building behind them, and the wind died down, and the knocking door became still and quiet for a time. As did their spirits.

Somewhere, a dog barked.

Being a Tale of Four Souls
July 4, 1976-December 6, 1976
And
August 24, 2013-October 17, 2013